ALL THAT WAS LEFT UNSAID

Jacquie Underdown

ALL THAT WAS LEFT UNSAID
By Jacquie Underdown

A vicious small-town murder, two unusual suspects, one big lie…

Tina is terrified when mysterious handwritten notes appear in odd places around her home. She strives to uncover who is behind the notes, and why, but finds no answers. Until one gloomy night, she catches a familiar face watching her through her bedroom window.

Maddison remains in her loveless marriage for the sake of her two young children. Still wearing the mental scars her husband inflicted after his years of betrayal, she uses alcohol and prescription drugs as a crutch. This starts her on a rapid ride to rock-bottom.

Approaching forty, Isabelle marries for the first time. Life couldn't be better, except her husband is still on good terms with his ex-wife. Isabelle doesn't like his ex, especially when she starts making trouble for the newlyweds.

When a vicious murder is committed on a quiet street in this small, blue-collar town, all three women are caught in the riptide of an investigation. Two are suspects. One will lose everything. And someone is lying.

A tangled lattice of manipulation and deceit must be unravelled to discover who the true culprit is.

* * *

This book contains language, adult situations and references to sexual abuse.

TABLE OF CONTENTS

ACKNOWLEDGEMENTS

Phew! What an adventure writing *All That Was Left Unsaid*. I received plenty of help along the way and I wish to acknowledge everyone who played a hand in shaping this story.

Firstly, Stuart Halls. Thank you so much for answering all my questions about police procedure. The information you provided helped guide the entire story. Without your assistance, I would not have been able to write this book in the way I envisioned it. Any inaccuracies are entirely my fault (and may be due to a little fictional licence on my part).

Sue-Ellen Pashley, thank you, once again, for fielding my questions relating to psychology. I appreciate your continued support.

Alana Kenzler, thank you for reading an early draft and checking for any potentially embarrassing forensic mistakes. Your insight regarding the story helped immensely.

Liz McKewin, I appreciate your early guidance so much. Without your keen eye, the story wouldn't have evolved into what it did.

Big thanks to Annie Seaton for performing the final proofread. You truly are a gem. Your assistance means I can release this book into the wild with confidence.

As for my husband, Brad, and my children, thank you for not only understanding how my brain works, but accepting me and supporting me when I inevitably hit that no-return point in a manuscript, and I am mentally MIA until it's done.

My readers, without your continued support, I wouldn't be writing. Thank you, a thousand times over, for reading and enjoying my stories.

CHAPTER 1

Dead. Detective Inspector McKenzie had seen enough dead bodies to know. Although, anyone with half a brain would arrive at the same conclusion, what with chunks of skull spattered on the road like an exploded piece of pork crackle.

Plus, the victim's face was unrecognisable. Beaten with a blunt instrument. That blunt instrument was a wrecking bar, discarded on the road, bloody and only metres from the body. Blood oozed from the skull and pooled under the forearm like a spilled tin of heritage-red paint. Still warm to the touch.

Around the crime scene, the forensics team was arriving in vehicles. A fire truck had parked on the elbow of the road, silent but its lights were flashing. An ambulance waited on the opposite side of the intersection. The victim's car was parked horizontally across both lanes—the right-side bonnet crunched in and glass from a busted headlight spewed across the bitumen.

Already, onlookers were gathering around the taped perimeter, feigning horror, their indistinct chatter like a chorus of twittering birds. Inwardly, they were buzzing. Eyes wide and excited. *A dead body. A murder. Gasp, gasp.* Tightening down low in the pit of their bellies.

They felt that way because their lives were banal. If they worked with death, saw enough of it, they would know it was not remotely titillating. The scents, the sounds, and the intrusive memories that would resurface relentlessly over the years.

McKenzie eyed the victim's hair. His throat closed over, spasmed. He had never been good with hair. Something about the way the strands matted from congealed blood. But he forced himself to take it in. His partner, Detective Jenkins, let him have his moment. She was aware of his hair repulsion. McKenzie had admitted it to her one night in a warm, smoky bar over a dozen glasses of strong liquor. Said he couldn't touch his wife's hair anymore. Hated the way it spilled over her pillow when she slept.

Detective Jenkins had reacted with empathy. Real empathy earned after seeing and experiencing firsthand how a career like theirs could take its toll. Not the kind of fake empathy used to prevent embarrassing the other person because they'd admitted to something *weird*.

The weird hair issue had been around since the early days of McKenzie's career when he was practically a boy straight out of the police academy before he'd had the years behind him to tighten and tan his soft skin into a weathered piece of impenetrable leather. That's kind of how he looked now: skin like a well-used basketball, pale blue eyes that stared for a long time without blinking, and height, but with a slight slouch to his shoulders as though every crime scene pressed down on him that little bit more.

His hair aversion had started with a dead body, too. Her head half-sunken into a toilet bowl. A shock of red blood against glaring, unnaturally bright auburn hair. Hair still wet from stinking toilet water. Enough to turn anyone's stomach. Since that day, he had often wanted to stop women in the street, those who had dyed their hair gaudy colours, shake their shoulders and tell them to be more considerate.

A police officer interrupted—a virgin first-responder. "The station contacted me. A call was made to emergency services to report a car parked on the side of the road about half a kilometre away from here. A woman is behind the wheel. Spattered in blood. Not making much sense." He was jittery, speaking too fast, despite forcing himself to appear composed.

"I'll head there now," McKenzie said, then focused on Jenkins. "Get forensics up to speed. Then start on statements from witnesses." He pointed to the tall timber power poles flanking the street. "Contact the council to see if there are CCTV cameras around here. If not, let's get someone doorknocking these nearby homes, checking for personal security systems that may have recorded what happened."

* * *

The next location was entirely different. Back where the dead body was, the sun overhead had been unobstructed and beat down hard like theatre-room lighting. Everything was seen on a clear, bright spectrum.

But at this scene, there was a tall border of trees lining the road. The car was half in shade, half in muted light because the sun sat on the opposite side of the canopy, casting a long shadow. A woman was inside the car. The engine was still running.

McKenzie stepped out of his vehicle. Even the temperature was cooler. He noted the time on his watch. 8.37 a.m. His shoes crunched over gravel as he approached the red Mini Cooper. Convertible. Top down. Older model.

The bystander raced to him. A young man in a high-vis shirt and dirty jeans. His ute was parked across the street, one wheel on the gutter, the other three on the road. He had been on his way to a job across town but was grateful to be assisting with this rather than putting scaffold together under the blazing sun.

"DI McKenzie," McKenzie said as he kept on his way to the car. "Tell me what happened."

The young man skipped beside him, his lips trembling slightly from the surge of adrenalin. "I was driving. She was in front of me. Swerving a little. I thought she was on her phone. Distracted, you know?"

McKenzie nodded.

"But then she veered off the road, flung in here between the trees. I thought she may have hit one because she skidded to a stop and the front of her car is crumpled. I parked there" – he pointed to his ute – "and went to see her. She's high. Or maybe she hit her head. There's blood on her hands and all over her clothes. I asked if she was hurt. She couldn't string a sentence together. I called the police then. And an ambulance."

"Okay, thank you…?"

"Derrek. Derrek Peterson."

Sirens from an ambulance blared in the near distance.

"Hang back for the moment. But stick around because I'll need to get an official statement from you."

McKenzie stood beside the car, appraised the woman. A purse sat on the passenger seat. A coffee cup was in the centre cup-holder. She wore a skirt that was riding up to her mid-thighs. A white see-through blouse displaying the same colour lace bra beneath. Makeup. Pale pink lipstick. Hair clean and styled. Covering all that were big splashes of blood like someone had come along with a brush dipped in bright red sap and splattered it over her.

He introduced himself. Asked her name. But there was nothing sensical coming back, only slurred sounds, almost like a wounded animal.

Tremors started then, big convulsions that rumbled through the woman's body. Her eyes were glazed and vacant. Pupils, big and black. Her jaw clenched tight. Not the first psycho-stimulant induced episode McKenzie had witnessed. He was well aware that this could go south rapidly, particularly if she spiralled into cardiac arrest, which was the worst case but very real scenario.

"I'm going to make you a little cooler here," he said as he pulled gloves from his pocket, sank his hands into each one. The air-conditioning was set to low. "I'm going to turn these air-con vents in your direction." He slanted the vents so cool air was pushing towards the woman. He reached for her seatbelt buckle to unclip it but drew his hand away; she would be safer strapped to the seat.

"Hurry up," he whispered under his breath as the sirens grew louder with their approach. "I've got an ambulance on its way. You'll soon be comfortable and in good care. Shouldn't be too much longer." He placed his thumb and forefinger at her wrist. Her pulse was going insane.

His shoulders relaxed when the paramedics roared up the road and pulled onto the gravel. A man and a woman, dressed in blue-green coveralls, climbed out and rushed over with their bags and equipment. McKenzie exchanged formalities and the small details he knew in a gush of short sentences, then stood back.

Between questioning Derrek further, McKenzie kept one ear open to the paramedics as they assessed their patient. They were worried about the woman's body temperature—too hot—and her erratic, racing heart rhythm. Soon, they wrangled her out of the car, laid her onto a gurney and strapped her in as she shook and trembled. They were saying things like 12-lead ECG, IV fluids and a cooling blanket.

Within moments, the back doors to the ambulance were closed, sealing the woman inside. As the van roared away, sirens blaring, lights ablaze, McKenzie marched to his car for the scenes-of-crime tape to start cordoning off the area.

Of course, he was wondering if the woman was linked to the victim found a short distance away. A scene was coming to life in his mind. A mild traffic accident. Both climb out of their car, but one reaches under the passenger seat for a wrecking bar first. For defence. She may have been scared. She may have been threatened but fought back hard. Or perhaps the reverse was true—purposeful intent to harm. Road rage gone wrong.

McKenzie considered the details, never one to rush to a conclusion. In that instance, with that case, he was right to take his time. Wait for the evidence. Connect *all* the dots.

CHAPTER 2

A month ago…

Maddison often fantasised about killing her husband. Over the years, she had stabbed him in the heart with a sharp kitchen knife. Sometimes she would spike his food with poison. Other times, she would suffocate him with her pillow. Hardly original, but fantasies with the same result, nonetheless.

Maddison had her reasons. Good reasons. And just because she fantasised about murdering Ben, didn't mean she would go ahead with it. If that standard was applied to all fantasies, there'd not be a married couple left standing on the planet.

That particular day, she was on the rowing machine in the gym. A little after noon, most days, Maddison would do a thirty-minute cardio blast. Not some half-arsed meander on a pretend rowing boat, but a workout so extreme she had been known to pass out from exhaustion. That's why she did that workout at that time when the least number of members were in the gym.

While sucking in breaths like her life depended on it, a deep lactic burn in her shoulders and thighs, she watched her husband at the front counter talking to another staff member. Belinda. A new aerobics instructor fifteen years Maddison's junior.

Right now, a double murder fantasy was playing out, committed with an eight-kilogram kettlebell swung at just the right angle and speed to clobber both their skulls, one after the other.

Maddison had a dark side. Those little fantasies sounded meek and mild when restrained to the confines of her mind, but when spoken aloud, they shed light on the disturbing nature of those thoughts.

Eight times that double murder scene played in Maddison's mind and each time her breathing grew more laboured until she was practically barking. Only when a bulky man doing bicep curls cast his eyes in her direction did she quieten.

Near the front counter, Ben's mobile rang from in his pocket. "Excuse me," he said to Belinda.

"I'll leave you to it," Belinda said and scampered away. She had recently moved from a tiny town. One that made Gladstone, populated by thirty-odd thousand residents, comparatively huge. All she wanted was a chance to work; there wasn't much of that for aerobics instructors in the dusty, red-earthed expanses of Winton.

So far, Ben had been a good boss to her. She cast a glance at Ben's wife sweating away on the rowing machine and was distracted by the wide, unsymmetrical set of her glazed eyes. Belinda believed that someone's eyes were the best indicator of sanity, so there had to be something deeply wrong with Maddison.

Ben pulled his phone from his pocket and answered. "Ben speaking."

"Sabrina Collins calling from Gladstone Primary Private School. I would like to arrange a meeting with you and

Maddison regarding Ruby. I'm afraid she's been the object of bullying. Nothing we can't handle. But I'd like to nip it in the bud as soon as possible and eliminate any chance of escalation."

"What kind of bullying?" Ben asked, his words clipped. Ruby was only nine. She had inherited her mother's small frame—the tiniest arms and legs—hardly capable of warding off bullies.

"A group of girls sprayed water on Ruby's lap and told the class that she had urinated herself."

His palm slid down his face. "You've got to be kidding me?"

"I'd prefer to discuss it face-to-face, so nothing gets lost in translation."

He blew out a long breath, suppressed an angry growl. "We'll be there soon."

"I was hoping perhaps after school. Three-thirty?"

"Is Ruby okay, though? Should I pick her up?"

"She's fine. We've handled it. The other students' parents have been notified and we'll be talking to them individually."

He pressed his palm against his forehead, closed his eyes. "We'll be there at three-thirty."

"Thanks, Ben. I'll talk to you then."

He ended the call, shoved his phone back in his pocket and took a moment to breathe deeply for five seconds in, five seconds out. Only when the rage waned from a jagged searing beneath his skin to a slow current, did he speak to his wife.

There was no convincing Maddison to stay put until three-thirty. Her protectiveness for their two children was like a mother lion on steroids.

Maddison, still dressed in her sweaty, sour-scented gym gear, arrived at the school barely twenty minutes later. With Ben in tow, she pushed through the administration building's front doors and beelined to the desk where Vanessa, a young receptionist in her early twenties, waited. Vanessa's cheery smile fell away as she noted Maddison's rigid stance, scowling face and the crazed tide of rage that ebbed behind her wide eyes.

"Bring my daughter, Ruby Brooks, here immediately," Maddison demanded. The other ladies in the small office lifted their heads from their keyboards and glanced in her direction. "We'll be taking her home now. I want to speak to Sabrina this second or the police will be involved."

Vanessa bit back her sharp reply, understanding that violence may be the realistic outcome of a forked-tongued response. "Sabrina is in a meeting at the moment, but I can book you in for an appointment—"

"I don't think you understand. I won't be taking no for an answer." Maddison's mind was filled with angry questions: where had the teachers been when these little bitches squared up against Ruby and squirted water all over her lap and where were they when they paraded her into the classroom and announced to the other snarky little shits that Ruby had urinated herself? She wanted answers, explanations.

Vanessa reached for her phone. "I can arrange for Ruby to be brought to the office if you think that's best."

"It is best. And I would like to speak with Sabrina now." Maddison's voice was rising. Ben placed a hand over her hand like a charmer approaching a rattlesnake, but he didn't say anything; he wasn't that stupid.

His wife calmed for the two seconds she was distracted, but she soon flicked his hand off, cast a murderous expression his way, then focused again on the receptionist.

Ben stepped closer to the desk. "Best you get Ruby for us. As for Sabrina…" Before he could finish, Maddison had spun away and was storming up the hall to the principal's office. "Damn it," he groaned under his breath and followed.

"You can't go barging in there," Vanessa called out after them.

Maddison had a vague awareness that she was overreacting, that her mind was spitting up old pain, anger and resentment, tainting this new but only remotely connected situation, and yet she couldn't stop.

She slammed the office door handle down, shoved the door open, startling the principal and a young couple with their daughter who were sitting opposite the principal's desk. All turned to face Maddison with various expressions of shock and curiosity.

"Maddison?" Sabrina barked. "I'm in the middle of a meeting. I'll be with you in a few moments."

Maddison shook her head. "Not good enough." She slapped her chest with her palm. "My daughter has been emotionally tormented and ridiculed because of you and your staffs' incompetence. I deserve answers now."

A big-bodied nine-year-old girl sitting between her mother and father, eyes already wet with tears, looked at Maddison and said in a meek voice, "I'm sorry. I didn't mean to upset Ruby. I was just playing—"

This drew all of Maddison's attention and her head flicked around so she was facing the child. "You're the bully?"

The little girl shook her head. "I didn't mean to be a bully. We were just having fun."

"Fun?" Maddison roared. "Humiliating another student is fun for you?"

The girl's face grew bright red, her bottom lip trembled, and she burst into tears.

The father's nose wrinkled. "You're going overboard, don't you think?"

"If this little fat bitch of yours—"

"That's not appropriate under any circumstance—" the mother interrupted.

"—even thinks about looking at Ruby, I will come in here and gut her like the overfed piglet she is. You got it?" Maddison's head was shaking. Her throat was raw from screaming so loud.

Two hands gripped her arms. Not aggressively but assertively.

"Maddison, look at me please," Ben said.

Maddison blinked, snapped out of her rage, and turned to face her husband.

"Let's go. You've said enough," he whispered in a low, soothing voice.

She turned back to the people arranged in the cramped office. Stunned faces. The father was red with rage, his leg bouncing, hands clawing the armrests to hold himself back. Tears were filling the mother's eyes as her daughter cried against her chest. The principal's mouth was flapping open and shut, rage in her gaze.

Maddison smoothed the hair from her face, held her shoulders back, chin high. "I've said my piece."

"You most certainly have," Sabrina said. "Get out. Now!"

Ben threaded his fingers with Maddison's, tugged her out of the room, and led her down the hall to the administration area. She flicked his hand away as soon as the door closed behind them.

Ruby was seated on a chair in the corner of the small waiting room, eyes wide, frowning. The poor girl had no idea what all the fuss was about. Her friends had played a funny prank on her that morning and now it was like they had all murdered someone with the way the teachers were reacting.

Ruby and her friends had been filling up their water bottles when Miranda had accidentally sprayed her with water and Ruby noticed that it looked like she had peed herself. They had all laughed so hard until they had tears in their eyes. Ruby hadn't laughed like that for a long time and it felt so good.

They had shuffled to the classroom and shown the other students. The kids laughed, not at her, but with her, and for a few moments, she was the most popular girl in grade four.

But now, the adults were crazed and acting like it was a crime.

Maddison ran to Ruby, crouched before her, and caressed the hair from her daughter's face. She kissed her forehead. "I'm so sorry this happened to you."

Ruby's brow crinkled. She shook her head. "I'm fine."

Ben lightly squeezed his daughter's shoulder and kissed the top of her head. "You sure?"

13

Ruby nodded. "Fine. Can I go back to class now? Mrs Bracken is reading a Roald Dahl book and I want to hear what happens to the giant."

"I don't think that's best, honey," Maddison said. "We'll take you home now. Give you a chance to relax."

Ruby frowned.

"Maybe we can stop on the way home and buy the book for you?" Ben suggested.

Ruby jumped to her feet, grinning. "Yes, please. It's such a great book."

"You can tell us all about it on the drive home," Maddison said, rising to her full height again. She took her precious daughter's hand—such a tiny little girl. All skin and bones and big joints. No height to speak of.

A tight foreboding filled Maddison's stomach for how she had behaved there today. But no way did she regret it. She would not adhere to social conventions when it came to her children. In her mind, that jealous little bitch inside deserved to cry for what she had done.

CHAPTER 3

Tina Brooks' daughter died three years ago. The anniversary fell on a Friday. The smallest of concessions in an otherwise black day. She would be able to keep herself busy at work, then she had the entire weekend to bunker down and cry.

To that second, the intensity of Tina's grief was equal to the chest-splitting, hollowing out that had come upon her when her daughter's much-too-small timber coffin sank beneath the earth and her little girl, only days away from her fourth birthday, was inside.

Irretrievable beneath tons of dirt was the one person who had taught her how to love with her whole heart—an intensity of love beyond all others. Tina often dreamed of clawing away that dirt, opening the timber box and cradling bones to her chest. Bones were better than nothing.

That day, she went about her rounds in a fog of grief, delivering package after package to the front doorsteps of Gladstone residents. Mostly middle-class suburban houses. In the newer estates, built during the more recent boom, were the cookie-cutter, slapped-up-as-quickly-and-as-cheaply-as-possible houses. The older estates held the commission homes cum fixer-uppers.

The more central suburbs were where the grand old Queenslanders stood, a mixture of peeling paint and asbestos. A few quality houses here and there. The big, flashy homes sat on top of the town's hills, most glimpsing the alumina refinery's sprawling tangle of orange-dusted steel.

Late February was hot and humid, but, for Tina, that was secondary—a patch of sweat under her arms, down the centre of her back, between her breasts and legs. It wasn't death. Not even close.

Death consumed her life. Every day since the funeral, when she awoke, Death was there too. When she flipped through photographs of her daughter, Death was right there with her. He invaded her home, memories, sleep, joy. He was there when she laughed. He was there at the end of every moment, cloying, loud, larger than ever when she went more than an hour without thinking about it. Death was like night. But even night had stars.

Her daughter, once full of life, no longer existed without Death. Interchangeable. If someone had said to Tina before she fell pregnant that at some point very soon, she wouldn't be able to think about her child without Death smashing through her chest and exploding her heart between His bony fist, leaving behind a cavern of hurt so deep, so present, it would make her unable to draw a full breath, she may have rejected motherhood.

Maybe. That's the devious cunning Death possesses— you can't know how He feels until He's there. And once He's there, He never leaves. In some cases, He retreats to the corner of the room, stays quiet, doesn't interfere much, but at other times, He sits his big, solid bones down on the centre of your chest and induces claustrophobic suffering.

Tina finished her day of work when the sun was still bright, though lower in the sky. No shadows yet. They would encroach after she dropped her van off at the delivery exchange centre, jumped into her car and drove the twenty-five minutes to Boyne Island along the winding coastal road, bordered by hills of rock, spinifex, banks of mangroves and the blue-green Pacific Ocean.

Much to Tina's relief, at that time in the late afternoon, the lawn cemetery was empty. She parked her car, cut the engine, and closed her eyes for a few moments. Inside her was a storm. Lashes of sharp rain needled against the underside of her skin. Cyclonic forces raged in her chest. Blunt and heavy. If she focused too hard on that hot darkness that dwelled inside her like a living thing, aching to take her over, she would become its prey. That violent beast had had its way with her too many times those past three years. It was brutal, merciless, and after each encounter, she was left scarred.

Not today, she thought as she climbed out of the vehicle. She was going to stay in charge. She was going to dictate her grief, no matter how forcefully it wrenched against the brittle chain barely holding it back.

Back out on the main road, which carried motorists between Gladstone and Boyne Island, the rhythmic whoosh didn't let up as cars passed in a long, end-of-the-workday stream. Every single person was oblivious of the cemetery, let alone Tina.

Tina's gaze moved to her daughter's headstone like it was a magnet and she the opposite polarity. Each step toward that erect, blonde rectangle of sandstone magnified the roar of emotion. Her breaths grew heavier but thinner, as though there wasn't enough air.

At the foot of the grave, she sank to her knees on the soft green grass, exactly a coffin's distance from the headstone.

Never would she forget the diminutive size of that timber box. Jarring. Uncanny. Wasn't right. Nothing about that day or any day since had been right.

Purple posies in a glass milk-bottle vase had been left beside the grave as well as a brown teddy bear with a tartan ribbon circling its neck and a bunch of natives adorned with a colourful tie. Someone had already been there.

Tina's neck tensed, making her head shake. A thin line of irritation traversed her limbs for the intrusion. But, of course, her ex-husband would have visited there today. She knew Chris well. He would have taken the week off work, driven to the cemetery early. His new wife would have joined him and probably rubbed his back as he cried.

Tina rearranged the flowers and teddy, setting them off to the side, pulled the white, stuffed unicorn from her handbag and placed it front and centre at the head of the grave. She rummaged around for the small, pink tealight, positioned it beside the unicorn and lit the wick with a lighter. A pointed, orange flame wavered in the humid afternoon breeze.

She stared at the blades of grass, the flame and the engraved letters of the headstone. *Kadie Brooks*. A tear rolled from her chin and landed on her leg. With that one tear, the chain broke, the cruel fangs of grief bit down hard until all she could do to protect herself was to roll on her side beside her daughter and wish she were inside that tiny coffin too. Death almost suffocated her.

When the cemetery was cast in complete darkness and the birds had stopped their cawing and chorusing, Tina uncurled, dusted the shards of grass from her clothes and drove the forty-five minutes to home.

Gladstone was a regional town. Industrial, mostly. The powerstation's three tall smokestacks intruded upon the mountainside skyline. The port was shared by long coal conveyor belts, wharves and big cargo ships. All were lit up like tiny cities at that time of night.

Beyond that was the harbour where islands dotted the horizon and dolphins often arched in the whitewash as recreational boats cruised about. Big white fuel storage tanks invaded the shoreline. To the north of there were huge LNG plants. Tina lived just beyond that in the tiny town of Yarwun.

After parking in the carport at the side of the house, near the water tank and shed, she climbed out of her car. Her legs weighed more. Her shoulder muscles ached. Her eyes were red, puffy and tired from the torrential tears.

"Damn today," she growled as she kicked off her work shoes, arranged them neatly on the front porch, perfectly in line with each other, then unlocked the door and went inside.

She flicked on lights as she walked through the foyer and into the living room. When her finger slowly lowered from the light switch, goosebumps blossomed across her forearms. The thin hairs prickled. A slither down the back of her neck.

She froze, held her breath, looked around.

All seemed normal. Everything in its place.

She shook her hands and told herself it was all in her head. She was merely tired and emotional and really should eat something, even when food was the last thing she could stomach.

When in the kitchen, she flicked on the light and eyed the room. The sink was clean. Nothing was on the benches that didn't have a purpose. Again, the slinking nail down the back of her neck. An eerie sense someone was there, or, at least, had been there.

"Hello," she called out. Her voice was weak, hoarse in the silence. Hearing the edge of fear in those two syllables, heightened her fear more.

She went to the back door, just off the kitchen, tested the lock, then rushed up the hall to every room and cupboard, turning on lights, checking each vacant corner and surface. Her throat was tight. Muscles tense. With a flurry, she yanked at the windows, testing their locks. Not one lock budged.

All was as she had left it that morning.

She sank onto the end of her bed, pushed her face into her hands. She was over-emotional, waiting for a monster to jump out from the darkness like it had that day three years ago.

Grief clenched her throat, made her eyes burn and gloss. But she didn't cry. She had nothing left. Today had been the longest, hardest day for her. All she wanted was to slip into the unconsciousness of deep sleep and stay there until she didn't hurt so much.

CHAPTER 4

Isabelle Brooks wandered into the kitchen and shoved her favourite mug under the coffee machine. As the aromatic, brown goops of espresso trickled into her cup, her lips curled into a half-smile.

Isabelle Brooks. Had a nice ring to it. She had been wearing that surname for eight weeks now and couldn't be more willing to show it off. All her business cards had been changed at the hairdressing salon she owned. Her bank cards. Her driver's licence. Any official document, she happily circled or wrote *Mrs* rather than the *Miss* she had contended with for too many years.

The espresso finished dripping, and Isabelle set about frothing milk. Again, that slow creeping smile. Her clients at the salon constantly teased her about it. Their hearts were warm and full to see their hairdresser wistfully happy and in love after fifteen years of singledom.

They had watched over the years as Isabelle's dating life never got off the ground. After falling pregnant and giving birth to her daughter two months after her sweet sixteenth, her path took a different course to those her age.

She never completed her final year of high school but gained maturity and had responsibilities a school could never have taught her. Her life rushed ahead a decade past her friends, so that always meant she was out of sync with them. It created an obvious divide—the girl who got pregnant in high school versus everyone else.

Her daughter's father was never in the picture. He sent a little child support for Julliette here and there, but nothing past her seventh birthday. Isabelle didn't chase him for it— she preferred the ease that came with not having him in their lives.

She dated on and off for six or seven years after Juliette was born, but men who were barely adults themselves were not willing to take a backseat to a child. Not willing to father another man's daughter. That's when she had decided to go solo. Just her and Juliette.

In those following years, she finished a hairdressing apprenticeship, earned a business diploma from the local TAFE, then eventually opened her own salon.

She guided Juliette through high school, and now university—the life Isabelle had always wanted for herself. Boyfriends were unavoidable for a young woman who had inherited her mother's good looks, but early motherhood wouldn't stunt her daughter's life. Isabelle had made certain Juliette was aware of contraception from the time she was a teenager. Unlike her own mother who had been too afraid to mention the word *sex*, let alone caution her about any other traps young women could fall into.

But children eventually grew up and took control of their own lives. That's all Isabelle had ever hoped for Juliette. Even though her daughter still lived with her, she spent more and more time out of the house as she studied, worked and explored her social life.

Sitting on her own most nights, waking to an empty bed, in an empty house, the space between Isabelle and the walls grew a little too big. The silence beneath the pad of her feet on the tiles as she moved about was startlingly loud. An expanding void in her womb.

She was aware of the years moving by like a blur of landscape seen through a speeding car's window. Prophecies filled her mind of sitting in front of the television, with grey hair and deep wrinkles, a warm blanket across her frail knees—alone.

But that nightmare changed when a handsome, rough-around-the-edges tradesman came into her salon for a haircut. As she had run her fingers through his dark hair, snipping and clipping, and looked into his kind blue eyes, she had realised it was now or never. If she didn't jump into the dating game, she would never do it.

Chris had sat in Isabelle's chair and tripped over his words when he spoke to her for the first time and allowed her to maternally wrap the cape around him, her long fingernails brushing his skin. Her salon held the pungent scent of hair dyes and shampoo. She was dressed in tight white pants and a white singlet top that had highlighted her tan and toned arms. Silky blonde hair, so long it skimmed her waist.

He would soon learn he was nine years older than her, and she was well above his batting average. When she had asked him out for a coffee, the shock was like a stinging slap to his head.

In the days between that haircut and their first date, he had been so nervous. But his tension vanished when he had sat across from Isabelle in a small, intimate coffee shop and she had smiled at him, set her chocolate brown eyes on his and talked and talked and talked.

She was one of those people. Could talk to anyone, anywhere about anything. They didn't have uncomfortable silences. But sometime after that, Chris had come to appreciate silence and wanted maybe one or two moments without words.

Isabelle filled her cup with frothy milk and sipped her coffee just as Juliette rushed into the kitchen. "Good morning."

Julliette smiled, kissed her mother's cheek. "Good morning. I'm late."

Isabelle checked her watch. "Seven minutes late."

"I know. It's my stupid hair. I washed it last night with a new conditioner. Today, it didn't want to do anything it was told."

"You should have come and got me. I would have helped you out."

Juliette shrugged. "I thought I'd let you get in some time with your *husband*." The musical way she said *husband* was like that of a child teasing their younger sibling about a boyfriend.

Isabelle lowered her eyes to her coffee, a whimsical smile gracing her lips. "I appreciate that."

Chris was home that week. He worked twelve days on, eight days off, fly-in fly-out roster to a mine site in Northern Queensland where he was employed as a mechanical fitter.

Their marriage was still very much in the honeymoon phase and that was reset twice a month by Chris's work schedule. It was true what they said about absence making the heart grow fonder. Every time Chris came home after twelve days away was like the start of their honeymoon all over again.

Not that they'd technically had a honeymoon. Isabelle was thirty-eight. Chris was forty-seven and this was his second marriage. Neither of them wanted to make a fuss. Chris hadn't wanted to marry again but eventually agreed when Isabelle said they wouldn't have to have a ceremony or an expensive trip away, just a simple signing of the marriage certificate with a minimum number of witnesses and a sole registrar.

Chris was that type of person—simple. That's what Isabelle loved about him. He was always the one person. Never wavering. No matter the circumstance, she always knew who she was coming home to.

Isabelle tipped her coffee into a travel mug with a lid. "Here. You take this. Looks like you need it more than me."

Juliette kissed her mum's cheek again, eagerly took the hot coffee. "You're a saint. Have I ever told you that before?"

A laugh. "You may have. Now go."

Juliette drank deeply from the travel mug, grabbed a banana from the fruit bowl and skipped out of the kitchen. She still had a semester left of her communications degree, but two months ago, she had landed a paid internship as a public relations and communications officer at the alumina refinery. Jobs like that, in that town, were gold, but if you didn't know someone who already worked there, trying to get your foot in was near impossible. Isabelle was so proud when her daughter, out of hundreds of applicants, had earned the position.

She quickly made another coffee, poured it into a spare travel mug, and tiptoed to her darkened bedroom. She opened the door. Chris's breathing was slow, rhythmical. He was on his stomach, naked backside in the air, sheets tangled around his legs. Tall and fit. Looking at her husband, even eighteen months into their relationship, had her wanting to climb back into bed with him. But her salon took priority.

She leaned over, kissed his stubbled cheek. "I'll see you this afternoon."

He smiled, eyes never opening, and slurred, "Have a good day."

* * *

From one side of Gladstone to the other was only fifteen minutes, so Isabelle arrived at her salon in ample time. She unlocked the doors, put cash in the till, heaved a load of towels out of the dryer and dumped them on the front counter. There, she logged onto the computer while folding the laundry-powder scented towels.

When she noted that her appointment book was full, her shoulders relaxed. Hairdressing wasn't where the money was at. Far from. As it was, she didn't declare any sales that were paid with cash. If she were forced to pay tax on that part of her income too, she would have closed the doors a long time ago.

That kind of stress and strain was an obsolete concern now that she had Chris in her life. He earned a great wage, much more than she had first assumed. She had known miners in Australia worked ridiculous schedules, and their job came with real safety risks, not to mention the amount of time spent away from their families, but she had never realised they were compensated well for all that. She wouldn't admit that to anyone, but it had been a cherry on top.

Not that they shared their finances, even since getting married and Chris moving in with her. But Chris paid for his share of living expenses and was generous when they had weekends away or went out for dinner and drinks. That was enough to alleviate the lifetime fixation Isabelle had on making ends meet.

A blissful tangle of joy filled her chest. A part of her wondered why she hadn't found a man to fall in love with years ago. And then her logical brain intervened, reminding her that she had tried. Numerous times. But all her attempts bore no romantic fruit. No, with her early start to adulthood and responsibility, the fast-tracked mature head on her shoulders, she'd had to wait until the potential Romeos caught up.

CHAPTER 5

Maddison stood in the centre of the living room and announced, "Bedtime."

Riley groaned from his place on the carpet, stomach down, his iPad before him, finger darting over the screen. Ruby was sitting next to Ben, her head resting on his lap as he stroked the hair from her forehead. Now and then, she would laugh at something she found funny on the TV, then look up at her father and he would smile down at her.

Maddison clapped her hands. "Come on. Up you get."

The children kissed their father goodnight, then snail-paced it to the bathroom. They were used to this routine and always took their time, dragging out the few sweet moments of wakefulness remaining.

When Maddison heard the tell-tale sounds of her children sprinting down the hallway, giggling and chatting, she followed them to their bedroom. A spacious room. A single bed for them both, each butting against opposite walls, leaving a big space between that had been hijacked by toy cars, racetracks, colouring books, pencils and dolls. Riley's bed had a colourful coverlet with computer game characters. Ruby's was soft yellow with cartoonish kittens.

She tucked Riley in first, kissed his cheek. Her fast-growing eleven-year-old boy. Her firstborn. He looked so much like his father—same fair hair and pale green eyes—and yet he had inherited Maddison's petite frame.

She stroked his fringe off his forehead and smiled. "Good night. I love you so much."

He grinned, flashing his recently earned new tooth that had now grown to about half the size of the others. "I love you too."

Sitting on the mattress beside Ruby, Maddison kissed her daughter's brow. "I'm proud of how you're coping with what happened today." Ruby was a smaller replica of Maddison—short, petite and with long dark hair and brown eyes. She looked younger than her age and had an unwavering expression of sweetness like she could never do or say a thing wrong. Not always the case, though.

"What happened to Ruby?" Riley asked, sitting up, pulling out his freshly tucked-in sheets.

Maddison frowned. "I told you. She had a nasty bully do something very mean to her today in front of the class."

Ruby's brow furrowed. "It's no big deal. It truly wasn't."

"Dad said I should punch bullies in the nose if they be mean to me," Riley said, emphasising the word 'punch' with a sharp jab of his fist out in front of him. "Then kick 'em in the balls."

Maddison sighed. "Honey, you would go find a teacher and tell them what happened. But something like this will never happen again." Not if she had any say in the matter. "Now both of you lie down. It's bedtime."

As the kids settled in their beds, Maddison looked away, not quite ready to admit that they would have to go to another school because of what she had done.

Only a couple of hours ago, a no-nonsense letter from Sabrina Collins had landed in both Maddison and Ben's email accounts. It stated that Maddison's threatening behaviour breached the students and parents' school and community guidelines. The safety of the children at Gladstone Primary Private School was paramount. Maddison would be granted one-time access to collect her children's belongings from the administration building but would not be permitted on schoolgrounds going forward, and if she did, a restraining order could be sought. Therefore, it was strongly advised Ben and Maddison seek alternative schooling options for their children.

"I love you so, so much," she said to Ruby. "If you need to talk to me about anything, I'm right here, okay?"

Ruby nodded. "I love you too."

Maddison got to her feet and smiled at her children, though it appeared out of sync with the rest of her emotionless features.

On the way to the basement home-gym, she passed Ben who was still sitting in the living room. He turned to look at her. "All okay?"

"Just getting in a workout before bed."

His eyes widened. "Another one?"

"Well, I could sit on the couch, eat chocolate and get fat if you'd prefer that?"

"I would prefer you to be happy." He sighed, eyes closing for a moment. "And, maybe, now and then, to spend some time with me."

"That would not make me happy."

He drew a deep breath, attempting to fill the dark void her offhand comment carved out of his chest. "You don't want to talk about what happened today?"

She shook her head. "Nothing to talk about."

His palm slid down his face. "You threatened to kill a little girl."

"And she deserved it."

"Maddison, think about it." He pointed in the direction of the school. "What you did and said was not rational. Not in the slightest. You're spending hours every day working out. You're bombing yourself out each night, just so you can go to sleep."

"And who's to blame for that, eh?"

"It doesn't matter who's to blame." His voice was more forceful than he had intended, so he softened it, yet the strain was obvious. "I think you need to talk to someone. To clear out some of this painful past you're carrying around."

"I don't want to clear out the past. And I'll handle my life the way I choose."

He waved his hand as if to say, 'do what the hell you bloody well want then'.

And she would. She marched down the stairs, slammed the door behind her, put headphones on and blasted techno music into her eardrums.

For the next two hours, she did leg presses, calf raises, deadlifts, bicep curls, tricep dips, chin-ups, press-ups, shoulder presses, and sit-ups until she nearly vomited. She yanked her headphones off, threw them across the room and lay there on the bench, forearm over her eyes until her nausea and dizziness settled.

When able to move again, she crawled on her hands and knees up the stairs, her legs unable to hold her weight. At the top, using the wall and door handle, she dragged herself up onto her feet. Each shuffled step ignited pain so great she bit down on her lip to stop from crying.

In the kitchen, she leaned against the wall beside the fridge, panting. She pulled out a bottle of sauvignon blanc and reached into the cupboard above for her stash of Zolpidem and Diazepam—a hypnotic and a relaxant prescribed to treat her insomnia.

She shook as she popped the tablets from their casing onto her tongue, then drank deeply from the wine bottle, only stopping when the heat of the alcohol burned her throat and she coughed.

Her leg muscles trembled and ached, almost gave way beneath her, as she staggered up the hallway to her bedroom. Ben was still in the living room watching whatever TV show he was currently obsessed with. His life could be summated by three activities: running his business, time with the children when he arrived home, then when the kids were asleep, TV. He would come to bed sometime after she was already lost to oblivion.

Their relationship hadn't always been like that. On their wedding day, as their carefully curated playlist had blared in the packed reception hall, she had circled her arms loosely around her new husband's shoulders as they danced. When she stared into his green eyes, the intensity of emotion she held for him burned like a fire within her and filled her heart to overflowing. In his gaze and the set of his face, his fierce love for her was reflected. She had been waiting for 'him' her entire life and there he was, in her arms, promising to spend the rest of his days with her.

Now, she could barely look at him. If not for their children, for her deep maternal instincts to give them some semblance of stability, she would be gone. And maybe, just maybe, staying in that dead marriage was a way to punish her husband day after day by sucking every last bit of joy out of his life.

Ben knew all that. He would never admit that to her, though, because he didn't want that punishment to end. His miserable marriage was the only thing that got him through each day, knowing that he was paying for what he had done. It didn't alleviate his guilt, but it made it bearable.

Ben was the type of man who could make women stumble over their words no matter how composed they assumed themselves to be. He was difficult to look in the eyes because he was the most handsome man most people had ever met.

None of that excused him but pointed to the historical fact that men like him, with abundant sexual opportunities, were the most difficult to make and keep monogamous.

In the early years of his marriage, he had resisted advances from women that other men would have struggled to turn away. Opportunities that came with the territory. He was a good-looking personal trainer and worked with many fit, attractive people.

But when he was thirty-one, along came Amber—a seventeen-year-old client who had been referred to him by her friend. Tall, athletic curves, long dark hair, plumped lips, big blue eyes. Beyond sexy and she knew it within every cell of her flawless body. Merely thinking about touching her, let alone kissing, let alone more, had made Ben so hard he could barely think straight.

Amber had ruthlessly flirted with him from the first moment they had met. And for a while, he had resisted. But over time, she artfully worked his willpower down to useless powdery dust.

One evening, after a training session, when all the patrons had gone home, he had pulled her into his arms, slammed her against the gym's window, and used her body like his life had depended on it. He sought that opiate again and again. Every moment alone, he spent it with her. In his office, on the gym equipment after hours, in his car.

But, predictably, the hormones and lust dissipated. Amber went from a perfect body that had once sent Ben into a sexual frenzy, to an annoying, overly chatty seventeen-year-old girl who liked to talk more about the dramas her school friends were engaged in than anything worthwhile. His rationality returned and they parted ways.

Until the next opportunity arose. Then another. And another. Year after year. By the time his wife had found out about his last indiscretion, he had been with at least fifty, maybe sixty, perhaps even a hundred different women.

Most of them were staff. Clients. Women he met at conferences or in bars. He'd screw them in the alleyways, dark corners or toilets of clubs. In taxis. Parks. Their bed. His bed. He didn't waste time on indecision; if an opportunity wasn't a sure thing from the get-go, he moved on to someone who was.

That wasn't his life anymore, though. He didn't do anything like that now. His last affair had been a lesson beyond lessons, so much so, he could barely get a hard-on these days. He wouldn't care if he never got an erection ever again.

Maddison was finding it much more difficult to move past that time in their marriage. She continued to dwell in the shadows cast by her husband. And so, they were always stuck back in time, his last conquest on repeat, over and over again. It droned like crazed circus music in the background of everything. All their decisions, reactions, and private thoughts stemmed from that day. All stemmed from the belief that Ben had once entertained about the importance of his genitals. Turned out, he was right—his genitals were important, just not in the way he had assumed.

Some people weren't analytical enough, self-reflective, nor willing to change their behaviour without life swinging a metaphorical wrecking bar at their face and forcing change to happen. Ben was that kind of person. He was getting help now. Saw a therapist every single week without fail. He didn't drink a drop of alcohol, nor take any kind of medications. He was dedicated to doing the work, no matter how hard it was.

His actions now propelled him upwards, away from that man he had once been. In many, many ways, he already was a better person for his wife and, mostly, for his kids. They had never deserved the older model.

When Maddison had painfully made it to her bedroom like she was a withered, sickened nana rather than the forty-one-year-old woman she was, she showered, crawled into bed, and laid back, looking up at the ceiling through the darkness. Even with the air conditioner running, the fan above her tiredly turning, humidity crept into the room and coated everything.

Outside, the streets were dark, illuminated by dull streetlamps. Quiet. Moisture was thick in the summer air. No breeze to shake the leaves in the big gum tree that stood tall in the neighbour's front yard. Families in the surrounding households were getting children to bed, having their evening showers or sitting together in the living room to watch TV.

That kind of normality didn't find a home in the Brooks' house anymore.

As the medication took effect, leading Maddison away from the uncomfortable dross of reality, her blinks grew long and slow. Her thoughts and emotions ebbed away, quietened. The next wave crept up without her even realising, swallowing her whole.

By the time Ben came to bed, blinking was like rubbing sandpaper over his eyeballs. He collapsed onto the mattress, climbed under the covers and watched his wife in the darkness. She was on her back, mouth open, snoring. He could scream, and she wouldn't wake.

He stroked a hand down her face. "I'm sorry. I wish I could take it all back. Every last moment. But I can't." And that was his agony; he couldn't change what had happened. What *he* had made happen. He just had to watch on as the aftermath fell around him like molten lead and bones spewing down upon them.

CHAPTER 6

Tina's house was a partially renovated Queenslander, set upon two-acres of cleared land and surrounded by arid bush. No light from streetlamps reached her property. On that night, a new moon hung in the air, offering little illumination. When Tina's eyelids snapped open with a start, her bedroom was smothered in blackness.

Something had awoken her. A sound. She reached for her bedside lamp and doused the room in dull light. Her heart was thumping hard in her chest as her gaze flittered around.

Nothing there.

She tilted her head. Listening hard. Listening long. Her loud breathing filled the silence. The corrugated roof ticked and clinked—usual sounds. Crickets. The odd caw of a lone bird still awake at that hour.

She was daring herself to get up and investigate, but she had seen enough movies to know that searching for danger always ended badly. But it was no more comforting to stay where she was and be chopped to pieces in the dark as she tried to go back to sleep.

One foot over the side of the bed. Then another. All the worst imaginings filled her mind: a hand shooting out and gripping her ankle, a man standing motionless behind the curtain with an axe, or a grinning lunatic tucked away in the darkest corner of the house.

She rushed to stand, leapt her next step and scurried into the hall, throwing on the light. One room after the other, she checked for unwanted visitors.

Nothing.

But something had awoken her. Something loud. She searched her sleep-laden memory for an answer. Was her name called? Was it a knock? Perhaps a scampering of footsteps across the timber floor? Small, light feet, quick as a greyhound. She couldn't pin down an answer.

Maybe it was a dream? Sure, that's one very reasonable explanation. Not the right one, but it was enough to ease her mind at that moment.

Tina turned on the light in the kitchen and went to the sink to fill a glass with tap water. She was hot and thirsty, so she gulped down the water. Her heart was beating wildly.

In her peripheral, a blur of colour sped past. She gasped, dropped the glass in the sink with a loud crash and spun.

But nothing was there.

She turned a circle.

Still nothing.

A hand to her head and a long, deep breath to calm her nerves. Only then did she notice the yellow sticky note stuck to her fridge door—a bright, small square against monochrome white. She owned sticky notes, but she kept them in her desk drawer in the room designated as her office. She never used them. Certainly not to then stick on the fridge. It would look too untidy.

Something was written on the note. She tiptoed to the fridge and read it.

Milk

Bread

Washing powder

Hand soap

The handwriting wasn't hers. Her brow furrowed as she read the list over and over again.

"What the hell is this doing on my fridge door?"

She stepped back. Tingles fanned down her neck and over her arms. Her stomach clenched with fear as realisation dawned—someone had been inside her home. She raced to the fridge door, ripped the note off, scrunched it in her fist and threw it across the kitchen.

She sought a rational explanation and eventually landed on a couple of panicked excuses. Maybe Chris had come over. He hadn't lived in that house for years now, but he did still own half of it. From time to time, he would stop in and help her with the lawn. Two acres of land was difficult to manage single-handedly on top of full-time work.

After their break-up, she hadn't the mental strength to move from the one place where all her memories were housed, and she didn't have the money to pay Chris out. They came to an arrangement where they would continue to each pay half of the mortgage payments. When they would sell in the future, Chris would get his money back. That's why he tried to keep the place maintained—to protect his asset.

But he never visited without her asking him to. Not that she was aware of. Then again, she had never changed the locks. Never a need. Not even a thought to. Maybe the ghostly presence lingering in her home the night she had arrived back from the cemetery was Chris's. He may have dropped by to look at Kadie's belongings in private.

But the note's handwriting wasn't his and it still didn't explain *why* he would write it.

Maybe a neighbour had called in while she was out. She wasn't strict about locking up the house. Not out there in the middle of nowhere. One of the older residents nearby could have dementia. Came walking. Disoriented. Entered her house. Made a note. And left.

Tina pressed her fingers to her temples, squeezed her eyes closed.

Perhaps it was a friend. Stopping by to help her out during that tough time. Either Mandy or Saskia. They would be worried about her. Probably checked the fridge and cupboards and wrote a list for her, knowing that grief would leave her scattered. They may have thought they were helping by ensuring she wouldn't forget anything when she visited the shops.

She would text Mandy and Saskia tomorrow and find out for sure.

The rational explanation was there, waiting for her to find it, but it was late, and she wasn't thinking clearly.

She kept all the lights on in the house and went back to her room. Despite the glow from her bedside lamp, she closed her eyes and, in time, managed to fall asleep.

* * *

Sunday morning, Tina was more rested than she had anticipated. The grief cloud had shifted. A sliver of sunshine had returned. After a shower, coffee and some Vegemite toast, she dared to pick up the scrunched note from the kitchen floor and unfurl it in her hands. The crinkled veins distorted the handwriting a little, but the certainty she had last night that this scrawl was unfamiliar, returned.

"What the bloody hell is going on?" she mumbled.

During Tina's marriage to Chris, they'd had many close friends, but Mandy was the only one remaining from that time. Mandy's husband, Trevor, had worked with Chris at the mine. Tina's other friends had slowly drifted away—the heavy, messy emotion of the last three years too much for them. She didn't resent them for it. Her own emotions were too much, so she could understand that others wouldn't have known how to deal with them.

Tina typed a text to Mandy.

TINA: *Did you stop by yesterday and leave a shopping note for me on the fridge?*

It took only thirty seconds for a reply to ping back.

MANDY: *Not at all. I've been flat out with work and kids. You know how it is. We should catch up for a coffee next weekend.*

TINA: *Sounds good.*

They decided on a place and time to meet before Tina started typing a text to send to Saskia. Saskia was an old friend from high school. They had lost contact until Saskia returned to Gladstone a couple of years ago after residing in Brisbane for a decade. She had missed the messiest part of Tina's life, which was most likely the reason they were still friends.

TINA: *Did you stop by yesterday and leave a note for me?*

Tina was almost through her coffee before Saskia replied.

SASKIA: *No. I'm spending the week camping at Moreton Island, remember?*

TINA: *Of course. Completely slipped my mind. We will have to catch up when you get home.*

SASKIA: *Sure. I'll let you know when I'm back in town.*

Tina sank onto a chair at her dining table. A small circular table with four seats that fit snugly within the kitchen area. She focused on the note again. How it got there was a complete mystery.

But as people were apt to do when they didn't know the real reasons why something was occurring, she readily accepted the next best answer—*she was in error*. She must have written it while tired and muddled. After all, that week had been the most exhausting and distracting of the year. It could also explain why the handwriting was unfamiliar and why she forgot writing it and pinning it on her fridge.

A one-off incident. Didn't warrant fixating on it. So, she wouldn't. And she didn't.

CHAPTER 7

Isabelle's legs and shoulders ached, and her eyes were dry and sore. She had barely been able to last another minute on her feet, so she left the salon early, delegating Renee, one of her senior hairdressers, to close up.

She drove home to her brick, three-bedroom lowset, situated in a suburb where original industry-workers' homes were built. Not what anyone would call upmarket. But until she had met Chris, she had paid her mortgage herself.

Thankfully, she'd bought her house before the second big boom had hit the town—during the construction of three LNG plants. An influx of blue-collar working men, some with families, many without, converged on Gladstone. Out-of-town investors flocked to buy properties while the rents were soaring. Residents raced to get into the market. A firehose of lending. Mortgage brokers won awards for simply turning up to work. House prices and the cost of every single service in town went through the roof.

During those five years, renting was impossible for some. The buyer's market was unattainable for anyone not earning the big bucks on the gas project. Some original residents left. Outsiders took their place, changing the face of Gladstone.

But like a prick to a taut, overinflated balloon, all that ended when the gas plant construction was complete. House prices crashed and rents bottomed out almost at pre-boom levels. Businesses closed down. Workers left town in the thousands.

Isabelle had ridden the wave up and down.

Chris's big, black ute was parked out front on the street when she drove into the single, covered garage. She had offered the garage to Chris when he had moved in, but he refused, said it didn't feel right to come in and take it over.

The scent of smoke and the undercurrent of roasting meat was strong in the air when Isabelle went inside. Chris had spent the afternoon in the backyard with the barbeque. That's one thing those old houses had going for them—they were situated on big, spacious blocks of land. A smile flittered across Isabelle's lips. She had never had anyone, since she was sixteen, to take care of her. As a single mum, a business owner, and with her parents living three states away in Tasmania, that's just how it was. Sure, she ate out some nights and some lazy Sunday mornings, Juliette had made her Vegemite on toast and a cup of coffee, but that was as far as it went.

She kicked off her shoes at the back door and joined Chris on the patio. The scent of caramelised meat and smoke intensified. A new passion of his.

He had got suckered into watching hours of meat smoking YouTube videos. Nothing much else to do when alone in his donga each night while in camp at the mine. Last Christmas, he had bought himself a smoker and, on his days off, he would prepare slow-cooked pork ribs or brisket, sometimes roast lamb or grilled steak.

When married to Tina, he didn't cook. Never even considered it. Their marriage had been traditional—he hadn't known there was another way to exist. He hadn't wanted to know. He liked Tina taking care of him.

He mowed the lawns when needed and fixed things around the house—usually months, sometimes years, after being made aware of the loose hinge, stuck window, or leaking tap. And he earned the lion's share of the money, so that's where his obligations ended.

Tina never complained, so it wasn't an issue. Maybe. That's what he told himself. Truthfully, he had an inkling their situation may have benefited him more, but he didn't change because he never had to.

Repeating that same mistake with Isabelle was not an option, though. That morning, like most days he was home, he vacuumed, loaded the dishwasher, and made their bed. Small tasks that filled him with a sense of pride, especially when Isabelle flashed a big, appreciative smile and thanked him. If he had smiled and thanked his ex in the same way, maybe their marriage would have survived.

After a quick change into shorts and a singlet, Isabelle joined Chris outside on the back patio.

"Hello there," Isabelle said, kissing his cheek as he fumbled with probes that pierced a piece of meat wrapped in aluminium foil on the barbeque plate.

Smoke and the acrid scent of burning charcoal filled the air. Her stomach swirled a little and she swallowed hard.

"Hi. You're home early," he said.

She nodded, swallowed again. "I'm exhausted. So unlike me."

"I hope you're not getting sick."

"That's the last thing I need."

"Go sit down. I've got dinner covered."

She didn't need her arm twisted and sank onto the cushioned seat of the new outdoor setting Chris had recently bought. Hers had been an old set that she had owned for fifteen years. The heritage green enamel had chipped off, revealing the blackened and, in places, rusted steel beneath. But mostly, it had hurt to sit on. Like a cold rock.

"What are we having tonight?" she asked, trying to summon some enthusiasm. Usually, she loved everything he cooked, but that afternoon, the smells were making her salivate and not in a good way.

"Beef ribs. Got another hour or so to go." He turned to her and frowned. "Your face is very white."

Her throat was thickening. A slight gagging sensation. "I don't feel great. It's the… I'm sorry, but I can't handle the scent of that charcoal. Smells noxious."

He grimaced, bent to look at the big pack of briquettes sitting beside the barbeque. The thick paper bag ruffled. "It's the same brand I always use."

She got to her feet. "I might go sit inside."

"I hope you don't have a stomach bug or something."

She stopped mid-stride. The last time she had experienced sensitivity to odours, she was pregnant. Her mother had kept an empty glass bottle—clean and dry, but it had once contained crushed garlic—in the cupboard near the drinking glasses. The scent of garlic had subtly lingered, so every time she had opened the cupboard, it would waft out and make her gag. That's how Isabelle's mother had known her teenage daughter was pregnant.

She shook her head and laughed.

"What?" he asked, a wavering half-smile.

"I was thinking about when I last felt like this. I was fifteen and pregnant. Can you imagine if that's what this is?"

His eyes widened. "It's not possible, is it?"

She shrugged. "I'm thirty-eight. It's certainly possible, but highly unprobab..." She trailed off. Just before the wedding, her contraceptive pill packet had fallen behind the side table, unbeknownst to her. By the time she was able to book an appointment with her doctor to arrange another prescription, five days had passed. When Chris arrived home from the mine, she was back on track, but it would have been enough time to affect her fertility.

"What?" he asked.

She waved his question away. "Nothing. I'm sure it's just a stomach bug."

The backdoor screen opened, and Juliette bounded out. Her blonde hair was tied up in a high ponytail. She wore the yellow high-vis shirt and bottle-green trousers that all workers at the alumina refinery had to wear. Her hastily toed-off boots were left outside the front door.

When no greetings or even a smile was offered her way, she frowned and looked between her mother and Chris. "Have I interrupted something?"

Isabelle shook her head. "No. I'm not feeling well. That's all. I was just heading inside for a shower."

Juliette lifted her hands in a warding off gesture. "Don't come near me with your germs. I haven't earnt any sick leave yet."

Isabelle laughed. "So bloody dramatic."

* * *

After Isabelle showered and changed into her pyjamas, the tight sickliness in her throat had loosened. Chris ushered the beef ribs inside on a metal tray, covered in aluminium foil to keep them warm while they rested.

Isabelle's empty stomach growled. Maybe that's all it was—hunger confused as nausea.

The three of them sat down to eat. She eyed the food. Baked potatoes and a big garden salad. "This looks delicious."

"Smell okay?"

She lowered her nose closer to the ribs and inhaled. "Beautiful."

"Sure does," Juliette said. "I'm starving."

Chris grinned, gestured to the food. "Well, dig in. There's plenty there."

Since Chris had moved in, there had been an unexpected but wonderful change to the dynamic in that house. Men brought a different energy, which was a new experience for Isabelle. Especially someone like Chris who was eternally laidback and unflustered. He marched along with life at the same speed, no matter the rhythm of the circumstance.

Isabelle cut into a beef rib and forked some into her mouth. It was tender, smoky, gamey and covered in spices. "Yum," she said with a grin and reached over the table, resting her hand on top of her husband's.

"I agree," Juliette said. "Next time you're cooking, let me know because I'd like to watch the whole process, so I can learn how to do it."

Chris sat taller, chest puffed. "Sure. The next Saturday I'm home, we'll cook a brisket."

Juliette finished the mouthful she was chewing. "You're on."

* * *

Isabelle headed to bed early. She could not keep her eyes open any longer. After showering, Chris joined her. He always came to bed when she did. Another Chris-generated difference in her life, but one that increased the magnetic pull between them.

He drew her into his arms and kissed her lips. His blue eyes met hers. "Still not well, hey?"

"Just a little tired." She rolled out of his embrace and stared at the ceiling, frowning.

"You're worried?"

"A little," she whispered.

"About what?"

"About the potential that I could be pregnant." She glanced at him. "About what that would mean for us."

"It means we'll be parents. What else could it mean?"

She sighed. "I'm worried about how you'd react to that. You're" – she gestured to him – "older than me. We've never discussed children. I assumed we were both on the same page that our time for such things was over. Yet here we are with the real possibility."

He reached for her, a gentle hand to her chin, nudging her to look at him. "Issy, I'd be over the moon if you were pregnant."

She blinked, lips falling open. "You would?"

He smiled. "You have no idea how happy it would make me."

She sat up then, ran fingers through her hair. "I thought you'd be... I don't know... angry?"

His brow furrowed. "I'm not sure how I ever gave you that impression."

She shook her head. "I'm not sure either. Maybe I just assumed. But you'd be happy?"

"Extremely."

She rested back on her pillows, smiling. "Well, that's a big relief." The last thing she ever wanted was to raise another child on her own. But abortion wasn't in her nature either. She knew the love of a child. The joy they brought, even when, because of circumstance, there were more doubts than hopes that a baby could be a blessing. "But no use getting ahead of ourselves. I may just have a stomach bug."

He kissed her cheek. "I'll buy a test tomorrow, so we rule it out, okay?"

She smiled. "Sure. Thank you."

"Now go to sleep," he said. "And get a good night's rest."

As Chris attempted to fall asleep, his chest was tight with excitement. His stomach looped with hope. More than anything, he ached to hear from Isabelle's lips tomorrow that the result of her pregnancy test was positive.

CHAPTER 8

Maddison slowly sat up and rolled her legs over the side of the bed until her feet touched the soft carpet beneath. A deep throbbing ache in her muscles. She winced as she got to her feet. Her mind was gluey, hazy from the drugs, but was screaming at her to get busy—go to the gym before the kids woke, head out for a run, something—but walking was unbearable. Anything more strenuous and her thigh muscles would collapse. She wasn't sure once she hit the ground if she would be able to claw her way back up.

Ben was in the kitchen, sitting on a stool at the breakfast bar, a coffee to his right, and *The Courier-Mail* spread out before him. He still liked the real thing—the scent of paper and ink, the ritual of leafing through the pages. His brain worked better with print; it hadn't rewired quickly enough to take in digital articles.

He lifted his gaze when she shuffled to the coffee machine. "You feeling okay?"

She shook her head, too tired and too sore to don her facade of 'everything's fine'. "I can't bear to tell the kids they have to go to a new school."

Ben closed the paper. Slouched. "I know. They were settled and changing will be disruptive. But, you know, they're kids. Good kids. Happy, sociable kids. They'll make new friends, and, in a few months, they'll feel settled again."

Tears glossed Maddison's eyes. She was a terrible mother. As much as she tried not to be, she always screwed it up. Never usually to that extent, though. "I'm going to talk to Sabrina today. See if I can change her mind."

Ben's neck and shoulder muscles clenched. A tic in his jaw. "I'm not sure that's a good idea."

"I've got nothing to lose."

Sabrina could get the police involved, he thought, but he didn't say it out loud, not wanting to add to Maddison's worries. It bemused him how she couldn't understand that what she had done yesterday crossed huge boundaries. "Leave it alone, Maddison. There's no coming back from it. Let's just concentrate on enrolling the kids in a new school. The gym has cover for the whole day, so I can sit the kids down once they're awake and let them know what's happened. I can drop by the school this afternoon to collect their things. Who knows, it may work better for them in the long run. Breanna always says how good North-West Primary is. All three of her kids go there—"

"I don't give a damn what Breanna has to say about anything!" She threw her empty cup in the sink. "I'm their mother. She has zero input."

He lifted both hands, suppressed his sigh. "Fine. I was just saying." He should have known better than to talk about any of their female staff outside of work. No greater trigger in that household.

"I'm going to shower, then I'm heading to the school to see if there's something I can do. I'll get on my knees and beg if that's what it takes." She strode away, mumbling under her breath, "Sabrina Collins would love to see that, wouldn't she?"

"I'll come too then."

"I don't need a babysitter," she snapped from over her shoulder. "Besides, someone needs to stay here with Ruby and Riley."

He pursed his lips. If yesterday's performance was any indication, his wife most definitely did need a sitter, but he wasn't about to tip her over the edge again by admitting that.

* * *

Maddison's cheeks were hot, blotchy, as she sat in the principal's office across from Sabrina. Two plastic bags full of Ruby and Riley's schoolbooks and stationery lay at her feet. Her throat was constricted, achy, her stomach a tensing mass of nerves.

Sabrina's obvious disdain unsettled Maddison, but she remained steady because her children's happiness was on the line.

"Firstly, I want to apologise very sincerely for what I said yesterday. It was not okay, and I do not feel proud of it."

Sabrina frowned. "I would hope not. As it was, I had to talk Mr and Mrs Rankin out of involving the police. They knew about your *past*, so they were kind enough to show some understanding."

Maddison cringed. Gladstone wasn't that small but trying to hide anything was impossible. The friendship chains were too incestuous, and gossip spread like an STI at a swingers' party.

"There's no excuse for how you behaved. In all my years as principal, I've never witnessed anything like that. I've had parents punch each other in the hall. I've had kids scream at me. I've had parents scream at me, but never have I had a mother threaten to gut a nine-year-old child."

The nest of nerves in Maddison's belly expanded. "I apologise." Her words were weak and soft.

Sabrina shifted in her seat, gritted her teeth. "I accept your apology."

Maddison swallowed hard, trying to loosen the painful contraction of her throat. "I hate that Ruby and Riley are being punished for something that wasn't their fault. Is it possible that they can stay here?"

Sabrina's eyes widened. "The safety of my other students is paramount. I don't take any pleasure in your children being the inadvertent victims of this decision, but that rests on your shoulders."

"I would have expected a little more compassion."

An eyebrow rose. "Likewise."

"My children have been through so much. They can't take this—"

"They're both very resilient," Sabrina said. "I'm sure they'll do well in whichever school you find them a placement."

Maddison leaned forward, ignoring the strain on her muscles as she rested her elbows on the desk and splayed her hands on the tabletop. "Please, Sabrina. I can't do this to them."

"I think this is more about you than them. They'll be fine. But, as for you, I recommend getting some professional help." Sabrina rose to her feet, walked around the desk to the office door and opened it. "Now, if you'll excuse me, I have a very big job I need to keep on with."

Maddison implored Sabrina with her gaze. "Is there nothing I can say to change your mind?"

"We have policies outlining our zero-tolerance stance on the type of behaviour you displayed yesterday. Good luck with finding your children a new placement elsewhere."

Maddison slowly stood, lifting the bags as she did, pain pulsing through her body. When she came closer to Sabrina, she lowered her voice to a harsh whisper. "You're a nasty piece of work, aren't you? See that's the problem with women like you. You get a little bit of insignificant power and you think you're better than everyone—"

"Get out!" Sabrina roared, her face turning bright red.

"Calm the hell down. I'm leaving anyway." Maddison straightened her skirt, held her head high and shuffled down the hall with as much dignity as she could, considering the blades twisting in her muscles with every step.

She didn't look at the smug-faced receptionist as she pushed through the doors, out into the school carpark. Only when she was in her car, hands gripping the steering wheel, did she scream at the top of her lungs until her throat was on fire. Anguish bled out in a gush of tears.

* * *

When Maddison arrived home, she didn't go inside to face Ben or the kids until she was composed. She squeezed eyedrops into each eye to banish the tear-stained redness. A trick she'd learned over the years trying to hide the pain that lived inside her bones.

She was fast finding that anger was more difficult to stifle. But, then again, anger was merely a loud, sharp manifestation of suppressed fear or emotional pain. The physical presentation of anger didn't hurt as much as the darker, more intense emotions causing it. Anger was a great tool to avoid the storm beneath, but it possessed its own unique, harsh consequences.

Ben was sitting with the children at the breakfast bar. Each was eating cereal and milk from a bowl. Ruby and Riley were dressed well, hair brushed neatly, but in day clothes, not school uniforms as they should be if not for Maddison.

"How did you go?" Ben asked.

She shook her head, forced a tight smile so as not to worry the children.

Ruby's shoulders slumped in time with her harrumph. "Why do I have to go to a new school?"

Ben leaned across the bench and patted Ruby's hand. "I told you why, honey."

She forcefully threw her spoon into her near-empty bowl. The metal clanged against the china. "I didn't do anything wrong, though."

Maddison rushed to Ruby, held her head to her chest and stroked her hair. "I know, sweetie. Sometimes these things happen, and we don't like it, but we just have to get on with it anyway. But none of this was your fault. Not one bit."

It was Maddison's fault, but she couldn't admit that out loud. She may have lost faith in herself, but she did not need her children to do the same. They needed strength and stability and a leader at the helm they could trust.

Riley wrinkled his nose. "I don't want to go to a new school. I didn't even get to say goodbye to my friends."

"We can invite them over after school to play anytime, mate," Ben said.

Riley crossed his arms and pouted. "Still not fair."

No, life was not fair. If Maddison had learned that earlier and more gradually, perhaps that truth may not have been so overwhelming. Maddison stood up taller and clapped her hands. "All right, enough of this moping around. We've got the day off, let's go to the beach for a swim."

Ruby and Riley's eyes widened. They tried so hard to stop from smiling, but their glee won in the end.

"Yess!" Riley said, punching the air above his head.

Ruby rolled her eyes at her big brother and grinned. "Sure, I guess we can go to the beach."

* * *

From outside observers, the Brooks family looked like any other happy family as they spent the morning in the sun at Tannum Sands Main Beach. The water held an all-year-round sub-tropical warmth. For hours they ventured in and out of the blue-green ocean, jumping over waves and paddling deep. On the beach, they moulded the hot sand into shapes as the briny breeze blew their hair around their faces.

The kids slept on the thirty-minute drive back into town, their heads lolling against the windows, mouths open. They were bright-eyed again the moment Ben parked the car in the garage. He sent them to the shower to wash the sunscreen and sand away and dress into dry, clean clothes because that afternoon, they had their first interview with a prospective primary school.

Ten minutes before they were to leave, Ben went to his bedroom for a belt and found Maddison sitting on the end of the bed, face in her hands.

He sat beside her, and she flinched at the unexpected intrusion.

"Oh," she said. "I didn't realise you were here."

"Let me handle the school interview, okay?" Maddison parted her lips to intercept, but Ben kept on. "You relax. Take a bath or nap or do some yoga."

"You don't trust me?" she asked.

He grimaced and bit back his sharp reply. "That's not it at all. I think you're dealing with a lot and I'd like to take this burden off you."

Maddison nodded, knowing she had hit a wall. That happened from time to time, but more and more lately. "Fine."

He leaned in to kiss her head, exactly like he would have in the earlier years of their marriage. Maddison shifted away and stood before his lips could meet her skin.

A deep, resounding throb in the centre of his chest. He missed the intimacy of that small act. He missed the willingness she had once shown him. He had forgotten how her body felt against his.

With a sigh, he got to his feet and strode silently out of the room.

CHAPTER 9

C hris went to the chemist after Isabelle had left for her salon. He scanned the shelves for a pregnancy test, found one that said all the right things on the box, and headed to the counter to pay for it. His heart was racing. All his efforts were used to hide the excitement that dwelled inside him from reaching his face as the young check-out clerk processed the transaction.

When home, he tucked the pregnancy test beside his rows of underwear and socks in the drawer Isabelle had cleared out for him when he had moved in. All day, he thought about it in there. He imagined when Isabelle would come home, disappear to the bathroom, only to emerge sometime later with an answer. Every time he reached that part, his stomach would flutter.

For the rest of the day, Chris did everything he could to distract himself. He went to the gym and worked out, then did a little grocery shopping, so he could prepare something for dinner. Besides smoking meat on the barbeque, his prowess in the kitchen was limited. In the early days after separating from Tina, he had delivered some disastrous results and made himself severely ill twice. But, eventually, he got a little better. At least he didn't over- or under-cook everything now. If he followed a video showing each step of a recipe, stopping and starting when needed, he fared okay.

After that, he cleaned—loaded the dishwasher, made the bed and cut the lawn. He even thought about heading out to his old property to mow for Tina. He had once done that a lot. A part of him didn't feel right leaving such a big job for her to take care of. She worked more days than he did in a calendar year. The hours weren't as long, and she didn't have the tedious flights he had to contend with, but still…

When Isabelle had discovered that Chris still mowed Tina's lawns and did a little maintenance, she hadn't approved. Not that she ever outright said so, it was more the way she had reacted. Her expression was tight when she spoke about it. A small hint of disbelief in her tone. Then, for the rest of the afternoon, her replies were shorter and abrupt.

The last thing Chris wanted was to fail at his second marriage, too. Divorces were brutal. His was one of the hardest times in his life. So, he took the hint and reduced how often he visited his former home. And if he did go, he kept it to himself.

Tina didn't give him grief about it. But, then again, Tina was never the type of person to be petty like that anyway. She had been through so much in her early life and earned a perspective he hadn't seen in anyone else. A perspective he still respected after all these years.

He wondered how Tina would take the news if Isabelle was pregnant. She wouldn't be happy. Not even a little.

There he went again, getting ahead of himself. He had to keep in mind, even though it would dull the polish on his excitement each time he did, that there was a huge chance this pregnancy was a false alarm. And even if Isabelle were pregnant, he couldn't live his life according to how Tina may or may not feel about matters. That relationship was dead. He was still alive and racing in a new direction.

Sometimes, only sometimes, the pace of his new life was too fast. He missed the quiet, familiar, comfortable speed he and Tina had operated at. With her, he had been himself from the beginning, and he had only sunk deeper and deeper into authenticity the longer they were together.

Over their marriage, they had grown to think the same. Grown to depend on each other so much that after he had moved out, it took months and months to break the habit of reaching for his phone to call her, or her being his first thought when he had gossip or wishing her warm body were right there beside him when he awoke alone in his bed each morning.

He had missed *them* with every aching part of his heart for a long time.

None of that meant that he didn't adore Isabelle. Love Isabelle. But she was still new. He hadn't hit that comfortable point. He was still trying to be someone else— the man he thought she wanted him to be. He farted quietly. He used toilet spray after going. He put the seat down. He was testing how crude he could go with his jokes. He still needed to find the limit to how relaxed Isabelle would allow him to be.

What he was sure of, though, was that he wanted this baby. He wanted this baby so much. He was already envisioning teaching his boy or girl how to kick a footy and ride a bike. Weekends fishing for barramundi at Awoonga Dam or heading out in a tinnie to Curtis Island for the day. Gladstone was a great town for a kid to grow up in. He was one to know; he'd lived there his whole life.

* * *

Chris was sitting on the couch, his leg bouncing up and down as he watched the golf and intermittently checked on the pastabake he had in the oven, when the garage door opened around six. His grin extended across his face, but when Isabelle came inside, smelling of hair dye and perfume, he hid his excitement.

"Hi," she said when she met him in the living room and kissed his cheek.

He still couldn't believe how he had managed to meet and marry a woman as beautiful as her. "Hi. Good day?"

She sighed and sank onto the couch beside him. "Busy. Not that I'm complaining."

"How are you feeling?"

"Still very tired. Even a little nauseous this morning. But it was better by about mid-morning."

"Did you have morning sickness while pregnant with Juliette?"

"Every single day until about four months into the pregnancy."

"I bought a test today." He got to his feet. "Come on. Let's do this because I can't handle the suspense any longer."

She giggled. "If I knew you were this impatient, I would have snuck home at lunch and done the test then."

"That would have saved me from a very, very long day."

When in their bedroom, he opened the drawer and handed her the box. "Pee on the stick thingy. Wait five minutes. If there're two blue lines, you're pregnant. If there's only one, you're not."

"That easy?" she asked with a brow raised and a small grin.

"That easy." He shooed her out of the room. "Go now before Juliette gets home."

She hastened her pace to the bathroom. "I'm going."

Five minutes later, Isabelle returned. Her face was ashen. Chris's heart thumped hard. She held up the stick and he had to step closer to see.

Two blue lines.

Pregnant.

He sucked in a deep lungful of air, eyes widening. Awe filled him from his toes to his head. He and his beautiful wife had created life. "I'm so pumped!"

Isabelle's gaze flickered over her husband's face and his smile, studying every facet for inauthenticity, but she couldn't find any.

All day, she had been lost to a moment almost twenty-two years ago when she had told her seventeen-year-old high school sweetheart, Trent Farrow, she was pregnant with his baby.

He was tall and muscled from rowing club. Took care of himself—styling his dark brown hair every day and he always wore clean and ironed uniforms. She was desperately in love with him. Had said again and again that she would run away with him if that's what it took. She honestly believed she would die of heartache if they were to ever break up.

One afternoon, she had invited him over before her parents arrived home from work. It would give them some privacy to talk about their changed future. She still hadn't dared to tell her mum and dad about the baby. She wanted Trent to be by her side when she finally did.

They sat together on Isabelle's bed and Trent had kissed her lips, her neck, his hands greedily running over her breasts. She pushed him away, straightened her shirt. "I didn't ask you here so we can fool around." Not until she had told him her big secret.

"Well, what is it?"

Her heart had fluttered like a frightened bird in a cage. Her lips were dry. The hormones, she realised later, had made her emotional and her eyes gloss with tears.

"Trent, I have some news."

He nodded, gestured with his hand that she tell him.

"I'm" – a forced smile – "I'm pregnant."

He laughed. "Pull the other one."

"I'm not joking." She trailed her fingers across her flat stomach. "I'm pregnant."

His face drained of blood and he was left as pale as starched white sheets. His quick gaze flicked from her eyes to her stomach. His lips twisted, pulled down at the corners. A slight crinkle of his nose.

No doubt about it, he was not happy with the news. He was not happy with her. His reaction hit her like a punch. She had not anticipated such a response.

He jumped to his feet, his mouth curling into the contorted shape of revulsion, and pointed at her stomach. "I will have nothing to do with *that*. If you want to keep it, that's up to you. If you want to get rid of it, that's up to you, too. But do not tell my father. As far as anyone knows, we were over before this happened."

She stared, lips parted. "We're over?"

"I'm going away to university next year, Issy. I can't have a kid."

"Well, you're having a kid. We're having a kid. I can't change that fact."

He shrugged. "You could. As I said, your call. But as far as I'm concerned, not my problem."

He strode to the bedroom door, turned one last time and glared. The revolted expression on his face had stuck with Isabelle for years. But not so much as the anger and shame Trent's parents had blasted her with a few weeks later when they had eventually discovered the truth.

Isabelle had spent much of her life thinking she was disgusting for falling pregnant so young. That to bring a child into this world was shameful. To witness the opposite in Chris's expression was eating away that long-held humiliation.

"You're truly happy?" she asked.

Chris nodded, drew her to him and cuddled her to his chest. When he spoke, his voice was husky and choked by tears. "I can't even find the words to tell you how happy this makes me."

She looked up at his face, into his glossy eyes and smiled. "Good. I think I'm happy, too."

CHAPTER 10

Saturday morning, Tina set about cleaning her house. Routine. With the stick vacuum, she hoovered across the floorboards of the hall, ensuring to get close against the tracks because dust would accumulate there otherwise. Old houses like hers, surrounded by bushland, were magnets for dust.

Into the office, she pushed the vacuum over every part of the floor, then pulled the connector off, added the small attachment she had in her pocket and poked it into the windowsills, sucking up dead flies, small bugs and cobwebs—again, a standard out there.

She wouldn't change it. Living on a big property, the seclusion and birdlife, the quiet pace of the tiny town, offered refuge. When she and Chris had inspected that house together fifteen years ago, they had both met each other's gaze and silently said that they were in love with it. The years there were mostly good. They had always wanted their own slice of land to grow vegetables and fruit trees. Raise chickens.

Out in the vast yard, the large rectangle vegetable gardens had grown over years ago. Only weeds and the odd stubborn pumpkin grew there now. The chicken coop, once filled with six fat hens that would scratch for worms in the cooler afternoons, was empty. A wild dog had gotten to each of the chickens one night after she had forgotten to return them to the secure confines of their cage early enough.

Some of the fruit trees still bloomed each season—the ones hardy enough to survive only on rainfall. But the fruit would fall to the ground, unpicked, filling the air with sweet-scented decomposition. How easily dreams could fracture when they were no longer nurtured.

Tina turned from the window to leave, passing her scant-used desk. Sitting on the desktop were three sticky notes all in a neat row. Faint scrawl across each. She gasped and dropped the vacuum's handle. It crashed to the ground at her feet.

She glanced around the room, listened hard. Only regular morning sounds of the house, insects and birds.

"What the actual hell?" she barked and marched to the desk, snatching up each note.

The first note read: *Hear no evil.*

The second note read: *See no evil.*

She could already anticipate what the third would say before she even looked at it.

Speak no evil.

A slight tremble in her hands as she read and re-read the notes, over and over, shuffling them like cards before her eyes. Enough was enough. Someone was playing games with her, though she couldn't understand what type.

She raced out of the room, grabbed her phone off the kitchen bench with shaking hands, and dialled the Gladstone police station. An officer called David May spoke to her for fifteen minutes as she explained in a rush of words what had been happening.

The officer asked her to fill out an online report, but, at that stage, there was little that could be done. No damage. No theft. No indication of who could be responsible. He suggested she change her locks and organise a personal security system.

When she ended the call and filled out the report, she searched for local locksmith listings. She dialled the phone number of the first business that appeared and hit dial. After a quick conversation, the locksmith said he wasn't available until next Tuesday morning. But she couldn't wait another three nights without assurance that she was somewhat safer in her own home.

"I think I've someone entering my house while I'm not here," she pleaded. "Or it could be while I'm sleeping. I live on my own. I'm scared. Please, can you doublecheck if you can fit me into your schedule today?"

A long silence, then his gruff voice returned to the phone. "I'll call in late this afternoon."

"Thank you. Thank you so much."

She took a seat on her office chair, face in her hands, wondering who could possibly be behind the notes. The only person she hadn't asked was her ex. She would not put the conversation off any longer.

When Chris answered the phone, familiar construction noises were in the background.

"Hello," he said, somewhat surly.

"Hi, Chris, sorry to call at work…" She parted her lips to ask her next question, but it was obvious that he wasn't responsible for the notes. Not if he was a thousand kilometres away. "It seems silly to call you now because you're at work, so it couldn't be you."

"What are you talking about?"

She sighed. "I've had someone breaking into the house. They're leaving weird notes around the place. I had one left on the fridge. Now I have three in the office. I was wondering if you may have been using the key to get in—"

"Why would I do that?"

"I don't know." She pulled on her earlobe. "I'm at a loss. I've contacted the police. They were no help. I wanted to make sure it wasn't you, that's all."

"It's not me."

"Okay. Yeah, I realise that now."

"I don't know what else I can do from here."

"It's fine, Chris. It's not your job to sort it out. I'll deal with it. I'll let you go. I know you're not allowed to use your phone during work hours."

A noisy exhalation. "It's fine. If you need help, I'm there, okay? It's just hard when I'm working so far away."

She did her best to hide the waver in her voice. "Yeah, I understand. Thanks."

"Let me know if it keeps up. Maybe I can install a camera or something when I get back."

"Can't hurt."

"I'll call when I'm home. We'll arrange a time."

"Sure. Thanks. Talk to you later."

She ended the call, placed the phone down and rubbed her forehead. All she could do was hope that whoever was doing this, stopped.

* * *

Mandy was already waiting at the large coffee shop for Tina, sitting at table and chairs located in the outside seating area. Tina forced a smile and waved, still not quite able to shake her jitteriness after finding those last three notes.

69

"You okay?" Mandy asked. She was a tall, muscular woman. Her soft-spoken voice and timidity were at odds with her stature.

Tina took a seat, nodded, then shook her head. "I…no. There's something really strange going on."

Mandy crossed her legs, leaned closer. "What is it?"

"I've been finding weird notes around the house."

Mandy's brow furrowed as she shook her head slightly. "I don't understand. What do you mean by *weird notes*?"

Tina explained the circumstances surrounding the notes and what each of them said.

"What could they mean?" Mandy asked.

Tina shrugged. "You know as much as I do. The first one turned up on my fridge last Sunday. The other three were on the desk in my office this morning."

"And you don't know how they got there?"

"Nope."

"Bizarre. Really, really bizarre."

"I'm getting the locks changed this afternoon," Tina added.

"I'm sure there must be some kind of rational explanation for the notes, but, until you find out what that is, changing the locks is a good idea." Mandy didn't feel like that was enough, though. Intuition hinted there was something particularly unhinged about all this. "Do you want Trevor to come over and check around for you? Like, maybe in the ceiling space."

Tina's heart thumped. "The ceiling space? I never even thought about that."

"I've heard creepy stories about people living in the ceilings or attics while the occupant has no idea at all."

Goosebumps spread along Tina's arms. She shivered. She had heard similar stories, especially one spooky account of an older lady living in a man's roof. She would creep out at night for a drink and something to eat from the fridge and was only caught after the occupant installed cameras.

It wasn't out of the realm of possibility that someone could be hiding in Tina's ceiling. She was a small-sized woman living on her own. She shivered again. "My God, can you imagine that? How unnerving."

"I'm sure it's nothing, but he'd be happy to take a look." Mandy's husband loved an opportunity to play the Good Samaritan, especially when he had an audience.

"I'd appreciate that."

Mandy's smile was sympathetic as she pulled her mobile from her handbag. "Shall we handle it now?"

Tina shook her head. "Not yet. I need some normalcy for an hour or two."

Mandy patted Tina's hand and nodded. "I understand. Let's have cake with our coffee today then, shall we?"

Tina giggled. "You read my mind."

They each ordered coffees and a slice of lemon meringue pie for morning tea. Over the next hour, Tina managed to talk about life—work, new recipes she had found, local gossip—and listened to Mandy in turn. But her mind remained fixated on the last three notes. Their conversation kept circling back to her worries.

"What could it possibly mean?" Tina asked. "A random shopping list and now *hear no evil, see no evil, speak no evil*. I can't make sense of it."

"Me neither," Mandy agreed. "They're totally disconnected. Maybe the recent notes are hinting that you know something you shouldn't? Or saw something?"

Tina rested back against the chair and crossed her arms. "Could be. But I can't think what."

"Maybe you were dropping off a parcel while something big was going down inside a house. And the people involved believe you may have seen."

Tina's eyes widened. "That could be a possibility. But why be so cryptic?"

Mandy laughed. "See, this is why I could never be a detective." Mandy worked in childcare—more concerned with shaping young minds rather than understanding criminals.

"Could be an old patient, perhaps?" Tina suggested. "Someone holding an old grudge. Might explain the lack of sense the notes are making." Tina had worked as a psychologist at the local hospital when she had first met Chris. She had studied hard at high school, earning grades that won her a scholarship to study for her four-year degree on campus in Rockhampton.

After completing her Bachelor's, she studied an honour's year. But eight years into her career, she'd suffered serious burn-out and quit.

Mandy's brows shot higher. "Could be. Like the scene in that movie where the patient threatens to shoot his psychiatrist."

They both burst into laughter, not because that scene was funny, but how absurd it was to expect something like that in a town like Gladstone. And Tina hadn't worked in that profession for nearly a decade now. Besides, in the movie, the patient's actions were blatant—a gun right in the psychiatrist's face. The notes appearing in Tina's house were subtle. Covert.

Tina blew out a breath, started to gather up her phone and bag. "Come on, let's get Trevor to check this ceiling space so we can rule out that terrifying explanation."

* * *

Trevor stood on a tall ladder, only his long legs showing as the rest of him was poking up through the manhole into the hot, musty ceiling space. With a torch, he shone arcs of light across every conceivable space and dark corner to make doubly sure nothing sinister was living in the roof.

"No evidence anyone has been up here," his muffled voice called to Tina and Mandy who stood at the feet of the ladder. Even from down there, the heat from inside the roof drizzled upon them.

"Thank God," Tina said, a hand over her heart.

"There's a frighteningly large snakeskin left behind, though, and a lot of rat shit."

Tina cringed, cheeks flushing. "I've got some baits under the sink. Hang on a second." She rushed to the kitchen and retrieved an unopened box. She couldn't even recall when she had bought them. Probably Chris had years ago.

She passed the box up to Trevor and he threw the rat baits haphazardly across the ceiling space, then climbed down. He closed the manhole lid, making sure it was securely in place. Beads of sweat lined his forehead and dripped down his chest. "Might get some funny smells coming from up there once the vermin start munching on those baits."

She groaned, a hand on her cheek. "Something to look forward to."

"But better a dead rat than a live one."

"Very true."

Mandy hugged Tina. "I'm sorry we couldn't be more help."

"That's okay. I'm glad that the ceiling theory didn't turn out to be the right explanation."

"Me too," said Mandy.

"Thank you both so much for coming out here. And Trevor, for looking up there for me. I appreciate it."

Trevor winked, smiled. "Not a drama. Any time you need us, call, okay?"

"I will. Thank you."

Once Mandy and Trevor left, Tina stood, arms crossed, at the front window and peered out, convincing herself that the locksmith wasn't going to show as he had promised, and she would have to spend another night alone without the added protection of new, working locks. But soon enough, a white ute with *Ando's Locksmiths* printed on the side came roaring up the long, gravel driveway.

The locksmith was grimacing as he parked and climbed out of his ute. The first professional rugby league game of the season was on later that night and he didn't want to be rushing around before he sat down on his armchair—which after much use now moulded to his backside—to watch it.

But if Tina got chopped up by an axe tonight because he was busting to get home to watch football, he didn't want to cop the community backlash that would be inevitable, so he had forced himself to drive the twenty minutes out there at the end of a long day.

He was a short, red-faced man with a bulbous double-chin and a huge stomach. As he went around the house, changing the two doors' locks and inspecting the locks on all the windows to ensure they were fully operational, he was rude and impatient, dismissive of Tina's fears, and much more concerned with the cold beer waiting in the fridge for when he arrived home.

By the time he was finished, it was almost dark, and he was sweaty and breathing heavily. Tina apologised and was overly thankful, which helped soothe his irritation a little. But the moment he climbed back in his car knowing he had to drive another twenty minutes to get home, his anger had returned afresh.

Tina watched the locksmith speed away along the gravel driveway, kicking up dust and rocks. When the ute turned right at the end of the yard and roared onto the main road, she shut the door and flicked the new locks closed.

Every second with that horrible man had been worth it knowing she had an added level of protection.

CHAPTER 11

Maddison finished her work-out on the rowing machine, then pottered around the gym, wiping down the elliptical cross trainers and treadmills thoroughly with disinfectant. Still dressed in her knee-length tights and a short crop-top that exposed her protruding ribcage, she drove to the primary school to collect her kids.

Unwilling to mingle yet with the other parents, she waited in the full-to-bursting carpark. As she sat there, hands gripping the steering wheel, her heart beat a strong, fast rhythm. Accompanying her children to their new classrooms that morning and leaving them there had practically destroyed her. She had spent the rest of the day seeking any distraction.

When the afternoon school bell rang, she headed to the shelter shed where she had arranged to meet her children. Riley was first to arrive, his too-big backpack slung over his small shoulders. She studied her son's face for any grief, any anxiety—all the emotions that were raging through her—but he smiled when their eyes met. She forced herself to mirror that expression as he ran to her and wrapped his arms around her bony hips.

"Hey, Riley, how did you go today?"

"Good."

"You like your teacher?"

"Yep."

"Make some new friends?"

He nodded but his gaze was darting around, more interested in the goings-on in the schoolyard rather than Maddison's worries.

Ruby appeared at the top of the shelter shed and burst into tears. She ran to her mother and wrapped her arms around her, shoving her face into her hip.

"What's the matter?" Maddison asked.

Ruby looked up, eyes bloodshot and wet. Her lips were twisting. "I want to go back to my other school."

Maddison crouched so she was at Ruby's height and cuddled her daughter tight. "I know, sweetie. Did something happen?"

"No, but I like my other friends better."

"No one was mean to you?"

Ruby shook her head.

"Was the teacher nice?"

Ruby nodded.

"I don't understand. What are you crying about?"

A sob burst from Ruby's throat. "I want my old friends." She was overreacting. Today hadn't been so bad and she had met some new friends already. A girl called Juniper, who had shown Ruby dance moves. She knew all the words to songs that Ruby hadn't even heard of. Juniper was such a beautiful name. Juniper had said that she loved Ruby's name too.

"Oh, honey. I'm sorry. But I promise it will get better. You've got to give it a little time." Maddison held her children's hands. "Come on, you two. Let's go home. I'll make you some afternoon tea and you can sit down and relax."

Back at the house, Maddison prepared some sandwiches and fruit, presented them on a platter and placed it on the coffee table in front of the television. The kids had calmed down on the way home, talking between themselves about all the facilities their new school had. They were most impressed by the eight-lane twenty-five-metre swimming pool and the basketball court with its strange, soft flooring rather than the gravelly bitumen one at their old school.

But Maddison's stomach had roiled with guilt for ripping Ruby and Riley out of the school they were comfortable in and putting them in a bigger, public school with lots of unknown faces and all new teachers.

She let her children stream a movie while they ate. When sure they were happier and distracted, Maddison strode up the hall to her bedroom. She closed the door behind her, leaned back against it and groaned.

Her stomach was hollowed out, pained with nerves. Her chest was tight and hot. She was to blame for this. She should have handled the bullying incident like a normal put-together mother instead of running her mouth off at a nine-year-old kid like she was some kind of deranged psychopath.

She marched to the full-length mirror and glared at her reflection. A sickly sensation in her throat to see her horrible body. Short. Ordinary. Her breasts now sagged a little. Wrinkles had formed on her upper arms and the front of her neck. She had creasing in the centre of her chest from sleeping on her side. Her face had aged, lines appearing around her eyes. She clawed at the skin on the sides of her stomach, bunching it into her fists.

"You're disgusting!" she spat at the mirror. "Horrible, disgusting woman. Old and ugly. No wonder your husband screwed other women when he had you to come home to each night."

She smacked her forehead with her palm. It stung. Her cheek then, the slap loud in the silent room. A burning pain filled her face. She clenched her fist, punched her cheek with a *thud*. Her breathing was heavier as she beat herself over and over, grunting, thumping. Both fists now, smashing at her face, hard enough to turn her vision a bright white at the edges.

She barely heard the door open. Her fists fell to her side and she tried to control her breathing. "Yes," she said, not turning, but her son could see her reflection in the mirror as he pushed his face through the slightly ajar door.

"Mum, can I have a popper, please?"

"Sure," she said, controlling the rasp of her voice. "You go grab one out of the fridge for yourself and Ruby."

"Were you hitting your face?" he asked.

Still looking away from him, she closed her eyes. "Of course not. There was a mozzie. It landed on my cheek, so I slapped it away."

"Did you kill it?" he asked.

She nodded. "Yep."

The door shut and Riley's footsteps scampered down the long hall, fading as he drew further away.

Maddison fished her mobile from the pocket in her gym pants and crumbled onto the end of her bed. She dialled her friend, Lucy.

When Lucy answered, she asked, "Keen to go out for drinks tonight?"

* * *

Maddison had spent the afternoon with an ice compress pressed to her face trying to stave off bruising and swelling. A pale purple-green discolouration had surfaced under her eyes and across her cheekbones, but she hid it behind a layer of makeup by the time Ben arrived home from the gym.

He noticed. He always noticed. "What happened to you?" he asked as Maddison changed in the walk-in robe.

"Dermarolling went a little wrong."

He leaned against the doorframe and crossed his arms. "Dermarolling?"

She nodded, threaded both legs into a tight-fitting pair of jeans.

"Looks like someone gave you a flogging. You sure you're okay?"

She rolled her eyes. "If someone had given me a flogging, you'd hear about it."

"If you say so." He was humouring her to save an argument, but he wasn't sure how long this could go on before he intervened. What that intervention would look like was beyond him. He was unable to comment, criticise, suggest, sometimes even speak, let alone intervene on something so momentous as his wife hurting herself.

That wasn't the first time Maddison had done something like this. She constantly worked out to the point of being unable to walk, let alone function properly for the next few days. He had interrupted her dermarolling her legs, concentrating on the one spot until her skin was inflamed, red and bleeding in places. He had noticed patches at the back of her head where she had pulled out chunks of hair.

"You heading out, are you?" he asked, forcing his voice to sound nonchalant.

"With Lucy."

"Where to?"

She popped her head through her tight t-shirt. It surprised him to see how much weight she had lost over the past couple of years. Maddison had never been tall, but she had once had a fuller body. Now she appeared childlike and it was jarring.

"Dinner. Then drinks somewhere. I don't know yet."

He nodded, sighed. "I'll see you when you get home."

* * *

Maddison met Lucy at their favourite restaurant that offered great food and cocktails. It was within walking distance to a pub that opened late on Thursday nights.

"Hi, gorgeous lady," Lucy said, hugging Maddison, a huge smile on her heavily made-up face. Lucy was a couple of years younger than Maddison. She once worked as an aerobics instructor at the gym until she had resigned to become a business trainer with one of the local banks. Maddison had been devastated to see her go, but she also couldn't begrudge Lucy seeking more than a casual salary after her divorce.

Lucy, in a word, was *tidy*. Long blonde hair. A fit, toned body. Single. One of only two single friends Maddison had.

Maddison had stopped asking her married friends to join her on a Thursday night for drinks. They soon discovered that an alcohol-fuelled bender with Maddison wouldn't end well. Not that they'd ever admitted that to her. No, they came up with believable excuses instead like sick children, a headache, or a school event they had to attend.

The small restaurant had a dozen or so patrons at that time. Maddison and Lucy were directed to a table for two on the outside deck. A sea breeze gently blew stealing the day's summer heat. Gladstone didn't have a roaring weekday nightlife, so the streets below were mostly vacant except for the odd car now and then.

"What happened to you?" Lucy asked, pointing to Maddison's face.

"It's not that noticeable, is it?"

"Well, not to someone who doesn't know you. It looks like you've been punched." Lucy gasped, both hands covering her mouth, eyes widening. "My God, Ben didn't, did he?"

Maddison waved her hand. "No. No. I tried dermarolling with a longer needle than should be applied to the face. It didn't end well. Just a bit of swelling."

"That's not good, Mads. You're not to use it again if this's the result."

"It's already in the bin."

"Good." Lucy crossed her legs as she reached for the drinks menu. "So, what do you feel like? Should we have a wine or a couple of cocktails?"

Maddison didn't need to look at the menu to know what she wanted. Something that would be hard-hitting. "A Long-Island iced tea."

Lucy rolled her head back and laughed boisterously. "I like the way you think."

A quick trip to the bar and they settled back at their table, drinks at the ready.

"So, fill me in. What's been happening with you?" Lucy asked. "I feel like we haven't caught up in ages."

Three months had passed since they had last had dinner because Lucy had found herself a new boyfriend—a colleague at the bank—who had, understandably, taken up much of her time. But the relationship came to a crashing end a couple of weeks ago.

"Same old," Maddison said. "Except, I did change the kids' school. I wasn't happy with the one they were at. There was a bullying incident the school didn't handle well. Ruby and Riley enjoyed their first day at North-West today. It's leaps and bounds ahead of the other school—it has a pool and a really good music program. Breanna, from our gym, do you remember her?"

Lucy squinted as she thought. "Yes, I think so."

"All three of her kids go there. She recommended it highly."

"I'm glad they're fitting in well. So, what was the bullying incident?"

"Just some horrible little girls being mean to Ruby."

"Poor Ruby. Is she okay?"

"Perfectly fine. I sorted it all out. And she's made some great new friends already. Best move I've made."

"I'm so happy to hear that."

Maddison rested her elbows on the tabletop, leaned over her straw and sipped her cocktail. "How about you? No word from Justin since the big breakup?"

An eye roll. "He texts now and then. But I stand firm that we're over." Lucy shrugged. "We weren't too serious to start with in all honesty. We'd only been seeing each other for a few months. He's acting like we'd already tied the knot."

"How are things at work? Not too tense?"

Lucy waved her hand dismissively. "It's tough sometimes. But he's going to have to get over it. Or leave. The latter would be nice."

Maddison laughed. "No one new on your radar?"

Lucy grinned. "Free as a bird."

A deep pulse in Maddison's stomach. Sometimes—more and more as the years rolled by—she wished she were free as a bird. But she wasn't naive enough to know that she wasn't in the best mental shape. Supporting herself and two children, even holding down a full-time job outside of the gym, was near impossible.

The more she fell apart, the more imprisoned she was in her marriage. And the more imprisoned she became, the more she fell apart. As time passed, it seemed increasingly difficult to ever break the downward spiral she had fallen into.

Maddison hid her discontent. Even though Lucy was one of her best friends, Maddison did not reveal her inner torment to the rest of the world unless her emotions broke loose like they had in the principal's office. "Plenty of fish in the sea."

Lucy laughed. "We're talking about Gladstone here. Unless some twenty-five-year-old tradie wants to hook up with a forty-year-old woman, the second-hand pickings are slim. There're reasons women leave their first husbands. I don't want to be the sucker second-wife who gets the new and improved version until the man is comfortable again and lets his belly out."

"I hear ya." Although, Maddison quite liked the idea of becoming complacent in a relationship. She quite liked the notion of relaxing into her own body and not trying so hard to meet some real or imagined expectation. She quite liked the delusion she often fantasised about that she and Ben had made it to those heights in their marriage rather than the cold reality she endured each day.

She sucked deeply on her straw until her glass was empty. By the time she arrived at the bottom of her third Long Island iced tea, the restaurant was slightly wavery around her. When she spoke, she had to sound her words around her thick tongue.

"Should we eat?" Maddison asked. "I'll be on the floor if we don't mop up some of this alcohol with food."

Lucy held her hand in the air to catch the attention of a waiter across the other side of the room. He saw her and marched over. A young man—maybe twenty-one. Tall, fit-looking.

"Well, hello," Lucy said, eyeing him up and down.

His neck flushed pink. "Are you ready to order?"

"That depends what's on the menu," Maddison said, grinning and the tip of her tongue moving against her straw.

He cleared his throat, leaned between them and opened the menu. "All in there. Let me know when you're ready." And he strode away.

Lucy and Maddison looked at each other and broke into laughter.

"Too young?" Maddison asked.

"Much too young. He was horrified."

"Mortified."

"Couldn't get away fast enough," Lucy said.

The smiles fell from their faces. Maddison sighed. "It sucks getting old. Screw dinner. Let's just get shit-faced. I don't care if someone has to carry me out of here." Maddison pointed to Lucy's empty glass. "Another?"

Lucy grinned. "You read my mind."

By the bottom of drink four, Lucy and Maddison made to leave. They linked their arms around each other for support, held their chins up high and swaggered out of the restaurant. When on the street, they dissolved into giggles knowing how they would have looked to the other customers there, but they were too full of alcohol-induced merriment to care.

A few hundred metres up the hill was a bar that also masqueraded as a night club. During the boom, every nightspot was open late most nights of the week and was filled with out-of-town workers. But a sleazy slant had also crept in—strip clubs and titty bars catering to the blue-collar crowd. Everyone was cashed up and had nowhere to go.

All the businesses in town thought they'd be flush with cash and patronage forever. Maddison and Ben had fallen for the short-lived delusion too.

The streets were almost empty. The gauzy glow spilling from closed shop fronts and streetlights lit their path along the cracked pavement. All the ten or so patrons in the pub turned to look when they entered the darkened, blue-tinged room. Music pumped loudly from the speakers and altered Maddison's heartbeat. She cast a glance to the empty dance floor on their way to the bar where they ordered another cocktail. Sex on the Beach or something like that.

A group of younger men were playing pool. Two men in business attire were at the bar, deep in conversation. A couple sat at a tall table, drinks in front of them.

Maddison and Lucy carried their cocktails to a table and shuffled onto a seat. The only problem with places like that was that now their conversation had to be conducted at the level of shouting just to hear each other.

The night moved on at a flurried pace. From bar to table, dance floor to the bathroom, back to the bar, over and over. Every time Maddison stood, her balance grew less reliable.

Her dance moves were a series of jumps and hand pumps in the air, her hair swaying from side to side as she rocked her head to the beat.

Each time she went to the bathroom, the louder her ears rang in the silence and the harder she plonked onto the toilet seat. No matter what she drank now, it all tasted the same.

Her vision was a blur of colour. Her surroundings a cacophony of sounds.

Deep into the night, she seemed to come awake again and remember where she was. The two businessmen were now sitting with her and Lucy. She looked around, unsure when that had happened. More people had arrived too. A younger crowd. Scantily clad women in high heels, with fake lips and breasts. Barely adult men in jeans and good t-shirts.

One of the businessmen—Thomas—had his hand high on her thigh. She gazed at him when he leaned closer to speak to her. A strong jaw and defined nose. Interested brown eyes. His hair was full and well-groomed. He smelled like expensive aftershave.

He repeated himself when she didn't answer. "How long have you owned the gym?"

She blinked. "Oh, um, ten years."

"That's a well-established business. You must be good at what you do."

She shrugged, nearly mentioned that her husband was who had made it successful, but she didn't want to reveal that to him right now. "I am."

Thomas smiled and she vaguely remembered a conversation where he had said he was an accountant. Explained the interest in her business. His hand skimmed higher towards the apex of her thighs. An unanticipated bolt of arousal. It had been so long since that hot, aching sensation had filled her belly.

She cast a glance at Lucy who was kissing the other businessman.

Thomas laughed. "They've got the right idea."

Maddison looked into his eyes. "You think so?"

He gravitated closer until his lips were a fraction away from hers and kissed her. For thirteen years, Maddison had not kissed another man's lips. She had never even imagined another man's lips. Ben had been more than enough until he wasn't. And by then, she was too broken to want for anyone else.

Her mouth opened and his tongue dipped inside, stroking against hers like silk. A tight, squeezing pulse of need through her veins. Muscles clenched, blood swamped lower and ran hotter. Breaths were deep and rushed as she kissed him back. Her hands raked through his hair. She was off her seat, pushing closer against him, craving his touch. His arms slung around her waist, pulled her between his parted legs.

She couldn't get enough. So long. So long since someone had touched her. Wanted her. His hand slipped down her waist, over the curve of her backside and squeezed. Lower his caress traced the slopes of her body until he was feeling between her legs.

Hot. Breathless.

She reached for his hand and that's when she felt it—a wedding ring. Like he was a scalding ember, she dropped his hand, broke free from his mouth and stumbled backwards.

"You're married?" she shrieked.

His brow furrowed as he chuckled. "Yeah, and so are you."

Her lips parted on a long exhale. He was right, her accusation rang true both ways. But she wasn't the one on a business trip playing up, seeking out the first easy target that came along, while the wife and kids were at home.

But she did have children and a husband, and they were at home, tucked up in their beds, and she was in a seedy bar, kissing a stranger.

Her head was spinning around her as she tried to keep her balance. Without warning, her stomach convulsed, and she vomited all over the ground only centimetres from Thomas's polished leather shoes. Her stomach clenched again, and another torrent of colourful liquid streamed from her mouth. Again, and again until the floor was a technicolour pool of acrid sick.

A rough hand gripped her arm. She looked up, expecting it to be Thomas, but it was a huge bouncer the size of a silverback. His arms were as thick as both of Maddison's legs.

"Out," he said through gritted teeth. "Now!"

"I'm sorry," she said and tried to catch the next stream of vomit in her hands.

"For God's sake," he growled. "Get out." He shoved Maddison forward, but she slipped in the vomit and nearly fell over, but he reached out, snatched her arm, squeezed tighter and yanked her upward towards him before she hit the ground.

Stumbling beside him, he all but carried her onto the street. Lucy followed after them.

"Taxi rank is that way," the bouncer said and strode back to the bar shaking his head.

Lucy was frowning. "Bloody hell, Mads, you couldn't tell that you were going to vomit?"

"Obviously not," Maddison said, barely able to shape the words into intelligible sounds.

Lucy shook her head, shuffled a hand through her hair. "I'm so embarrassed. I don't think I've ever been more embarrassed in my life."

"Get the hell over yourself! Seriously."

Lucy's eyes widened. "We're grown women. There comes a time in our lives when we don't projectile vomit all over the floor of a bar."

"Don't you dare patronise me."

"Maybe I have to. I think this" – she gestured at Maddison – "is too far. You've got vomit all down your shirt. Jesus, Mads. When is enough enough?"

Maddison rolled her eyes only because the thought of speaking was too much when she could barely see straight, let alone think straight, let alone stand upright. All she wanted to do was crawl into bed and die.

"I love you. I do," Lucy said. "You're my best friend. And I'm happy to go out with you. But every time we do, it always ends with me putting you in a taxi because you're too smashed to walk."

"Well then, don't go out with me. Simple."

A taxi pulled up and Maddison crawled into it. Lucy buckled her into the backseat and told the driver of her friend's address.

"Bye," Lucy said and shut the door. Even in Maddison's state, she recognised the finality in that single word.

The trip home went by in a blur as Maddison weaved in and out of unconsciousness. The next thing she knew, Ben was lifting her from the taxi into his arms, apologising to the driver, then carrying her into the house.

When in their bedroom, he attempted to change her out of her vomit-covered clothes, but she slapped his hands away. The scent of booze and spew saturated the air.

"I kissed a man," she said defiantly, trying to hold her chin up high. "He wasn't you and I don't even care."

Ben didn't say anything, simply grabbed his pillow and strode out of the room to spend the night on the couch.

CHAPTER 12

S unday afternoon, Tina had mentally prepared herself to tackle the mundane task of piloting the ride-on lawnmower over the huge expanse of dry but too-long grass. Up and down, back and forth, stopping now and then to refill with petrol and change the catcher. Dust spewed from behind the mower.

She enjoyed being outside in the warm afternoon sunshine, breathing in the woodsy scent of fresh-cut grass, amidst the calm stillness of her property. The only issue she had was that driving the mower reminded her of her day job, endlessly touring the same route every single day.

When she finished up, the sun was setting and a cooler evening breeze had settled in, rustling the leaves on the tall gum trees in the bordering bush. In a dry summer, twigs and leaves were shades of rust and brown and eucalyptus-scented detritus would crackle underfoot.

If the tropical rains descended, the thirsty dirt would soak up every last drop and take it deep beneath the surface, then sporadic bursts of grass would sprout across the ground like a rug. Leaves would deepen from fawn to pale green, but the green hints never lasted too long.

Early into a dry autumn after a long, hot summer, the colour across her property, extending deep into the bush, were shades of beige. That's how it looked now.

Tina hosed the mower down from the tap connected to the water tank, then parked it in the four-bay shed that had once been home to myriad tools, spare parts and materials for projects Chris would work on during his days off. He had made some of the furniture that still stood in the house. Beautiful, durable pieces—TV unit, bookshelf, and a desk— from expensive hardwood. Pieces that could never be found in commercial furniture stores. She wondered if he made furniture for his new wife. She couldn't imagine he'd have the room.

The shed smelled like hot steel, fuel and hard work and she was consumed with nostalgia. Of carrying a beer out for Chris in the hot afternoons. Seeing the pleasure on his face to be thought of and taken care of. She missed those years in her life and grieved those memories like each were little deaths.

Tina stretched high for the roller door handle, jumped and used her weight to drag the door closed with a loud metallic clang. She locked it with a padlock—something she never usually did—but with what had been going on around there, she wasn't taking the chance for anyone to hang out in dark places biding their time.

When done, it was late, though the orange glow behind Mount Larcom still offered some illumination. The evening chorus of birdsong was dying down as the birdlife found tree limbs to perch in for the night. At the water tank, Tina slipped off her runners and set them aside before she turned on the tap. The water was refreshing as she washed away the grime and sweat the afternoon in the yard had yielded.

She switched off the tap and shook her hands, tiny splatters of water flicking around her. Gripping her runners, she started back to the house. Her feet crunched across the dry grass, but only a few steps away from the shed, a rustle sounded from the bush.

Turning fast, she surveyed the bushland. Nothing stood out in the shadowy tangled mass of tree limbs and debris. She smiled to herself, at her creeping paranoia. It would be an animal of some kind. A kangaroo—they often appeared at twilight, bounding across the yard to congregate in small groups as they munched on grass. She waited a moment longer as a chorus of crickets and cicadas burst into song around her and there was a flurry of flapping wings as birds took flight, squawking and rushing from something.

She kept her eyes focused, but the afternoon sun was sinking fast, and the small gaps and spaces in the bushland were dark. Too dark to see anything. Tree trunks morphed into thick limbed bodies. Her heart thudded hard. She blinked, shook her head slightly, and they reappeared as ordinary, unthreatening tree trunks. The small gaps between a bunch of leaves were two eyes staring. She glanced away, looked back, and they were leaves again.

She was being ridiculous. Her mind was trying to convince her that something was there, watching her, even though there was nothing but gnarled bushland. She turned away, facing the house, only for the rustle to sound again.

She smirked and didn't look back for a few paces, but the crackling grew louder, and her grin fell away. A hastening slap of footsteps across the grass heading towards her. Her skin tingled. Pulse raced. She spun and looked.

Black feathered, wide-spread wings rushed at her, flapping in front of her face. A gobble, then fast clawing across the grass as the scrub turkey darted away.

She leaned over, exhaling a long gush of air, hands on her knees. "You've got to be kidding me. You stupid bloody turkey."

She shook her head, marched back inside, slammed the front door behind her and set the locks. For the rest of the evening, she tried her hardest to banish the slow-burning fear. It had only been a scrub turkey in the end, but it had set off her fight-or-flight response.

After an easy dinner, she sat at her laptop in her office and navigated to an online forum. She hadn't been able to find an explanation for the notes appearing in her home, so maybe someone else, with an outside perspective, could.

When logged into the forum, she typed what was happening to her onto a board called 'Strange Occurrences'. Within moments, replies appeared.

Reaper69: *If you don't have security—get it. Set up cameras. Catch the intruder red-handed. That way you've got evidence.*

Naysayer92: *I've heard of stories like this. A man was finding everyday objects in strange places around his house. Like the bleach in the fridge and fruit in teacups. Turns out his gas heater was leaking high levels of carbon monoxide and slowly poisoning him. He was the one moving the objects but had no memory of doing so. Check your heater.*

Mescaline: *Stay off the drugs!*

CrumbitCroombit: *A strange story hit the news in Australia a couple of years back about an entire family who became* *paranoid and fled their property believing something or someone was after them. I reckon they had heavy metal poisoning, like lead or something like that, and it was slowly making them crazy. If you still have old lead plumbing or paint in your house, get a heavy-metals blood test.*

Personification101: *Poltergeists ooo-ooo-ooo!*

Tina read the comments. In the end, over thirty people had replied. Most were telling her to set up cameras facing entry points. But some suggestions were a little left of centre. She didn't have a heater—they were useless in Central Queensland. But she did have an old water tank. It could be possible the pipework contained lead. Her main drinking supply came from that tank.

It wasn't too absurd to question if she were writing these notes herself while in some sort of stupor. Disguising her handwriting. It would explain the lack of evidence—apart from the notes—of anyone entering her house. A blood test was worth her peace of mind.

But until she could book an appointment with a doctor, then wait for the results, she was going to install a camera as Chris had suggested.

Her stomach lurched when she envisioned an uninvited guest moving through her house. Tingles fanned over her arms and the back of her neck. The person could be watching over her while she slept. Standing at her doorway staring. Peeping through the windows on an evening as Tina watched television. Outside right that second.

She spun in her chair, looked out her office window. All was black.

Goosebumps sprang up along her skin and she shivered.

Maybe the worst thing was her imagination.

She typed a quick text to Chris.

TINA: *Hi. Just wondering if that offer is still open to install some cameras for me?*

His reply came back a few seconds later.

CHRIS: *I'll be back in Gladstone Saturday. I'll pick up a couple of cameras and stop by Sunday morning. About ten-thirty?*

TINA: *Thank you. See you then.*

She sighed with relief and flopped against her chair. She had to get through until next weekend, then hopefully she would have some answers.

CHAPTER 13

Isabelle sat on the end of her bed, her jeans laid out beside her. Chris had arrived from the airport around noon and was now in the shower.

Nerves nested in her belly. Once she and Chris were dressed, they would be taking Juliette to the local Thai restaurant for dinner to tell her she was about to become a big sister.

She found it so odd that Juliette was five years older than she had been when Juliette was born, and only now was Isabelle finally getting around to giving her daughter a sister or brother. For over a fortnight, she had sat with the news, had a doctor confirm her result, and yet she was still viewing it through a surreal lens.

She lifted her jeans from the bed, pulled her feet through the legs, then stood to tug them over her hips. She buttoned them up—already a little tight. Only for another couple of months would Isabelle get away with wearing jeans. Maternity pants would need to be added to her shopping list soon.

She sat back down. When she was pregnant with Juliette, she didn't have the luxury of such things as 'maternity' clothes. She had made do with her small wardrobe until she no longer fit into it, then her mother bought her some cheap, but colourful, dresses, which she'd cycled through in the latter months of her pregnancy and then until her figure finally returned after giving birth.

No one had mentioned to her that the by-product of nine months of pregnancy was going to be a big jelly belly that would linger for a long time afterwards. She had naively packed in her hospital bag the clothes she had worn before she was pregnant, but when she had tried to dress into them, she was unable to do the zippers up. Tired, disheartened, and tearful, she had rummaged through her bag for the cheap dress she had worn into hospital and had to go home in that.

Now that she was nearly forty, she doubted her body would return to its usual shape as quickly as it had all those years ago. Maybe it never would. She placed a hand over her stomach and found she didn't care either way because there was joy and laughter ahead of her. It would all be worth it.

She wasn't forgetful enough to have done away with the memories of the difficult, tiring, and stressful times that babies inevitably lumped upon parents. But now she would have a husband to help. Help that would fit in with a fly-in, fly-out schedule, nonetheless, but it was more help than she'd had with Juliette.

As punishment or a lesson, she wasn't sure which, her mother had not lifted a finger when Juliette was a new baby. Isabelle had been afforded a roof over her head but nothing else. Maybe that was more than some women across the planet had, but it had stung. All at once, she had created her own little family and yet was abandoned by the only other family she had ever known and loved.

When she had enough funds to move out, she did, making sure there were three big state borders between her parents in Tasmania and her home in Queensland. She never returned. And as Juliette grew and Isabelle established their new life, her parents visited now and then. They loved

Juliette, that was obvious, but the damage they had wielded upon their own daughter was never forgotten.

She wondered what they would think about this new pregnancy. Her parents had visited over Christmas and met Chris while they were there. One night, they had quietly taken her to the side and admitted they liked him very much. She had anticipated they would. Chris was effortlessly likeable, and they were probably grateful to see their daughter finally in a relationship. But a tight band of resistance sat in her belly every time she imagined picking up the phone and telling them about her pregnancy. Scars were not only physical. That's why she was so nervous about telling Juliette, too. She had been conditioned to view pregnancy as a horrible crime. A condemnable act only bad girls made happen.

Tears filled her eyes.

"Everything okay?" Chris was standing in the doorway, a towel around his waist, bare-chested. His face was contorted with concern.

She quickly wiped her eyes, tried to find a smile. "I'm okay. I just realised why I've been so nervous about this pregnancy. I've been in two minds."

Chris sat beside her on the end of the bed. He smelled of steam and soap. "Yeah?"

"I was made to feel like I'd committed murder when I fell pregnant with Juliette. And then punished every day after by my parents in their own way. I was thinking I was still that young girl. I kept imagining Juliette hearing the news and being upset with me. Like I'd let her down."

His brow furrowed as he shook his head. "You've no reason to feel like that at all. This baby is the best thing that's happened in my life. Juliette's going to think so, too. I've no doubt."

She wiped her fresh tears away. "I know. I just needed to be reminded of that."

A tightening again in her belly. Despite rationality telling her that Chris was most probably right, there was still a chance that Juliette might not see the news as favourable.

* * *

The Thai restaurant was a rabble of chatter and movement, full of patrons. It smelled like spices and seared meats. A waitress piloted the three of them to a table at the back of the room, close to the kitchen. Juliette sat opposite her mother. Isabelle next to Chris.

Chris's shoulders were relaxed as his elbows rested on the tabletop, fingers laced together. He was a little distracted, though. He was wondering how he was going to meet with Tina tomorrow morning to install the cameras without telling Isabelle about it.

Not one bad intention sat beneath that thought. He was genuinely worried for his ex and if this was a way to put her mind at ease, to make her safe somehow, then he had to help. Omitting to tell Isabelle was similarly innocent. He didn't want to unnecessarily worry her as Tina was a sensitive topic.

Isabelle squirmed in her seat. Her hands were twitchy. Words fast as she said, "Really busy in here tonight, isn't it? Hope we don't have to wait too long for our food because I'm hungry."

Juliette smiled at her mother. "Everything okay, Mum? You seem a little wired."

Isabelle looked at Chris for reassurance, but he was peering out the window at a group of people about to make their way into the restaurant.

"I'm fine. I…" She ruffled a hand through her hair. "I've some news I wanted to share with you."

Juliette's brows arched high; she leaned forward. "Really? I was wondering where this impromptu dinner invitation had come from."

Again, Isabelle looked to Chris for backup; he was smiling warmly at her now. "Um… I'm…well, I'm pregnant." She swallowed hard, waiting for a response.

Chris, still smiling, placed his hand over Isabelle's.

"What? Like, for real?" Julliette screeched. "You're going to have a baby?"

Isabelle nodded. Chris did too.

A slight quirk at the corners of Juliette's lips, then she burst into a full-blown grin. "Oh, my God. How exciting!"

Isabelle sat back against her chair. "You think so?"

Tears wet Juliette's eyes. "Yes. I'm ecstatic. I'm going to be a big sister. The *best* big sister, I can tell you that right now."

Isabelle laughed, blinking fast, trying to stem her happy tears to see the joy in her daughter's face. Genuine joy.

Juliette pushed her chair back, the legs scraping noisily against the tiles and sprang to her mother's side, wrapping her arms tightly around her. "I have wanted a sister or brother forever." She released her grip, went to Chris and cuddled him tight. "Congrats. You've made me the happiest person in here tonight."

Chris laughed. "Glad to hear it."

When seated again, Juliette couldn't subdue her smile. "I think we need celebration drinks. But alcohol-free for you, Mum. Can't be guzzling the champagne in your condition."

As the night progressed and they ate, drank and celebrated the news, beneath Isabelle's relief and genuine joy, a niggle of guilt festered. Guilt for not having done this earlier. Guilt for putting her life on hold for too many years.

She had all that she could have ever wanted or needed at that moment, but some time-hardened part of her heart regretted not being fully present and completely open to her vivacious, youthful years where life was felt and experienced at such pace and vibrancy. Ways life didn't play out now that she was older. What a waste. Baby or not, new husband or not, she would never get those passionate years back.

* * *

By the time Isabelle arrived home and climbed into bed beside Chris, she had tied a rope around the part of her mind that grieved for her past and deeply missed her youth. She wouldn't make the same mistake now. She wouldn't reach age sixty and look back to her late thirties and realise just how young she still was and how her focus upon her past and who she no longer was had stopped her from experiencing who she was now. No, she was going to embrace everything.

She wrapped an arm around her husband and kissed his cheek. "I love you so much."

He grinned sleepily. "I love you too."

"You've made me the happiest woman I've ever been."

He kissed her forehead. "Back at ya."

CHAPTER 14

Maddison woke to the sound of her children's footsteps as they scampered from their bedrooms down the hallway. As soon as her eyes opened, memories from the night before rushed in, followed by a squeezing, churning rise of her stomach contents.

She threw her legs over the side of the bed and staggered for the ensuite. A metre from the toilet bowl, she vomited all over the floor and wall. Sidestepping the unpleasant mess, she made it to the toilet and aimed her head over the bowl before another wave hit her. She hung there, staring until her stomach was empty and all she had left to do was dry heave.

When she was able to stand tall again, she flushed. She was shaking, her eyes and nose watering. At the sink, she rinsed her mouth and splashed her face with cold water before looking into the mirror. What stared back was not her. She shook her head, unable to reconcile this pale, gaunt, ageing woman in her reflection with the version of herself she saw in her mind.

A mournful groan. She looked away. No wonder Lucy was upset with her. She was an embarrassment. After she cleaned the bathroom floor, finishing with strong-scented disinfectant, she scrounged in the bathroom cabinet for painkillers to dull the thumping aching in her temples. She swallowed two down, then tiptoed back to her bedroom to find her phone.

She called Lucy, desperate to apologise for how she had behaved last night, but the phone went straight to the message bank. So, she typed a text message instead.

MADDISON: *I'm really sorry about last night. I screwed up again. Please, give me a call so we can talk.*

She placed the phone on her bedside table and lowered her face into her hands until the painkillers kicked in. When able to walk without feeling like her skull was splitting in two, she went to meet the kids and make them breakfast. At least it was the weekend, and she didn't have to drive them to school.

Ben always went to work early on Saturday, and he wouldn't be home until that afternoon. The vague taste of a memory flittered across her tongue. She flinched when it became fully formed. Last night, she had confessed to kissing another man. She groaned and doubled over, hands on her knees.

"What's the matter, Mum?" asked Ruby from the end of the hall.

Maddison stood up straighter, blinked the tears from her eyes. She forced a strained smile. "Oh, nothing. I felt a little sick for a second there, that's all. But I'm okay now."

"You want me to make you some toast and a cup of tea?"

Maddison's heart warmed for her little girl, but she was the one who was meant to be the grown-up. Shame, guilt, all those emotions, flamed in her cheeks. "That's such a lovely gesture, but I tell you what. How about I make you and Riley some pancakes and bacon instead?"

Ruby grinned wide. "Yes, please. I haven't had those for ages."

"Well, then it will be a treat for us."

Maddison hadn't been in any shape most mornings to do much for her children, let alone cook pancakes. For so long, she had been striving to maintain some sense of stability for her kids and yet what it took to maintain the facade that everything was okay, only ever achieved the opposite.

Ruby scurried to the living room to join her brother in front of the television. Maddison set about making pancake batter and layering bacon onto a tray to cook in the oven. By the time she had finished, she was sweating, exhausted and ready to vomit again, though there was nothing left in her stomach.

She placed the plate of pancakes along with maple syrup and bacon on the dining table and called Ruby and Riley in. They dived onto their seats, grins wide.

All the maternal parts of her were aching, begging her to take a seat beside her children and have a wonderful morning with them. A memory-making morning. But Maddison couldn't bear standing another moment. The scent of fatty bacon was turning her stomach.

"I'm going to have a lie-down," she said.

Her children looked at her as they loaded their plates with pancakes.

Riley frowned. "Aren't you going to eat any?"

Maddison shook her head. "Sorry. I'll have to join you next time." Then she hurried away, down the marathon-long hall to her bedroom, closed the door behind her and bee-lined to the bathroom. She stood over the toilet as wave after wave of nausea hit her, but nothing came up.

She crawled into bed, a dying woman, and slept between dashes to the bathroom. As she drifted off to sleep or fielded questions from her children, she repeated to herself, "I'm a terrible mother. The worst mother that ever was."

* * *

Later that afternoon, Maddison hauled herself out of bed. The pounding in her head and nausea had subsided, but she was still weak. She managed to sip water and hold it down.

"Come on, Ruby and Riley. Do you want to go for a swim?"

Her poor children had been locked in the house all day in front of the TV. She could have called Ben, but that would have meant admitting she wasn't capable of looking after their kids because she was too hungover.

When Ben arrived home, Maddison was resting on the banana lounge while the kids screeched, laughed, swam and splashed in the pool. He was pleased to see her awake, functioning. After the state she was in last night, he had been worried she wouldn't be in any condition to take care of the kids. But she hadn't rung him, so he took that as a good sign.

Many times, during his day, he had reached for his phone and nearly called, wanting to check in on them all, but never did. Maddison would have taken offence. They would have fought, and he didn't want that for his children. It was bad enough they had to endure two parents who never showed affection or had a nice word to say about the other.

Maddison could barely meet her husband's eye despite all her bravado last night. Today she was a shell, scarcely capable of life let alone courage.

Ben noticed but kept his comments to himself. He cheerfully greeted the children, yanked his shirt off over his head, and jumped into the pool to join them. As he romped around with Ruby and Riley, he didn't speak to Maddison. Not directly.

Afterwards, Ben and the kids dried off, then he sent them to shower and dress into clean pyjamas. He still hadn't said a single word to Maddison. Not even as she made dinner and they sat at the dining table as a family to eat it.

He didn't say anything as they negotiated the before-bed routine, then tucked the children in their beds for the night.

Deep into the evening, Maddison was making dandelion tea in the kitchen. Ben strode in and sat on a stool at the bench, watching her silently.

She slammed the jug down with a clank. "Please, enough with the bloody silent treatment. If it's some kind of immature punishment—"

"Punishment for what, Maddison?"

She swallowed, looked away. "Punishment for kissing another man."

When she turned to face him again, he was silent but grimacing, staring at his clasped hands.

"Well, what do you have to say?" she asked.

He shook his head, sighed. "I don't care about that."

A sharp, splintering sting in her heart like a snap of elastic flicking hard against her skin.

He cleared his throat, leaned in, green eyes shaped with concern. "I'm worried about you. Really, really worried."

She rolled her eyes. "Save me from your—"

"You're on this downward spiral and I think it's gotten way out of hand."

She crossed her arms over her chest. "Not you too. Bloody hell, Ben, I'm fine."

"You're not fine. Not at all. Have you seen your face this morning? What kind of message is this sending to the childr—"

"Don't you dare bring Ruby and Riley into this. They're fine. I'm fine. If this is some nasty way to make me out to be a bad mother—"

"For Christ sake, Maddison. It's not. I'm scared you're slowly killing yourself." There, he finally said it. He almost couldn't breathe.

She jolted, eyes widening. "I'm not killing myself."

"Aren't you?"

Maddison stared at her husband, read all the pain, shame, grief and fear in his eyes. It nearly broke the final threads holding her heart together because those exact emotions were what she saw reflected every single morning when she looked in the mirror. She understood the burden, the weight of all those feelings.

Tears tightened the back of her throat, pricked her eyes. Composing her voice as much as she could, she choked out, "I'm fine."

"I think you need help. I've told my therapist about you—"

"You had no right to do that."

"I have every right. This is my life. You're my life. She wants to help you."

Through gritted teeth, "I don't need your help. And I don't need your stupid, do-gooder therapist's help."

Maddison felt so trapped, she was almost suffocating. To simply exist, every single moment, was too much. She scooped her tea off the bench and started for her refuge downstairs in the basement. The cold, hard metal of dumbbells and weight bars.

"That's it, walk away."

She stopped, turned to face Ben wearily.

"Ignore it all, like always. Keep everything bottled up in that messed-up mind of yours. All this" – he said with a sweep of his hand around the room – "is the consequence of that."

Her nose wrinkled, mouth twisted. "Yeah, well, what's your excuse, Ben? I'm a hundred times the person you ever were. You don't get to take the moral high ground now. You never get to take the moral high ground. Ever—"

"Then leave. If you don't like me, leave!"

A violent burst of anger roared through her limbs. "You leave!"

Both of them knew they wouldn't. Couldn't.

Turning, Maddison marched downstairs to the gym where she exercised until the dumbbells fell from her hands to the hard floor with a *clunk*.

CHAPTER 15

Gravel and sticks crunched. The low rumble of an engine. Tina glanced out the living room window to find Chris's ute winding up the long gravel driveway. Still the same car he'd driven when they were married. Painful nostalgia struck her to see Chris behind the wheel, out there on the property again.

As Chris rolled down his window to allow the bushland scents in, he remembered the years when this drive was his favourite after a long, hot, tiring shift away. Tina would open the door, stand on the top step outside and smile and wave.

He looked ahead to the door, willing it to open, for Tina to come out, just like she once had. When she did, his shoulders relaxed and the eternal tightness across his chest eased. But she didn't smile, and she didn't wave.

Isabelle's face filled his mind, followed by thoughts of their baby, and he reminded himself that he no longer needed to see a smile or a wave from his ex-wife. Nor should he expect it. He had everything he wanted back at his house.

Though, living with Isabelle, in her house, still didn't feel like his *home*. Not while all of her furniture filled the rooms. Not while Juliette still came and went.

Chris had some room set aside for him in the cupboard-sized shed in the backyard, a couple of drawers in the bedroom and some hanging space for all his work uniforms in the spare room, but that was it. When the baby came, he hoped his bones and heart would settle into that home and family like it were his own.

In the passenger seat beside him were a couple of boxes. He'd stopped in at the local electronics store on his way and picked up two cameras that could be connected to an app on Tina's phone. She would be able to access real-time footage of the house whether she was home or not.

He contemplated what was going on with Tina. Unusual in a town this size. Almost unheard of for there to be any kind of crime. But after the last mining downturn, a decent number of residents found themselves in some financial difficulty. And like many regional towns, there was a lot of drugs getting around. Maybe a combination of those two found their way out there.

Ex-wife or not, though, he wasn't going to leave Tina in any kind of danger. Not if he could do something as simple as install cameras. He had told Isabelle he was going to a hardware shop to look for some new tools for work. All he had to do was mention *hardware* and her eyes glazed over.

Chris parked and lumbered up the short staircase.

Tina smiled. "Thanks for coming."

He held up the boxes. "Two cameras enough?"

"I would hope so. Maybe we can put one out here and another inside facing the hallway."

"Don't want them at the front and back doors?"

She shook her head. "I need to see what's going on inside."

"No other indication anyone has broken in since the locks were changed?"

"No. Thankfully."

He glanced towards the shed. "Do I still have a toolset in there?"

"Should do."

His attention wandered around the rest of the yard. "You mowed?"

She nodded.

He studied the overgrown gardens, the bare fruit trees, but didn't say anything about those.

Tina ran back inside for the key, then led Chris to the shed, unbolted the padlock and opened the roller door. She held the camera boxes for him as he searched for his toolset.

"No sign of anyone getting in here?" he asked.

"No signs anywhere. Except for the notes."

When they headed into the house, Tina poured them both a cup of coffee, leaving one on the kitchen table. Chris came in and out, lifting the mug to his lips to drink the hot brew while he installed the brackets and attached the cameras.

Finishing the last of his coffee, he eyed the neat kitchen with homesickness, remembering when he had once been so comfortable within that space. Knew where all the appliances were kept. Had shoved his head under the sink to fix a leaky tap once or twice. Would head to the fridge with the sense that he had every right to do so. Not like at Isabelle's where he still felt intrusive each time he opened the fridge door.

The kitchen was completely spotless, not a fleck of dust, which was standard for Tina. He glanced on top of the fridge; it amazed him how she managed to keep that surface clean when she wasn't even able to see up that high. A box of prescription tablets had been placed there. He shouldn't

113

question it, shouldn't intrude on her personal life anymore, but he couldn't help himself.

"You feeling okay?" he asked as he was packing up and she was clearing away the wrapping and white powdery residue from where he'd drilled into the plaster.

She hesitated before answering, not wanting to appear needy or like she was playing her victim card, but in the end, she went with truthful. "I'm not great. I think the stress has been getting to me. I've been feeling a little sick this past week. Headaches. Dizziness. Nausea. I'll have test results back early next week to see if I've been contaminated by something. Some people on a forum mentioned that heavy-metal poisoning can cause all sorts of paranoia."

He frowned, deep lines forming between his brows. "Where would you have been contaminated by heavy metals?"

She shrugged. "Maybe the paint or plumbing. Perhaps the water tank."

"Not possible. The piping is copper. And the tank is galvanised steel. Plus, the inside has been lined with a special membrane to stop that kind of thing from happening. The paint isn't lead either. Maybe it once was, but someone had renovated well before we bought the place."

An impatient sigh. "I don't know then. I'm trying to check every possibility off the list at the moment."

"It couldn't be some *boyfriend,* could it?" he asked, focusing on his feet instead of her eyes.

She restrained a smile for how difficult a question that was for him. A reasonable question. In three years, she should have moved on. Chris certainly had. But for Tina, she hadn't even gone on a date. Hadn't even thought about it.

She wasn't physically or emotionally ready for a new relationship. "No."

"Right, well, hopefully, we get some answers on these cameras. Or better yet, it all goes away, and you have no more trouble."

"I like the latter option."

"You don't need me to come back tomorrow for anything else? No leaky taps? Leaves in the gutters?"

"I think everything is up-to-date."

He tilted his head towards the door. "I better get going then."

"Sure. Thanks again for your help. I appreciate it."

"No problem. I'm a phone call away. Until next Sunday, anyway, then I'm back at the mine."

She opened the door for him and followed him outside.

His blue gaze met hers. A soft smile. "See ya later."

"Bye, Chris. Thanks again."

Tina remained on the top step until the rumble of Chris's ute's engine was but a hum in the far distance.

* * *

A wave of dizziness had overcome Tina, so she had spent the last hours of her weekend on the couch streaming movies. When she could no longer hold her tired eyes open, she showered, dressed into her pyjamas and climbed into bed.

She dreaded going to work tomorrow. Delivering heavy parcels in Central Queensland heat while feeling unwell was akin to torture. Needing to distract her mind for a half hour or so before sleep, Tina reached for a book that was sitting on her bedside table. She jerked her hand back and screamed when she noticed the sticky note attached to it. Scrambling to her knees, she crawled across the bed to the other side, climbed off, ran to the door and palmed the light switch, flooding the room with bright light.

Her heart was beating hard and fast. Her breathing shallow and quick. Her focus remained fixed on the glaring yellow note. There was only one entry and one exit to her room and that was via the hall.

She snatched her mobile, then the book, from her bedside table and went to the living room, switching on lights on the way. She placed the book on the couch and finally allowed herself to read the note.

I see you.

A stream of shivers ran up and down her spine, spread along her arms. Her throat was closing over as fear budded. Her muscles twitched. Teeth ground hard together.

Her first thought was, *Had Chris done this?* But after forcing herself to sift through her memories of that day, she was certain he hadn't gone into her room. He had been in her sight the entire time. So, whoever had come inside, had done so between the time she had made her bed that morning and now.

A tremble racked her. Her teeth chattered.

She was almost too afraid to look at the footage on her phone, but she had to. She needed to know if she should call the police and, most importantly, if she finally had proof that someone had been inside her home.

Fast-forwarding at triple speed, she zoomed through the recorded footage from the moment the cameras were set up till now. She viewed herself walking up and down the hall at various stages throughout the day, but not one other person.

No one.

She raced back up the hall to her bedroom window and lifted the frame, but the secured lock kept it firmly in place. Impossible to lock it on the way back out; it had to be done internally once the window was closed. Every other window was locked, too. She had double- and triple-checked them over the past week.

Tears filled her eyes because no other explanation remained. It had to be *her* writing the notes.

CHAPTER 16

Isabelle stood at the kitchen sink, gazing out the back window at Chris. His arm muscles flexed as he heaved big, round pots filled with soil and green bushy trees, positioning them around the patio's perimeter. The masculine energy of it all was stimulating.

Operating a business and being a single mother had left little time for outdoor maintenance. Isabelle's yard had never received more care than a teenage kid running a lawnmower over it every other week. Chris, in a matter of a few months, had turned it from straw to lush grass. The edges were trimmed and neat and the cut was even.

A hand floated to her stomach, and she smiled so wide her cheeks hurt. Imagining their life once the baby came into the world filled her with playful buoyancy. Witnessing Juliette's reaction had set her world right and given her permission to feel elated about this pregnancy.

She had even gathered the courage to call her parents. They were shocked, but they weren't unhappy either and that met all expectations that Isabelle had. A heavy burden of weight had dissolved the moment she ended that call.

Chris glanced through the window and caught her watching. She smiled bashfully, her cheeks flushing. "What would you like for dinner tonight?"

"Whatever you feel like. I'll give you free rein for the next nine months."

She giggled. He was trying to help, so she refrained from explaining that she would rather he decided for her. She wouldn't have asked otherwise. Her ability to make up her mind about things, especially food, was limited at the moment.

Isabelle finished loading the dishwasher and took a tray of chicken out of the freezer to defrost on the bench. A salad and grilled chicken were now on the menu for dinner, although, by that evening, she would probably feel like something completely different.

She cleared rubbish from the kitchen bench and pressed her foot onto the small garbage bin's pedal to open the lid. It flicked up more quickly than she had anticipated and a few loose papers that had been shoved on top flew out onto the floor. She dropped the rubbish into the bin, then swooped up the papers, noting with a glance that they were recent receipts. One was from a big hardware store for one hundred and fifty dollars. The second was from an electronics store for a little over one thousand dollars. Two security cameras.

"What did you buy security cameras for?" she called to Chris.

"Pardon?"

"Come here."

He stood at the backscreen door and she held up the receipt. "What did you buy security cameras for?"

"Oh, that's for Tina. She's been having some weird stuff going on at home."

Isabelle flinched at her husband's use of the word *home*. "What kind of stuff?"

"Someone has been getting inside and leaving notes."

Her eyes widened. "Really?"

"Yeah. I suggested I get some cameras and set them up around her house."

"So, this is where you were this morning?"

He nodded, looked away.

"I thought you said you were going to look for tools?"

"I did."

"But you didn't tell me you were also spending the morning with your ex."

He opened the screen door and stepped inside. It snapped loudly behind him as it closed. "It's not like that, Issy, and you know it."

"Did she pay you back for the cameras?"

"I can't expect her to come up with a thousand dollars."

Hands on her hips. "You do remember she's your ex, right?"

He sighed.

"You can't continue paying for stuff like this. Her life has nothing to do with you anymore. We're about to have a baby, and you're out spending a thousand dollars on Tina behind my back." She motioned towards the spare room that would soon become a nursery. "We could have bought a cot and a pram with that money."

"And we'll still be able to buy everything this baby will ever need."

Her rigid stance softened a little. "We need to start thinking about *us*. If she wants expensive cameras, she can get a better job."

A brow arched, a tic in his jaw as his teeth clamped tight together.

Her nose wrinkled. "What does that look mean?"

"Could you afford them? Without me, that is?"

"Don't you dare," she shrieked. "I don't ask for a cent from you."

"Nor should you have to. We're a partner—"

"You're not my knight in shining armour coming in with a full bank account."

"I never said I was. But don't ask me to desert someone who was once a big part of my life. One little payment isn't going to hurt you or the baby."

"I don't understand this relationship with her."

An angry sigh as he shuffled a hand through his hair. "Jesus, Issy. People don't always have to hate their ex. People can be civilised and get along."

"Do you still love her?"

He hesitated.

Her breath was stolen from her throat and her shoulders slouched.

"I don't have feelings for her in a romantic sense," he said quickly.

"Why the delay?" Her question was weak, hoarse sounding.

"Because I was trying to think of how to phrase it diplomatically."

"How about you try the truth rather than diplomacy. When do you go back to the mine?"

"Next Sunday," he answered, eyes narrowed.

"Right, well you can sleep at a mate's house until then."

"Don't be ridiculous."

She pointed at him with jutting motions. "No, you stop being ridiculous! Get your priorities in line. I will not be let down by a man again."

"And I won't be blamed for what some overzealous teenage boy did to you two decades ago." His voice was harsh and accusative.

"Get out. Now, before I slap your smug face."

He moved past her not saying another word. That was why they should have bought an entirely new place together instead of Chris shacking up in one Isabelle already owned. He had done nothing wrong and yet he was the one scurrying from there with his tail between his legs.

He was a grown man, not a seventeen-year-old kid, so he wasn't about to burden a mate with that petty relationship bullshit. He would find a hotel instead and wait it out.

CHAPTER 17

Maddison cut her nightly workout short. Her body could not take another self-inflicted beating. The toxicity of her hangover yesterday still lingered deep in her aching muscles. So, she sat there, on her workbench, staring, listening to the happenings upstairs until Ben, at last, went to bed.

Tiptoeing, she headed up the stairs, into the kitchen and pulled out a bottle of sauvignon blanc from the fridge. Delicious white wine, French grapes, made in New Zealand. Not that any of that mattered. She would gladly pour it from a cask if that didn't highlight something about her nightly habits she wasn't ready to admit.

Maddison had watched a show about the growing population of middle-aged women across Australia who drank themselves to sleep each night, yet still managed to wake in time for the school run and could function in their day job. By functioning in their lives, they could hide the underlying addiction problem from the community and themselves.

Maddison found one too many similarities to those women's stories but had managed to twist and mould her growing dependence on alcohol and prescription drugs into something less ugly. Something socially acceptable. Tolerable.

She positioned her wine on the table under the overhead lights, sat behind it and smiled wide as she snapped a selfie using her smartphone. She uploaded the picture along with an upbeat description on her social media feeds.

Quiet night in with hubby. #lovinglife.

As the likes and comments flowed in from old friends, family and people she barely ever saw in real life, she drank glass after glass of wine until she had squeezed the last drop from the bottle.

Her sobriety morphed into a lightheaded spin of thoughts and sight. She smiled again for the camera as she held up her fourth full-to-the-brim glass of sauvignon blanc, ensured a beauty filter was on, tilted her chin upward, and snapped a picture.

She uploaded the picture and clumsily typed: *Cheers, everyone! I hope you're all enlkoying your Saburday night. #lovinglide #Saturdaynightim.*

By the time she hit the bottom of that glass, her mind was muzzy. Each blink hurt as her lids scratched against tired eyes. She mechanically sought out her supply of Zolpidem from above the fridge, took two and stumbled up the hall for a long, hot shower.

* * *

Bright light behind Maddison's eyes. A poke at her ribs. The sound of a child's voice.

"Mummy, there's a lady here," said a six-year-old girl as she crouched beside Maddison.

Maddison dragged her eyelids open, squinted against the blast of sunlight and gazed into the face of the small girl. Big brown eyes stared down at her. The girl smiled.

"Come away, Natasha. Hurry! Come on now," came the high-pitched voice of Natasha's mother.

"Hello. You have priddy lipstick," said Natasha.

Maddison sat up. Her head was pounding. She glanced around. Grass beneath her palms. A swing set in the distance. The local park. Muted morning sun. She felt in her pocket for her mobile phone but came up empty.

Natasha's mother, dressed in a sunhat and white khakis briskly marched to her daughter, gripped the child's hand and pulled her behind her body.

"Are you okay?" the woman asked Maddison.

Panic rose in Maddison's chest, crept up her neck, into her cheeks. She shook her head in a jarring motion. "No, I don't think I am. Why am I here? How did I get here?"

"Is there someone I can call for you? To come and get you? The police?"

Her breaths were harsh and heavy. "No. No police. I don't think... should I?"

The woman shrugged. "I'm not sure. Are you hurt?"

Maddison scanned her body for injuries. Her clothes were intact. She was wearing pyjama pants and a singlet top. No shoes. She painfully climbed to her feet. The world tilted around her, so she stood very still, held her head exactly right until her balance was restored.

A hand at her temple to stop the throbbing. She swallowed down her surging nausea. Confusion. A tangle of memories that wouldn't become coherent tightened behind her eyes. The last thing she recalled was drinking wine in her kitchen. Heading to the shower. Then... then... nothing. Strange feelings and emotions but no concrete understanding.

A house. Familiar. But she couldn't discern whose. She shook her head. "Can you please call my husband for me? I need him to come and get me." Tears were thick in the back of her throat. Her chest was hot and achy.

The little girl looked up at her with wide eyes and a frown while the woman pulled her mobile out of her handbag. This was the lowest point Maddison had reached in her life. She told the lady Ben's phone number. After dialling, the woman held her phone to her ear, not willing to hand it over to a stranger in a park.

"Hi, my name is Sylvia. I'm at Henderson Play Park. Your wife is here. Yes, she's okay, just a little confused. She needs you to pick her up. Okay, good, see you soon."

"Thank you," Maddison said, tears falling down her cheeks. "I'm sorry to have—"

The woman waved her apology away. "It's fine. Don't worry about it." And she strode away, holding Natasha's hand tight.

Maddison made the long, slow walk to the edge of the park, keeping her head very still and her footsteps small. She sat on a short fence as she waited for her husband and silently begged the world to cease spinning.

Soon, the family car arrived and parked in front of Maddison. Ben was behind the wheel. The kids were in the back, which ignited anger so fierce if she were not so sick, she would have unleashed it. The last two people on earth she wanted to see her like that was Ruby and Riley. But Ben hadn't had any other options. He couldn't leave his young children at home on their own.

He threw the door open, raced to her side, helping her from the fence. "Are you okay?".

She burst into tears. "No. I don't think I am. I don't know how I got here."

He cradled her into his arms like she was a child and bundled her into the passenger seat.

"What's wrong with Mummy?" Ruby asked.

"She's a little unwell at the moment," Ben said, leaning over Maddison to buckle her up.

"Will she die?" Riley asked, his voice wavering with emotion.

Maddison wanted to assure her children that she would be okay, but she couldn't stop sobbing. Long, loud wails.

Ben kissed her head, closed the passenger door and ran around to his side of the car. No one spoke again for the entire trip.

When home, Ben turned the cartoon channel on for the children and then helped his wife to the ensuite for a shower.

As Maddison undressed, she glanced at her reflection. Her lips were covered in bright red lipstick, bleeding into the lines around her mouth, messy like a three-year-old had applied it. Revulsion twisted in the pit of her stomach.

When the water was set, Ben asked. "You're not hurt?"

She shook her head. Her whole body was trembling.

"Between your legs?"

She gasped, eyes going wide. Her hand flung between her legs and she patted gently at first, then harder as her bravery grew. No soreness. No fluids. She burst into tears and shook her head to answer her husband.

"Good." He gestured to the running shower. "Hop in. I'll make you a warm drink and something to eat. Call out if you need me."

"Thank you."

"It's okay."

"I'm going to get help," she said when Ben had reached the bathroom door. "I will. I promise."

He managed a sympathetic smile. "Good."

Ben strode out of the bathroom, leaving the door open behind him. Partway down the hall, out of sight, he leaned over, hands to his knees and exhaled with a groan. Tears sprang to his eyes. He hadn't cried for years. Nothing had been big enough. Not since...

He stood up, wiping his eyes, and shook the emotion away as he drew a deep breath in and kept on his way to the kitchen.

CHAPTER 18

Tina rushed to the front door of the silent Gladstone residence, knocked and called out, "Delivery!"

No answer. Most people were at work during the week. If not, there were tell-tale sounds of the television, music or exuberant children. She placed the package against the alcove at the front door and returned to her waiting van, the engine humming in the midday heat.

As she climbed into the driver's seat for the hundredth time that day, a text message *dinged* on her phone. She checked the screen. Her blood test results were in.

A subtle edginess in her limbs as she dialled the number. An automated voice outlined a series of options, then a receptionist answered.

"Um, hi, this is Tina Brooks. I just received a message that recent blood results were in."

"Okay, Tina, let me check your file here." The receptionist clicked and clacked at a keyboard. "Your results have come back negative. So, the doctor has marked in your file that she won't need to see you about this matter."

Tina slouched in her seat. "Okay, thanks so much."

She hung up, stared at the steering wheel for a long while. She didn't have heavy metal poisoning, but something was wrong with her. Since her appointment last week, her condition had worsened. It may be that a virus was doing the rounds or perhaps she had a minor underlying infection of some kind. For the rest of today, she would push through the fatigue. But tomorrow, she would call work to let them know she was much too sick. Give herself a couple of days to rest and recoup and if she didn't improve, another trip to the doctor was in order.

Tina reversed her van out of the driveway and darted along the road to the next property. She was back at square one regarding the notes. For her, the most frightening aspect to it was the anonymity and covertness. She knew well enough that the worst kinds of people operated under the cover of darkness.

She shuddered and shook her head slightly to toss that train of thought away. Simply too terrifying; she would never be able to sleep without one eye open again.

* * *

Tap. Tap. Tap.

Tina's eyes snapped open. She glanced around her dark bedroom at the shadows appearing like tall, misty forms keeping vigil from various standpoints in the room. But when she blinked, the forms became a regular shadow or a patch of discoloured wall paint.

Tap. Tap. Tap.

She faced the bedroom window, listening hard.

Tap. Tap. Tap.

There was someone outside the window. She gasped, palm covering her mouth, eyes wide. She stretched for the torch that was on her bedside table. A more discreet light, unlike her lamp that would draw too much attention.

Breathing heavily, she rolled out of bed, both feet pressing to the floor, and tiptoed to the window.

Tap. Tap. Tap.

She froze. Her heart beat out a hard, fast rhythm against her ribcage. There was someone out there. Every part of her twitched and tensed, urging her to scream and run, but she had to find out. She had to know who was doing this or she would go mad.

Creeping closer to the window, she stood to the side, back against the wall. Drawing on all her courage, she lurched, pushed the curtains back, flicked on the torch and blasted it at the windowpane.

A startled face stared at her. Tina's hand slapped over her mouth as she screamed. The person blinked, turned, then sprinted across the yard towards the side of the house.

The confrontation took mere seconds, but the adrenalin sparking through Tina's body had dragged out the incident making it feel like minutes. More than enough time with her sharpened senses to know who was out there.

Isabelle Brooks!

She made chase, sprinting out of her room, skidding around the corner into the hall, then dashed out the front door into the night. She was panting. Her senses firing. The outskirts of her vision blurred. A strange ringing in her ears.

A blur of colour and rustle of leaves near the bushland perimeter.

Tina jumped down the stairs, raced across the front yard towards the sound. "I saw you, Isabelle! I saw you," she screamed as she navigated the uneven ground. "What are you doing here? Why are you doing this to me?"

When she made it to the boundary, all was quiet, only the choral hum of cicadas, crickets and flapping wings as a few startled birds took flight. Tina shone an arc of torchlight into the scrub, steadily from left to right and back again, but she couldn't see anything.

In the distance, a car engine rumbled, followed by wheels skidding, then the noise faded as the car edged further away.

"Damn it," she huffed and lowered the torch to her side.

She marched back into the house, barely able to believe what had happened there tonight. Her stalker was Isabelle. That didn't make sense whatsoever to her. She locked the front door and returned to her bedroom, snatching her phone off the bedside table. With unsteady hands, she typed a text and sent it to Chris.

TINA: *Tell your wife to stay the hell away from me!*

* * *

Tina's incredulity about what happened the night before had morphed into trembling rage by the next morning. She called her employer to inform them that she was too ill to make it into work. Then she sat at the dining table, coffee within arm's reach, and used her phone to access the footage from the two cameras.

Not one indication that Isabelle was either inside or outside the house. That meant one thing—Isabelle knew where the cameras were located.

It didn't necessarily imply Chris was complicit. Isabelle could have coaxed that information from him in general conversation. Though, if Tina did discover Chris had any inkling of what Isabelle had been doing, and he had done nothing to stop her, she would be in her car so fast, driving over there to give them both a piece of her mind.

A message notification dinged on her mobile and she flinched.

CHRIS: *Was this text message meant for me?*

Referring to the hasty text she had sent him during the middle of the night.

She typed a reply.

TINA: *Yes, it was. And if you don't understand why then you need to have an overdue conversation with your stalker wife.*

She didn't receive a reply.

Tina placed her phone on the tabletop, closed her eyes and tried to calm her growing rage. Her leg bounced up and down, muscles twitched. She couldn't stay there in her home acting all Zen-like as though that was going to somehow help.

Knowing who the stalker was had given Tina a small semblance of control. She had to send a strong message to Isabelle that she wouldn't be intimidated any longer. So, she got to her feet, dressed, then drove into town, parking a little way from Isabelle's hairdressing salon.

Tina climbed out of her car and rushed along the street, past the small offices and businesses. When she arrived at the salon, she pushed open the glass door. The *tink* of bells had all the hairdressers and their clients looking in her direction.

Hairdryers were whirring. Black capes were strung around customers. A couple of women were at the sink, water streaming over their hair. Another had a head full of thin foils. Upbeat music hummed from the speakers.

As Isabelle pasted bleach onto a strand of a woman's blonde hair, she lifted her gaze to look at Tina.

"I know it was you," Tina said, glaring unflinchingly.

Isabelle's brow furrowed. "I have no idea what you're talking about."

133

Tina turned her head, closed the door behind her, and walked back to her car.

* * *

The next morning, Tina woke early. She checked the house for strange notes, but she was certain she wouldn't find any more. Anger bristled across her flesh as she dressed and made herself a coffee.

The energy she had spent on Isabelle over the short time she'd known of her existence was miniscule. It hadn't been a huge shock when she'd learned that Chris had moved on to a new relationship. At that stage, they had been separated for about twelve months.

But knowing now that Isabelle—her ex-husband's new wife—was her stalker, amplified Tina's energy upon that woman a thousandfold. Every time she thought about the situation, and what she had been put through those past few weeks, a vibrating rage rumbled in her chest.

But one thing Tina couldn't understand was *why*.

She had been nothing but genial when it came to Isabelle. Not that they'd talked to each other much, but in a town that size it was impossible to avoid bumping into her and Chris on occasion. When she had, she had simply smiled and chatted casually about the weather with them. Never had she given Isabelle a reason to dislike her nor stoop to the depths of stalking.

Isabelle had to be unhinged. Could explain why she had never had a relationship until Chris came along. You could only hide your mental instability from your intimate partners for so long.

Tina knew Chris's mind well. He would look past any insanity for as long as he could. Maybe he would never take off his rose-coloured glasses and see what he was truly dealing with.

Either way, Tina wasn't going to sit idly by and let Isabelle get away with it. She would show her exactly what it felt like to be afraid because of someone else's vindictive actions.

Tina locked the front door behind her and climbed into her car. She drove into town, towards Isabelle and Chris's home, parking a few streets away on the arm of the road that was bordered by a nest of trees. She waited there as a sparse flow of cars drove past, occupied by people on their way to work or mums and dads doing the school run.

She waited for Isabelle's car to show. When it drove past, Tina pulled the steering wheel full lock, screeched onto the road, flipped a U-turn and trailed her. At the upcoming traffic lights, she manoeuvred beside Isabelle and stared at her through the passenger window. When Isabelle finally looked over, her eyes widened, and she hastily glanced away.

The traffic lights flashed green. Tina slowly rolled forward, letting Isabelle take the lead, then steered right to tuck in behind her car again. All the way to work, Tina followed, only driving away once Isabelle had made her way into the salon.

That afternoon, Tina came back, parked directly outside the doors to the salon and waited for Isabelle to finish. She trailed close to her car—only a quick push of Isabelle's brakes away from colliding with the bumper—and shadowed her all the way home.

Each time Isabelle glimpsed Tina through the rear-view mirror, Tina didn't dare show the gratification she was feeling for seeking her revenge. Instead, she narrowed her gaze and all but snarled at her through the windscreen. That way, Isabelle would think twice about ever coming to her home again.

CHAPTER 19

Isabelle strode out the door and headed around the front of her house to the garage. As the roller door was opening, a glint of metal in the distance caught her eye. Her shoulder muscles tensed, and she spun to look. Tina was parked on the side of the road a few streets away. The third morning in a row.

It was just her luck to have this sort of thing happen while she was trying to prove a point to Chris by kicking him out. A skulking foreboding moved through her as a thought struck: *Had Chris been staying with Tina these past few days?*

She shook her head.

Isabelle wasn't experienced when it came to men and how they thought. She had lived vicariously through her friends and clients, listening intently to their relationship stories. Men could be arseholes. They could be cheaters. But many of her friends were in happy relationships and had been for years. That was how she chose to view what she had with Chris—a happy marriage. But theirs had been a whirlwind romance. One minute they were having coffee, the next they were going on dirty weekends away, and then they were married. She wasn't certain that was enough time to truly know someone.

She darted back inside her home, the foreboding increasing, for it was becoming obvious that she had rushed too fast, too blindly, to fill her loneliness and settled with the first man who showed potential.

"Stop thinking like this," she growled as she rummaged through her handbag for her mobile. She called Chris and waited with the phone against her ear.

"Hi," he said.

She squeezed her eyes closed. "Hi. Where are you?"

"I'm at a hotel."

"You've been there these past few days?"

"Yeah. I was too embarrassed to explain the situation to a mate."

A slight twist of guilt in her stomach. "You haven't been with Tina?"

"Of course not. Look, Issy, I installed cameras for her. That's it. I hadn't seen her before that for months and months."

She sighed. "Well, Tina is parked a few streets from here. She's been following me to and from work every day. I don't know what she wants."

"Following you to work?" A bewildered tone.

"Yes. Tailing close to my bumper. She's frightening. I can't have an accident. What if the baby gets hurt?"

"I'll go talk to her. As long as you're okay with that?"

"Tell her to stay away from me."

"I will."

"I'll get Renee to open the salon this morning. Stop by afterwards. I think we need to talk."

Hesitation. "Right. Yeah, sure. I'll be there soon."

* * *

Chris spotted Tina's car. She was parked on the side of the road next to a row of trees. When he pulled his ute in behind her, he looked around, noting the clear line of vision up the hill to Isabelle's house.

Chris went to her, standing beside the driver's side window. Not that a window mattered when Tina had the top down on her Mini Cooper.

Tina frowned, met his gaze, seatbelt still buckled across her chest. She was pale. Thin. Her eyes were bloodshot. She was fidgeting.

"What's going on?" he asked.

"She obviously didn't tell you."

Two lines of tension sat between his brows. "Tell me what?"

"Isabelle's the stalker, Chris. I saw her outside my window on Monday night. She was tapping on the pane. I blasted her with my torch, and it was Isabelle standing there."

He laughed sardonically. "What? No way. That's not right."

"I saw her!"

"She wouldn't have done that."

"It was Isabelle. She then bolted away into the bush."

He sighed. "You don't look well, Tina. What's going on?"

"Don't gaslight me. I'm fine. I know what I saw. Your wife has been leaving notes inside my house. She has been tapping on my window in the middle of the night."

He shook his head, unable to grasp what he was being told. At least it explained the strange text message she had left him.

"Did you see her leave the house Monday night?" she asked.

He looked at the ground, bit down on his bottom lip.

Her eyes narrowed. "What?"

"I… ah, haven't been home. So, I couldn't tell you if Issy left the house or not."

Tina blinked.

"We fought. About you."

She pointed to her chest. "Me?"

"Yeah, she was upset about the cameras."

"I don't understand. What the bloody hell have I done to her? What have I ever done to deserve this?"

He lifted his hands. "Look, she's upset, sure, but it doesn't mean she's coming over to your house in the middle of the night and tapping on your window."

"And how would you know?"

"I know. Okay? Leave her alone."

Tina leaned closer to Chris, her nose wrinkling with her anger. "No, you've got it the wrong way around. She's to leave *me* alone. You tell her not to set foot on my property again. If she does, I'll call—"

"You don't dare touch a hair on her head. You hear me?"

Tina recoiled, sank back in her seat. She was going to say she would call the police, not hurt Isabelle.

"If you dare touch her, then I'll—"

The ferocity in Chris's voice was something she hadn't encountered before. Not in all their fifteen years of marriage. "Kill me? Is that what you're going to say?"

He took a step back, his shoulders sagging. "No, of course not. Look, Tina, Issy's pregnant. I can't have her getting hurt."

All vision faded as Tina's breath was thieved from her lungs like she had been trampled. "Pregnant?"

He regretted mentioning it.

"Your baby?"

He bit down hard on his resentment for being asked such a ridiculous question. "Of course."

Her lips twisted with rage. She was shaking. Eyes glossing. "Right, I see how it is. She can terrorise me and it's perfectly okay because she's having your baby—"

"That's not it at all."

"Sure. You know what? Forget it. Enjoy your life." She unlocked the handbrake, slammed her foot to the accelerator and the car skidded away, kicking up dirt and rocks behind her.

Chris groaned, put his hands on his head and looked up at the sky. Blue. Not a single cloud, which was completely at odds with his emotions.

* * *

Isabelle opened the door for Chris when he arrived at the house. She had spied on his encounter with Tina from the front window. With the way Tina had abruptly left, it didn't look like it had gone well.

"Hi," she said and stood out the way so he could come inside.

He was frowning. His brows were low. She wasn't sure if she had seen him upset like this before.

He stepped inside. "Hi."

"Do you want a coffee?"

"Sure. Thanks."

She led him to the kitchen. "How have you been?"

He shrugged, frowned even deeper. "As well as someone who has been kicked out of his house could be, I guess."

Her eye twitched. She resented his answer, though he was in his rights to gripe about it. She turned away from him, concentrating on pouring milk into a metal jug. "So, what is Tina doing parked down the road?"

"She thinks you're her stalker."

Isabelle spun to face her husband, eyes wide. A small chuckle. "You've got to be joking. Why the hell would I stalk *her*?"

"I'm not sure," he said with a shrug. "I can't make sense of it."

"She's utterly lost her mind."

"Did you go to her house, Issy? Tap on her windows?"

A derisive laugh. "Why would I do that?"

"I don't know. I wasn't here to vouch for your whereabouts. But she swears black and blue that she saw you outside her bedroom window on Monday night."

She slammed the jug onto the benchtop, milk nearly splashing over the lip. "As if. How could you even think that I would do something like that?"

"I don't know what's going on. I'm hearing two conflicting stories from people who have no reason to lie. I don't know what to believe."

"How about your wife? The woman carrying your child."

He sighed. "Look, I just told her about the baby. Believe me" – he focused on his linked fingers – "she's suffering enough. So, if you were, perhaps, dishing out some kind of punishment, then please stop."

She gasped, nose wrinkling. "How dare you! Seriously, Chris, how bloody dare you!" She pointed towards the front door. "I've had enough. Get out! Now! I don't need this in my life. Get out! Go!" she screamed, shaking with anger.

After so many years living independently, only herself and Juliette to worry about, she wasn't used to some third party lugging their bag full of emotional landmines, throwing them all over the house and expecting her to sidestep them. Eventually, she was going to hit one. Too many this past week.

Chris held both hands up in surrender. "I believe you. I'm just saying."

"Well don't. You have no right. Go! Leave! I can't even look at your face."

"For fuck's sake, Issy. You can't just keep throwing me out."

"It's my house. I'll do what the bloody hell I like."

He nodded with resignation as he stood. "Exactly. And it will always be this way, won't it? You screaming at me to leave *your* home. Might be the reason you so adamantly wanted to keep this house." His fist slammed down hard on the benchtop. "Gives you the upper hand every fucking time!"

She didn't say anything. Stared until he dropped his gaze, turned and walked out. When the front door slammed, she jumped. Her pulse was speeding like a bullet train. She stood there in her kitchen, trying to catch her breath, trying to stem the tears that were flooding her eyes, until his car engine started, then hummed away as he drove off.

She snatched the metal jug off the bench and threw it across the room. It hit the opposite wall, crashed to the floor, milk splashing everywhere. She sank onto the tiles beneath her feet, lowered her face into her hands and sobbed. She didn't want to be in a marriage where she had to continually argue her position to her husband. He should be on her side.

CHAPTER 20

The day of the murder…

Tina careened off the road and nearly ploughed into a bank of trees. She pulled the handbrake on, reached for her seatbelt with trembling hands to unbuckle it, but she couldn't coordinate her movements enough to manage the task. The outskirts of her sight were blackening, tunnelling her vision. The bark on the trees, the green leaves, her car's dashboard, were warping and waving.

Her heart was thumping so hard, she thought she could die. Ahead of her, a dark, crouched figure manifested between the tree trunks. The gloomy spectre edged closer to the car, growing more vivid and colourful with its slow advance.

Tina gasped as she finally made out what it was: Isabelle, on her hands and knees, crawling across the rocks and dirt. Her face was caved in, her skull collapsed in places and blood was pouring down her cheeks, chin, and neck. She glared at Tina with demonic eyes, a teasing snarl, then lurched at the car and roared like a monster.

Tina covered her face and screamed, bracing for the impact.

* * *

Tina woke in hospital. She was startled as she opened her eyes, meeting bright light, unfamiliar equipment and four white walls. Her head lolled from side to side, her breathing quickening, as she fought to understand her surroundings.

A nurse was beside her, unwrapping a blood pressure bandage from Tina's arm. She smiled warmly. "Hello, you're awake."

"Where am I?" Tina asked with a soft, hoarse voice. The back of her throat was sore, her tongue dry.

"You're at Gladstone Hospital."

She shook her head, panic rising in her chest. "Why? What's wrong with me?"

"Let me fetch Doctor Michaels and he can explain everything."

The nurse left the room and Tina's eyelids closed. She was woozy and blocking out the world helped to stem that sensation. The sound of footsteps had her snapping her eyes open again.

"Hi, Tina. Good to see you're awake," Doctor Michaels said as he stood beside the bed. "You're looking much better. How are you feeling?"

"Tired. Confused."

He silently studied her chart for a moment. "Your last ECG shows your heart rhythm has returned to normal. Your body temperature is good. Blood pressure is still a little high, but nothing to be concerned about. Do you recall what happened?"

She looked up to the ceiling. "I was driving. And then… then…" She shook her head.

"You were found in your car this morning, presenting with symptoms of drug intoxication. An ambulance transported you to the emergency department. We ran a tox screen, but it didn't pick up on any of the usual suspects. Have you taken anything recently?"

She frowned. "I don't take drugs."

"You're not on any kind of medication?"

"None."

"No vitamins or natural remedies of any kind?"

"No."

"No supplements? Maybe you bought something from overseas?"

She shook her head.

"As we don't know what specific drug we're dealing with, we had to treat your symptoms generally. You've been fed activated charcoal to ensure there was no absorption of the drug into your lower bowel. You should pass that with your next bowel movement. Be sure to drink lots of water in the meantime. We have ordered a broader tox screen to see if we can pinpoint what the specific substance was and how much you consumed. Knowing what we're dealing with will be much more helpful for your treatment but may also ensure you don't get re-exposed to it."

"I don't understand." Tears filled her eyes, but she blinked them away.

"Have you had any symptoms before this morning?"

She drew a shuddering breath inward, tried to return her mind to the past, but it was all so foggy. Only snippets of information were available. "Um, yeah, I've had dizziness and brain fog for a couple of weeks. I've been very tired."

He took notes. "Heart palpitations?"

She nodded. "Sometimes. Nothing I was worried about. I've been thirsty, a lot. And hot. I don't understand any of this. I don't understand what's happening."

"Until we know what you've ingested, all you need to do is rest. I'll keep the oxygen up overnight and a saline drip for hydration. We'll reassess in the morning."

She nodded, wiped the tears from her cheeks.

"Your clarity should return soon enough. Just give it a little time. Meanwhile, I want you to get a good night's rest. If you need help going to the bathroom or anything else, just press this buzzer here," he said, pointing to the switch above the bed connected to a long cord. "A nurse will assist you."

When the doctor left the room, Tina closed her eyes. Something dark and terrifying was lurking in the deepest recesses of her mind. Not much made sense at that moment except for one thing—she did not want to come face to face with that monster.

CHAPTER 21

The day of the murder…

Detective McKenzie's stomach was knotted as he stood on the front doorstep. He closed his eyes for the length of time it took to draw a deep, calming breath, then knocked on the door.

Jenkins was fiddling with her collar, not meeting his gaze. That was her way of getting in the zone. This was never easy. Ever.

After so many years in the job, McKenzie could handle a lot. Thick skin was real; it had to be. But informing family members about a death—let alone that their beloved relative had been murdered so gruesomely—was something no human with a heart could ever dissociate completely from. Sweat was already forming under his arms and across his brow.

Muted footsteps from inside, then the door opened with a rush.

A petite woman with long blonde hair stood before him. Her face was lined with worry. "Hi. What's this all about. I'm absolutely beside myself. Is someone hurt?"

"Isabelle Brooks?"

She nodded.

"I'm Detective Inspector McKenzie and this is Detective Jenkins. Perhaps it's best if we speak about this inside."

Isabelle raked a hand through her hair then gestured they come in. They stepped through the doorway and followed Isabelle to the living room where they sat on the couch beside one another, Isabelle taking the large chair opposite.

McKenzie leaned forward until his elbows were on his thighs, hands clasped. He cleared his throat and looked Isabelle in the eyes. "I'm sorry to inform you, but your daughter Juliette has died."

Silence.

A slight shake of Isabelle's head.

A delirious chuckle that soon morphed into a deep frown. "No. That can't be right. She's at work. She got a job at the alumina refinery. She's there right now." Isabelle got to her feet, looking around her. "Where's my phone? I'll call her, to show that you're mistaken."

"Isabelle?" Jenkins said.

"She'll answer. You watch."

"Isabelle," Jenkins repeated. "Please, come take a seat."

Isabelle returned to the couch and sat down like a robot. Her eyes were wide, frightened.

"I know this is an extremely difficult situation," McKenzie said. "We were called to an incident this morning, not far from here. Juliette was involved. When we arrived at the scene, it was too late."

Isabelle's face contorted as her denial was thieved by the realness of the moment. Two serious detectives with sombre frowns. It wasn't some cruel joke or disgusting mix-up. Deep down she was aware of that but letting her mind come to that conclusion consciously was impossible. "How? What kind of incident?"

"An autopsy and continuing investigation will offer more certainty, but at this stage, it appears that a minor car accident occurred. Juliette exited her vehicle, at which point, she was attacked."

Isabelle gasped, threw her hands over her mouth. She was shaking wildly. "Attacked? What does that mean? Who did this?"

"Juliette suffered injuries to her head, it appears to have been with a wrecking bar. We're still trying to establish who was involved. It's early days yet, but I assure you we will do all that we can to find that out."

Isabelle's head spun. She squeezed her eyes closed. Her heart was beating so hard, it was bruising against her ribs. A deep, violent throb of pain. Twisting in her womb. The brutality of that moment pummelled her, knocked her off her axis. She was no longer spinning around the sun that was her daughter.

Juliette was dead.

Someone had beaten her to death with a wrecking bar.

Only after a moment did Isabelle realise the deep, guttural groan filling the room was coming from her. Her eyes filled with tears. "No." Her mouth twisted, lips trembled.

Detective Jenkins went to sit beside Isabelle, wrapping an arm around her. Isabelle fell against her and cried the most mournful cry Jenkins had ever heard. She held her head high, blinked back the moisture in her eyes, not allowing herself to succumb to it all. If she did, it would sweep her away.

After a long moment, Jenkins slowly moved away and sat up taller. "We would like to ask you a few questions."

Isabelle didn't acknowledge the statement.

"Isabelle, I know this is extremely hard," McKenzie said in a warm voice.

"Who did this?" Isabelle asked. "Who would kill Juliette?"

"That's what we need to get to the bottom of."

Detective Jenkins stood. "I'm going to make a cup of tea for you. While I do that, Detective Inspector McKenzie is going to ask a few questions. Okay?"

Isabelle stared straight ahead but nodded.

McKenzie opened his notebook, lifted his pen from his pocket and clicked the end. Such a small sound but in the silent, emotionally charged room it was obtrusive. "What time did Juliette leave the house this morning?"

"Seven past eight."

"That's a precise time."

"Juliette's precise." Isabelle scrubbed a hand through her hair. "She's a very smart, capable young woman."

"Was she heading to work?"

Isabelle nodded, fresh tears falling down her cheeks.

"Was she going anywhere before work?"

"No. Never. She started at eight-thirty, so she had just enough time to drive across town and park at the refinery."

McKenzie made notes. "Did Juliette have a boyfriend?"

Isabelle shook her head.

"A recent ex?"

"She hasn't been seeing anyone for months."

"Did she mention if someone was interested in her?" he asked.

"No. She's been so busy with work and study. She hasn't had time."

"And she works at the alumina refinery, you said?"

"Yes."

"No troubles with any workmates?"

"No. None. Not that she told me." Isabelle's face was pale. Her eyes were red and watery.

"You're married, Isabelle?"

A deep breath. A nod.

"Your husband is…?"

"Chris Brooks."

McKenzie lifted his head, gazed at her. "He's not Juliette's biological father?"

She shook her head.

"What is Chris's relationship with Tina Brooks?"

"She's his ex-wife."

"Did Juliette have a relationship with Tina?"

Isabelle's brow furrowed. "Not at all. I don't understand why you're asking about her."

"Just trying to get an idea at this stage."

"Was Tina involved?" Isabelle asked. "Did she hurt Juliette?"

"Tina was found nearby. At this stage, we're unsure if she was involved in the incident."

"She's been stalking me every morning for the past week. If she hurt my daughter… If she so much as touched a hair on her head…" Isabelle lurched to her feet, glanced around the room erratically, then marched to the window, looking outside to where Tina had been parked the past few mornings.

"Isabelle?" McKenzie said.

Isabelle turned her head, met his sympathetic gaze. "Did Tina hurt Juliette?"

"Was there a reason for Tina to hurt Juliette?"

She shook her head, shrugged, and came back and crumbled into her seat like her legs had given out beneath her. "I don't know. I don't think so. No one would want to hurt Juliette. She's the kindest, most beautiful…" She broke off with a mournful groan, bending over.

Jenkins appeared in the entryway with a cup of tea in her hand. She went to Isabelle, touched her shoulder, making her flinch. "Come on now. Sit back. I've made you a nice cup of tea."

Isabelle robotically took the tea from Jenkins's hands.

Jenkins settled beside Isabelle. "You're doing really well. I know this isn't easy, but the more information we can gather early on, the more direction we have."

"Where's your husband at the moment?" McKenzie asked.

Isabelle glanced at him, frowned even deeper. "He's staying at a hotel."

"Is that usual?"

She shook her head. "We fought."

"Do you mind me asking what about?"

"He had bought cameras for Tina. He'd gone to her house to install them."

"You were worried about the cost? Or that he saw his ex?"

"Both." Her hand fell to her stomach. "I'm pregnant."

McKenzie and Jenkins looked at each other.

"Is Chris aware of this pregnancy?" Jenkins asked gently.

Isabelle nodded.

"He's happy about it?"

Again, Isabelle nodded, but her body trembled, and she spilled tea down her front. Jenkins reached for the cup, taking it from Isabelle's shaking hands and rested it on the side table next to the couch.

"I can't believe this," Isabelle groaned. "I can't believe it."

"Which hotel is Chris staying in?" McKenzie asked.

"I'm not sure. I don't think he told me."

"Is there someone you would like us to call?" Jenkins asked. "Chris? A family member? A close friend? Just so you have someone here to support you."

Isabelle's parents were first to come to her mind, but they were in Tasmania. By the time they organised flights, it could be hours, if not tomorrow before they could get there. Juliette's face appeared then, and pain surged anew like long-taloned claws were raking out her insides.

Only then did she think about Chris along with the ominous realisation that she didn't trust him, especially if Tina was involved in Juliette's death. What she did know for certain was that she didn't want Chris anywhere near her.

All she needed was for Juliette to walk through the front door in one piece. Nothing else would help; nothing at all.

"Yes." Her voice was soft, croaky. "My friend. Renee. She works at my salon."

McKenzie managed a warm, sympathetic frown. "Let's give her a call then."

CHAPTER 22

D r Michaels spoke with two detectives waiting in the hall outside Tina's hospital room. A full day had passed since Tina had been admitted. She lay on her side on the bed, knees bent towards her chest, eyes closed, dozing.

"Tina isn't fully lucid at this point," Dr Michaels said. "But she's in no physical harm if you would like to speak with her."

The two detectives strode into the room.

"There are some people here to see you, Tina," Dr Michaels said.

Tina dragged her eyelids open, rolled onto her back and pushed her palms into the mattress to lift herself into a seated position. Her head was woozy, her mind a patchy jumble of thoughts and memories.

"I'm Detective Inspector McKenzie and this is Detective Jenkins. We would like to talk about the incident yesterday. Do you think you're up to it?"

Tina glanced at the doctor, then back to McKenzie who was dressed in perfectly ironed grey trousers, a crisp white long-sleeved shirt and tie. The female detective wore black slacks and a flatteringly cut pale-blue shirt.

She cleared her throat. "Ah, I'm not sure. Maybe. My brain isn't working properly, but I'll do my best."

"Use that buzzer there to call me if you want to take a break," Dr Michaels said, then strolled out of the room.

McKenzie offered his partner the chair beside the bed and collected a spare chair from across the room. It was a four-patient room, but the other three beds were unoccupied.

Tina coughed. Her throat was so dry. With shaking hands, she reached across to the small table beside her that had a jug of water and an empty glass waiting. She clumsily poured a drink but spilled some on the tabletop. When she lifted the glass to her lips, drips fell onto the bed and down her white hospital gown.

McKenzie took a seat beside his partner. "How are you feeling now, Tina?"

"Not the best," she said with a weak voice.

"That's understandable. You were in quite a state when I found you yesterday morning."

Her shoulders drooped as she sighed. "I'm sorry I've caused so much trouble."

"It's fine. I'm glad the staff are taking good care of you here."

Tina placed her cup on the table, leaned her back against the bed, resting her head on the pillows. It was difficult to stay upright without feeling like she was about to tilt over.

"We would like to hear your account of what happened. You okay to talk about it?" Jenkins asked. She was noticeably younger than McKenzie. Had a less harrowed look to her deep brown, almost black, eyes.

"I can try. I'm still not feeling myself."

"I understand. Just take your time."

Tina linked her hands together over her lap. A smooth, pale blue blanket covered her legs.

"Chris Brooks is your ex-husband?" McKenzie asked, peeling open the soft cover of his notepad.

"Yes."

"You divorced a while ago now?"

"A few years ago, I think."

"You think?"

Tina pressed a hand to her head. "I'm sorry. My memories are so foggy. We separated, um, about two-and-a-half years ago."

"And he has remarried? To Isabelle Brooks."

She nodded.

"Why did you and Chris separate?"

She squeezed her eyes closed, swimming through the jumble of her thoughts. Her memories were connected with tar, some obscured, some vivid, some fleeting, disappearing like fine silk strands in a breeze the moment she reached for them. "We had our only child... um..." She hesitated, then sat bolt upright, blinking hard. "I can't remember her name. I can't remember." She hit the side of her head, once, twice. "I can't—"

"Take your time," Jenkins said.

Tina tossed her head from side to side, holding her breath and then burst out with, "Kadie! Kadie was her name. I couldn't..." Tears filled her eyes. Her nose ran. "I almost forgot. How could I forget? What mother forgets?"

McKenzie passed a look with Jenkins, then focused on Tina again. Her eyes were red and swollen, filled with tears. She was twitchy. Her hands wringing together. "You've been through some turmoil, Tina, I'm sure, under these circumstances, it's quite normal."

Tina wiped her eyes with her palms, breathing quickly.

Jenkins stood and picked out a couple of tissues from the box on the side table and handed them to Tina. "There you go. You just take your time there."

Tina dabbed her tears and blew her nose, trying to breathe slowly and calmly.

"Can you continue?" Jenkins asked with a soothing, sympathetic tone when she had returned to her seat.

Tina nodded. "After Kadie died, Chris and I weren't great. You know? Stressed. Grieving. So lost. Our relationship fizzled out."

"That's understandable. I'm sorry about your daughter," McKenzie said.

"Thank you."

"How did you feel about Chris remarrying?"

She shrugged. "We were over by then. I anticipated he'd eventually move on. I'm glad he was able to find some happiness again."

"What is your relationship like with Chris now?"

"Pretty good," she said. "We still talk now and then."

"No heated arguments or conversations?"

Tina shook her head, but then stopped herself and nodded instead. "We did argue recently."

McKenzie kept his expression neutral. "When was that?"

"Yesterday. No, um, the day before that. He came to speak with me about Isabelle. I told him she'd been stalking me. Tapping on my windows at night. Leaving strange notes inside my house."

"Isabelle had been doing that?"

She nodded.

"How do you know it was Isabelle?"

"I saw her. I shone torchlight directly on her face. It was Isabelle."

"Over what time did that happen?"

"The past few weeks. I called the police to help me, but there wasn't much they could do, so they told me to lodge an online report. I didn't know it was Isabelle back then. I didn't understand what was happening."

"The Gladstone Police?"

She nodded. "I spoke to an officer. Ryan, Peter, I can't remember his name."

"And this was what Chris spoke to you about?"

"Yes. But he didn't believe me. He didn't believe that Isabelle was stalking me."

"Was the conversation heated?" McKenzie asked.

"A little. Nothing major. I raised my voice somewhat, then sped away."

"Sped away? This conversation took place in your car?"

"Yes."

McKenzie's pen was poised on his notepad. "Whereabouts?"

"Um... a few streets from his house."

"His and Isabelle's home?"

"Yes."

"Why in that specific spot?"

She hesitated, swallowed hard, gaze focused on her lap, rather than the detective's eyes. When she finally looked at McKenzie, she was frowning, blushing somewhat. "I'd been following Isabelle to work. I wanted to show her that I wasn't intimidated. And maybe it was to give her a taste of her own medicine."

"Because of the stalking?"

She nodded.

"Anything else happen during that conversation? Something said that made you upset or angry?"

She wrung her hands together. "He told me Isabelle was pregnant."

"And did that upset you?"

"It did. I was sad he was replacing Kadie so easily. I felt like he was betraying her memory."

"Did you tell him that?"

"No. I just drove away."

"Did you go home after that?"

She nodded.

"Tell me about the following morning?" McKenzie asked, focusing on his notepad, leaving a silence hang in the small hospital room.

"My memories are patchy." She shifted on the bed, head shaking slightly, eyes darting around the room.

"You were found in your car on the side of the road, a few streets from Chris and Isabelle's home at around eight-thirty in the morning. Can you tell me why you were there?"

She squinted, looked off in the distance, searching through the black gloom of her memories. "I was driving somewhere."

The detectives remained quiet.

"I saw Isabelle. Yes, that's right, I saw her. She was in her car. Driving past me. She lifted her middle finger at me and smirked. I don't know if... or..." A hand to her head. She squeezed her eyes closed, trying to draw the memories from the sticky resin they were trapped in. Her eyes flashed open again as a thought struck her. "I was dizzy. So dizzy. I wasn't feeling good, and I think I just, I don't know, blacked out, maybe. It's hard to remember. There was an impact. My car hit her car. Isabelle got out. Yes, she got out and she was screaming at me. Such anger. I was frightened she would hurt me..." She trailed off, looked deep into her mind. "Something was wrong with me. I was too hot." She pressed a hand to her chest. "My heart was racing. I thought I was having a heart attack." She squinted. A blink, lashes fluttering. "I don't know what happened. I can't—"

"Take your time," McKenzie said. "See what else turns up."

Tina racked her brain, but behind her temples was an insistent pounding. The top of her skull ached. She reached for her head, pulled gently at her hair. "I don't know. I can't remember anything." Tears slid down her cheeks. Her chest was tight. A sick, slippery sensation of doom pervaded her belly and moved up her throat like burning vomit, choking her. "Something bad happened, didn't it? Something really, really bad."

She pulled her knees to her chest, hugged her legs and rocked. Loud, watery sobs filled the room. "Something bad. Something so bad." Each word was choked by tears, barely decipherable. "I don't know. I don't know. I don't know." She rocked harder, hugged her knees more firmly. "No. No. No. No. Isabelle was horrifying. Her face had changed into this... demonic thing." Snot and tears dribbled from her nostrils. "She was charging at me." She flinched, tore the sheets away, searched her body for an injury. "Did she hurt me? Is that what happened?"

"The doctor just told us you're physically unharmed. What else can you remember?"

After a long moment, an image formed in her mind. "I ran. I ran from her. I climbed into my car and I raced away. I was petrified she would follow me. But I couldn't see properly. There was something wrong with me. I couldn't see the road properly. These black spots were everywhere. And then" – she shook her head, narrowed her eyes – "I don't remember." She glanced around the hospital room as though seeing it for the first time, pulled the sheets high up to her chin and shook. "Did I hurt her? Did I hurt Isabelle?"

After a long silence, McKenzie leaned forward. "Isabelle is safe and healthy."

Tina's hand flung to her chest and she sighed with relief. "Oh, thank God. I didn't hurt her?"

"No, you didn't hurt Isabelle."

"I'm so relieved." She narrowed her gaze, brow furrowing. "I don't understand. Was it a dream? Was it even real?"

McKenzie glanced at his partner, then back to Tina. He was cautious of pushing Tina to incriminate herself at this stage when she was still obviously under the influence of some substance.

"Once you get medical clearance, we would like to continue this interview at the station."

"Why? You said Isabelle was safe."

"Just to make sure we've exhausted all available avenues."

She crossed her arms over her chest and frowned. "Um, okay."

"I'm going to read back my notes to you, but I'll get the doctor in the room before I do that. I'll need a signature to confirm I haven't misrepresented what you've told me today. You can, of course, clarify anything at any time."

Tina nodded. She had never been more confused in her life.

CHAPTER 23

A knock at Chris's hotel door. His heart skipped, hoping it was Isabelle. He was flying out to the mine in the next couple of hours and didn't want to leave what had gone wrong between him and his wife still broken.

He threw on a shirt and jogged to the door. Apprehension made his shoulders heavy. He prayed Isabelle wasn't going to give up on this relationship so soon. He was terrified of being thrust back into the aftermath of another separation. It hurt like nothing else to have a good relationship end.

Chris hauled the door open, but his brow wrinkled when he found a sharp-dressed man and woman.

"Chris Brooks?" the man asked.

"Yes, but—"

"I'm Detective Inspector McKenzie and this is Detective Jenkins. Do you mind if we come in and have a chat?"

He shook his head. "Detectives? What's this about?"

"Just a few questions about Juliette Stanley."

"Juliette? Why, what's she done?"

They peered down the long, empty hall. "It's probably best if we come in and chat about the matter."

He stood out the way and gestured they enter. He was staying in a small room, the bed taking up most of the space. There was a desk along the front wall with a single chair, but that was it as far as seating went. "I don't have anywhere to sit."

"That's okay. We can stand."

The detectives stood in the centre of the small room, their presence enormous.

"Have you been in touch with Isabelle recently?" McKenzie asked.

"We spoke a couple of days ago," Chris said. "Why? What's going on?"

Jenkins gestured to the bed. "Take a seat there, Chris."

Chris backed up and sat down, his gaze never leaving Jenkins.

"I'm sorry to inform you of this but yesterday morning, Juliette died. At this stage, we strongly suspect she was murdered."

Chris leaned forward, eyes bulging, and mouthed, "What?"

"I apologise for being the bearer of this news, but I assumed Isabelle would have told you."

He shook his head again. "No," he said, but it came out so weak it was barely audible. He coughed, attempted it again. "No. I haven't. I had no idea. Dead? Are you certain?"

"The victim's family still needs to formally identify the body, but it's, ah, a certainty."

"Oh, my God." He lowered his face into his hands. After a long moment, he lifted his head, gaze darting between the two detectives. "How?"

"She was bludgeoned with a heavy tool. We're still waiting on an autopsy."

His eyes were glossing. "I can't believe this. Oh, God. Isabelle. She must be beside herself."

"Is it out of the ordinary that she would keep this from you?" McKenzie asked.

Chris nodded, then shook his head. "I don't even know anymore. I would have thought she'd call me immediately. She's been on her own since yesterday?"

"A close friend has been giving her support," Jenkins added.

McKenzie glanced around the hotel room. A suitcase sat open on the luggage holder. Bright yellow reflective high-vis shirts and blue jeans filled the insides. "So, why are you in a hotel rather than the family home?"

Chris sighed, shoulders slumping. He was finding it hard to breathe. "Issy was angry with me."

"How so?"

He swallowed hard. His lips were trembling as he fought back tears. "She was upset with me about my ex." His eyes widened and he gasped. "You don't think I had anything to do with this, do you? Because I can tell you right now, I didn't."

"We're trying to gather information at this stage to get an idea of what took place. Juliette deserves that, don't you think?"

"Of course. And Isabelle." He got to his feet. His legs were unsteady beneath him. "Isabelle will be devastated. Have you seen her?"

Jenkins nodded. "We spoke with her yesterday."

"Was she… Jesus. Was she upset?"

"Understandably." Jenkins left out the worst of the details, though they had weighed on her all evening, then again, like hard jabs to her ribs, when she awoke this morning. The guttural keening, that was the part that had almost undid her. "Take a seat, Chris, and we'll be out of your hair soon enough," she said. "Would you like a cup of tea?"

He sat on the unmade bed, nodded. "Sure." Then he glanced at his watch. "I'm meant to be flying to Townsville soon. There's no way I can go. I need to be here for Isabelle. Juliette is such a good kid. I find it so hard to believe that she's..." His throat closed over, and his eyes glossed with tears. "I should give Issy a call. Go see her."

"Call when we're done here," Jenkins said, moving to the small kitchenette where there was a jug, a few cups and some teabags. She checked the tiny fridge for milk.

"What's your relationship with Tina like?" McKenzie asked.

Chris blinked. "What's that got to do with Juliette?"

"I was hoping you could help me out with that."

He focused on his lap, brow furrowing. "It's fine, I guess. Fairly amicable." Then he lifted his head, his lips parting. "Oh, is this about the stalking?"

"I'm not sure," McKenzie said, taking out his notepad and pen. "What do you know about that?"

Chris relayed to the detective what Tina had told him about the notes and Isabelle appearing outside her bedroom window. He explained how Tina had been trailing Isabelle to and from work. "I told her to stop it, but she assumed I didn't believe her."

"So, you do believe your wife was stalking Tina?"

"Of course not. I can't see Issy doing something like that. She didn't like Tina, I know that, and she didn't want me seeing her, but she wouldn't stalk her." He groaned, regretting ever questioning her over it.

"When you spoke with Tina about her trailing Isabelle, was the conversation heated?"

He shook his head, then sighed. "I don't know. Maybe a little. She was upset because I'd told her that Isabelle was pregnant."

"Right," McKenzie said with a nod, understanding how Tina, after losing her only child, would be upset by her ex-husband moving on so soon afterwards. McKenzie had two children—grown now and living their own lives. His eldest son was a solicitor, practising in Brisbane. The younger of the two, though in his late twenties, was an engineer. He still lived in town with his wife and two children. If anything had have happened to either of them, even now, let alone when they were young children, it would have broken him irreparably. He was certain of that.

"Tina had never been able to have children," Chris continued. "We tried and tried from the moment we were married, but it never happened."

McKenzie kept his expression impartial. "The young daughter Tina lost wasn't your biological child?"

Chris narrowed his gaze. "Do you mean like one of the miscarriages she had?"

Jenkins handed Chris a cup of tea. He gave a perfunctory 'thanks' but didn't turn away from McKenzie.

McKenzie shook his head. "Not a miscarriage. I believe this young girl was four when she died. Kadie Brooks."

Chris sipped the hot tea. It was comforting and warm in his stomach, soothing the storm of anxiety raging inside. "You must have your wires crossed. Kadie wasn't our daughter. She was my brother, Ben's, daughter. A horrible accident the way that all played out."

"Your brother's daughter?"

He nodded.

"Are you able to tell me what happened with Kadie?"

Chris drew a deep breath. "Ben and his wife, Maddison, they used to live on a property at Yarwun, two houses up from us."

"Where Tina still lives?"

"Yeah. Ben was meant to be watching his three kids while Maddison had gone into town to do the grocery shopping. I was at the mine, due home the following day. Tina was with Ben, in the bedroom…" He cleared his throat, looked down at his hands, never able to admit to this story without difficulty.

"Tina and your brother were having an affair?"

"Well, they both said it was only that one time. The worst timing possible."

"How so?"

"The kids were playing hide-n-seek. Kadie had… an accident. When they found her, she was already gone."

"I see. And this was how long ago?"

"About three years. It was messy. My marriage didn't stand a chance. I no longer speak to my brother."

"That would have been a very difficult time."

Chris sipped his tea again, his mouthful too deep. He swallowed quickly and winced as the hot water slipped down his throat.

"Do you know if Tina is on any kind of medication?" McKenzie asked. "Psychiatric medications, perhaps?"

He shook his head. "Not a chance. No way."

"Why are you so certain of that?"

"Tina's mother was a hippy, I guess you'd say. She was into healing with food and natural things. It was drilled into Tina's head while young. She hated drugs. Any form. She wouldn't even take paracetamol for a headache. She was like that through our whole marriage."

"Right," McKenzie said. "Quickly, before we get out of your hair, where were you yesterday morning between eight and nine."

He looked off into the distance and frowned. "Here. Asleep. I'd had a few drinks the night before—drowning my sorrows—so I was sleeping it off."

"Anyone here with you? A mate, a lover, a sex-worker?"

Chris shook his head. "I was alone."

* * *

When the detectives left, Chris headed to the bathroom and washed his face at the basin with cold water. He gazed at his reflection in the mirror. Pale. His eyes were bloodshot. A slight tremble in his hands.

That news had shocked him. He'd endured the aftermath of his niece's death only three years ago, and it was a nuclear hell for everyone involved. Ben and Maddison had taken the blow as hard as could be expected.

The anger Chris harboured towards his brother wasn't able to manifest loudly enough amidst all that grief. He was never able to scream and shout and blame his brother for his betrayal because Ben was experiencing a punishment far greater than Chris could ever wield.

Chris had attended the funeral, gave his condolences, said goodbye to his beautiful niece, and never spoke to Ben, nor his family, ever again.

Tina had been knocked off balance. It may as well have been her body inside that small casket and lowered into the ground. He'd never witnessed anything like that before. She went cold. No longer shed tears or showed sorrow. No joy or anger. Her face held the same expression no matter what they were talking about. And when they did speak, she would nod in all the right places, offer responses, but the timing was a little off, the replies slightly disconnected.

He could have forgiven her for the affair. He could have. He'd been partially to blame. Their marriage had spiralled into a rut. He'd taken her for granted. Always assumed she would be there, waiting for him when he got home after twelve long days away. But in the end, Tina no longer existed, only her shell remained, so there was no one to forgive.

When he had finally left the relationship, it was like leaving a stuffed doll behind.

That time in his life was difficult for a lot of reasons, but mostly because he never knew at any moment how he should be feeling. So many conflicting circumstances made his normal reactions and emotions inappropriate.

He contemplated the road that lay ahead of him and Isabelle and cringed. A crippling road, full of despair, full of pain unlike anything physical. He wasn't sure he had the wherewithal to shoulder that again.

He gazed into his solemn eyes. He loved Isabelle and he would have to carry this load with her regardless of his doubts. It would be a nightmare, but they would be stronger together. Maybe.

The baby was a godsend. At least there was some hope ahead. He held onto that thought, of eventually bursting out through the other side and holding his child in his arms.

He gathered his mobile phone from the desk and called his employer, informing them about what had happened and that he'd be taking the next couple of shifts off. That would give him a little over a month to be home with Isabelle.

After a deep, shaky breath, he called his wife. His heart raced as the phone rang and rang and rang. But no one answered.

He left a message. "I was told the news, Issy. I'm so deeply sorry. I'm utterly heartbroken. I can't even begin to imagine how you must be feeling." He hesitated when he was about to say he would go over there. But he wasn't certain she wanted that. If she did, he would have been one of the first people she had called. "Would you like me to come over? I've taken time off work. I can be there in five minutes if that's what you want. I have no words for how sorry I am."

He hung up, flung his phone onto the bed, lifted his face to the ceiling and cried.

CHAPTER 24

"I shouldn't remember that day," Maddison said to her psychiatrist, Dr Cheryl. "But I remember it more clearly than anything else in my life. Every single detail. I've heard stories about other people remembering death as though it existed in a haze, but not me. It's vivid. So vivid. I wake at night with the images of it in my mind as though it's all happening again right in front of me."

Upon hearing about Maddison's blackout and waking in a park, the doctor had designated her new patient a priority. That was their third session that week. The first two sessions, Maddison had skirted around the painful topic of Kadie's death, pretending that her husband's affairs were the real concern. But they never had been. They were big and bad, but they were nothing compared to her daughter dying.

"Is that where your use of alcohol and prescription drugs started?" Dr Cheryl asked.

Maddison nodded. "You can only feel that pain once in your lifetime. But to be blasted with it every single night, every single minute of my day, was unbearable. I either blocked it out or I…"

"What were you going to say there?"

She swallowed hard. "Or I would kill myself. But I couldn't do that to Ruby and Riley. I couldn't put them through that on top of losing their baby sister." Tears filled her eyes.

"I understand." Dr Cheryl leaned back in her chair, notepad on her lap, pen tip hovering over the page. "Tell me about that day, Maddison."

She tensed, jaw clamping shut—her body's way of telling her not to go there. But she couldn't wake up in a park again. She couldn't keep blocking that moment in time out because no matter how much she willed it, it never went away. It lurked in the background of everything. Like a monster, she had to turn and face it, to truly understand what she was dealing with.

Maddison closed her eyes, hid her trembling hands beneath her thighs, and, in a second, she was back there, that day her heart was ripped out of her chest.

The pounding heat of summer. The thick humidity that filled her every breath and coated her skin in a thin layer of sweat.

She pulled into the driveway, parked beside the house, opened the boot of her car and began piling shopping bags into her hands. If she were being honest, she'd admit that she had enjoyed her time alone those past couple of hours. Even though she was pushing a shopping trolley around a bustling grocery store, it was time to herself. She could barely shower, let alone go to the toilet in peace with three young children constantly on her tail.

She wasn't sure that she and Ben had known exactly what they were in for by having the children so close together. Barely eighteen months between each. It had sounded reasonable at the time, so her children could grow up as friends, but the reality of having three children, aged eight and under, was much different. Her house was mostly littered with toys and hastily discarded clothes. Food was pushed under couches by little hands. And noisy. At least three times a day, one of them was whinging, fighting or crying over something one of their siblings had or hadn't done.

Shopping with the three of them was torture, so she usually waited for Ben to have a few hours off from the gym on the slowest day of the week and duck away by herself.

She hauled bags up the front steps, lowered the door handle with her elbow, then shoved the door open with her foot. Her neck was straining from the effort. Her fingers sore from the tug of the heavy bags.

In the kitchen, Ruby jumped out from the cupboard, "Mummy," she said with a squeal and a smile.

"Hi, my darling. What were you doing in the cupboard?"

"Playing hide-n-seek, but no one find me."

"You've chosen the best hiding spot then." She groaned as she loaded the bags onto the kitchen bench. "Where's Dad?"

Ruby looked to the side in thought. "He in the bedroom with Aunty Tina?"

Her brows arched. "Bedroom?"

One big nod.

Maddison's stomach knotted. Alarm bells in her brain. "Wait here," she said to Ruby. "I need to ask Dad to give me a hand with the groceries."

"I can help," Ruby said and raced towards the front door.

Maddison walked up the hallway, each slow footstep to the bedroom door had her filling with trepidation. A hand on the knob, then she turned it slowly and pushed. Her focus zoomed to the space beside the bed.

Her husband's bare arse, his deep breaths filling the room. Beneath him, flat on her stomach was Tina.

Maddison screamed, her hand smothering her mouth as she did. Still to this day, she didn't quite understand why she had screamed. Perhaps it was the shock. The utter grotesqueness of the moment. The sordidness of seeing her husband's bare arse clench with every thrust into Tina.

Most likely, though, she had screamed because seeing her husband that way was so dissonant to every thought and every belief she had ever held about him. That one moment had fragmented the reality she had existed in since their wedding day all those years ago.

Most jarring was that Ben hadn't stopped, he continued for a while longer until he tensed and jerked with his release.

Maddison's expression twisted. She'd witnessed the tipping point. No return from that moment. Disgust was tightening the walls of her throat, making her want to gag. Her husband was a repulsive animal.

Ben, at last, pulled out of Tina and got to his feet. He was dressed in a shirt, his shorts down around his thighs, his erection jutting out until he pulled up his pants to hide it. Tina remained on the floor. Maddison looked at her sister-in-law, but no words formed in her mind. None adequate in that surreal moment.

With a huff, she spun away and marched down the hall. "Ruby, Riley, Kadie, come here please. Right now."

When she made it to the end of the hall, Ruby was walking through the front door, dragging a heavy shopping bag behind her.

"Go hop in the car please and wait for me. Where's your brother and sister?"

"I don't know," Ruby said. "Hiding still?"

"Go wait in the car."

Understanding the seriousness in her mother's tone, she dropped the bag and ran quickly out the front door to the carport. Riley appeared from behind the couch in the living room.

"Go wait in the car with your sister," she said. "Turn it on, so you have some air-conditioning. But don't touch anything at all. You understand me?"

He nodded and walked quickly towards the front door to join his sister.

"Kadie," Maddison called. "Come on, darling, we're going for a drive." Maddison raced around the house, looking in cupboards, under beds, behind curtains, in the washing basket, in the shower, under the kitchen sink, anywhere there was a four-year-old-sized space her daughter could fit. "Kadie, hide-n-seek is over. You must come out now!"

Ben met her in the living room while she was stupidly lifting cushions from the couch as though Kadie could be behind them. His face was still flushed and that made Maddison almost vomit.

Tina walked past them, not saying a word, not looking in their direction, and left via the front door.

"How dare you!" she spat at Ben. "How dare you! With your brother's wife. What kind of sick, twisted, desperate pervert are you?"

He lifted both hands in a surrender position. "I'm sorry. It just happened."

She slapped her hands over her ears, her nose wrinkling with her distaste. "Don't give me your gory details. I'm leaving. Where the bloody hell is Kadie?"

"I think we should talk about this instead of you running away."

She spun to face him, finger pointed. "You don't get a say. You don't tell me how I should be reacting to you screwing Tina while you're supposed to be watching our children." She lunged forward a step, struck him on the face, once, twice, three times as hard as she could until he caught her wrist. She wriggled her hand out of his clasp. A big red welt was already appearing on his cheek.

Maddison had thought a hundred times since then that she would happily relive seeing her husband screwing another woman if it meant she didn't have to endure what happened next.

Convinced Kadie wasn't hiding inside the house, she marched out the front door, looking around the yard for a hiding place. She checked behind the front bushes, all the while calling out for her. She checked in the trailer, in the shed, in Ben's car. As she headed around to the back of the property, bright colour pulled her focus.

Her gaze moved from the very back of the yard to the line of bordering trees. At first, she assumed Kadie was sitting in the tree, waiting. Perhaps she was stuck and couldn't get down. She marched across the yard, but the closer she got, the more she realised something wasn't right.

Kadie's feet were hanging down from the tree branches. Both her arms were limp at her sides. It took long moments to make sense of what she was seeing and allow the image to become a part of her reality.

Maddison sprinted. Loud, desperate screams of horror. Neighbours would recall later hearing that sound and knowing something was horribly, horribly wrong.

"Ben," she screamed. "Ben, get here now. Get here now. It's Kadie!"

Ben was already bolting across the backyard towards her.

When directly under the tree, Maddison started climbing, her nails digging into the gum's trunk as though she could claw her way up. Her heart was thumping so hard she felt the pulse in her ears. She could barely draw breath as her throat closed over with dread.

She already knew. But she still hoped.

She looked at Kadie as she clumsily sought branches to pull herself up on.

Ben was there then. He gripped Maddison by the waist, lifted her down and passed her his phone. "Call an ambulance," he panted. "I'll get her. I'll be able to lift her down with me."

His voice was the strangest she had ever heard. It made her do a double-take. She had never seen that pale, wide-eyed expression on her husband's face before.

Maddison's hands shook so much, she had to dial triple-zero three times before her fingers hit the right numbers. As the call connected, Ben was already up the tree, edging towards the branch Kadie was hanging from. She was hanging by her head, just beneath her ears.

As she told the calm woman on the end of the line what was happening, Ben gripped Kadie by the waist from the branch beneath, holding her with one arm as he forced the thick tree branches apart with the other. They tapered outward, the gap between them growing larger toward the thinner outer limbs. Where Kadie's head was stuck was much too narrow.

Maddison informed the operator of her address as Ben tried to break the branches when he wasn't strong enough to separate them. Ben lifted Kadie a little, her head falling heavily to the side, and gently moved her along the branches until they were wide enough for him to slip her through them.

As he lifted her down, her head fell back at such an unnatural angle, Maddison screamed and dropped the phone. Ben shuffled along the tree branches, Kadie in his arms, then shimmied down the trunk. Carefully, as though touching the finest of china, he supported Kadie's head and lowered her onto the grass.

"Hey, darling," he said, stroking a hand down her face. "Kadie, it's Daddy. I've got you. You're safe. We'll get you some help. Kadie. Open your eyes, sweetheart."

No response. She was pale.

Maddison had heard people say that dead people looked like they were sleeping, but that was not the case. Something had changed in her daughter's face, in the stiffening stretch of her small body as she lay on the grass. Her daughter wasn't there, only the flesh she once inhabited.

Dead.

The first time that word became conscious, Maddison's legs gave out beneath her. "Do something," she said breathlessly, barely able to get the words out.

Ben tilted Kadie's head slightly back, blew small breaths into her slack mouth, then gently felt along her chest, finding the right place, positioned his palm and began to pump. Kadie's limp body moved with each push.

"Come on, baby. Come on, baby," he said, voice strained.

Maddison watched her daughter, hoping with all hope, aching with all her body, wishing, threatening and demanding that her daughter open her eyes and sit up.

"Come on. Come on. Come on, Kadie," she whispered like a prayer.

The paramedics arrived, drove the van across the backyard, parking a few metres away. They set to work with such calm efficiency, Maddison worried that they hadn't realised the seriousness of the situation. But then she noticed the look that passed between them when they saw the condition of Kadie's neck.

Maddison's eyes filled with tears. Her lips trembled.

Time moved so fast as they worked on Kadie. Eventually, the male paramedic, tall and thin, dressed in blue-green coveralls, sweat sheening on his forehead, slightly out of breath, got to his feet.

He frowned when he stood before Ben and Maddison. "We'll wait for the police to arrive to see how we proceed here."

"Why aren't you trying?" Ben said angrily. "Why aren't you taking her to the hospital? Doctors could be helping her."

"I'm very sorry, but we've done all we can do."

Maddison shook her head, tears flooding her eyes. Resignation, like deep barrel waves, knocked her off her feet and she fell into Ben's arms. He held her face to his chest.

"I'm so sorry," the paramedic said.

Life seemed to rush out of focus then as though a barrier had slammed down to shield her, for to be fully present, to acknowledge with all her senses and awareness that her daughter was lying on the grass, dead, would have permanently destroyed her mind.

Even as the police arrived, inspected the scene and asked their questions, it was like Maddison was floating between it all. As the mortician carefully lifted Kadie's broken body onto a stretcher, and Maddison pressed a kiss to her daughter's cold cheek, she wasn't completely there. Her emotions were cordoned off behind a wall.

Even as the stretcher with Kadie's little body covered in a sheet was taken to the van, it was like she was in a dream.

The only thing that zoomed into focus was her husband's face. She looked at him, seeing every line, every freckle, every groove. Venom filled her mouth as she spat, "You're to blame for this."

Maddison broke from her reverie and sucked in a sharp breath as her surroundings filled her awareness. The psychiatrist's office. Since Kadie's death, she had never delved so deep into her memories of that day. Her heart was bruised, throbbing with the same measure of pain she felt those few years ago.

Dr Cheryl reached for some tissues and handed them to Maddison. When Maddison wiped her cheeks, they were wet with tears. She hadn't even known she had been crying. Her nose was running, so she blew it hard.

"Do you still believe your husband is to blame for Kadie's death?"

Maddison didn't hesitate. "Yes." She rubbed a palm over her mouth, noisily breathed through her watery nose. "But I think, maybe, I want to forgive him. Or kill him. Both impulses are as strong as the other."

Dr Cheryl offered a small, sympathetic smile. "I understand. Let's work on that together and see where it leads us."

CHAPTER 25

Detective Inspector McKenzie entered the small interview room. Four cream-coloured walls. A square desk and three chairs filled most of the space. He had spent hours in there over the years he'd been working as a detective, but murder, the most serious of crimes, wasn't usual in a town like this. Only eleven convictions in the past twenty years.

Tina Brooks sat in the chair, sidelong to the door. Her dark hair was tied back into a neat ponytail. Her face was pale, gaunt, eyes slightly downturned at the corners, as was her mouth.

McKenzie placed his folder onto the table, much more loudly than he had intended. Tina flinched, her gaze darting between the folder and McKenzie's face. She was terrified, he realised. A much different countenance to the one he'd faced in hospital.

He hoped fear didn't shut her down. She had the right to silence today, but if he approached the interview precisely, building a rapport, he should manage to get her talking.

Forensics and scenes-of-crime police officers had been working around the clock gathering photographic and video evidence, measurements, fingerprints and DNA samples from the two crime scenes.

Overnight, the results from the victim's stomach, bowel, bladder, bile, sputum and saliva samples were finalised. All tagged according to protocols to ensure the chain of evidence was intact. The last thing McKenzie wanted was any question of contamination. With a major investigation, the most he could hope for was a clear line of evidence to substantiate a prima facie case and bring perpetrators before a court of law.

Earlier that morning, McKenzie had endured the grave task of reading the Government Medical Officer's autopsy report, which indicated the victim died from blunt trauma to the skull, face and brain. No other signs of struggle. No blood or skin under the nails. No scratches. No drug use.

The Crash Investigation Unit had determined Tina's car was implicated in the initial collision with Juliette's vehicle—aligning with the information Tina had initially offered him while in hospital. The team had provided images outlining the exact path each car took before, upon, and after impact.

Fingerprints taken from the steering wheel of Tina's car matched the fingerprints on the wrecking bar left at the scene. He was still awaiting the results of forensic DNA samples taken from Tina's shirt, the victim and hair found at the scene. Tina's medical records would be forwarded today after a warrant had granted him access.

"Hi, Tina," he said as he took a seat on the chair closest to hers. He ran through the preliminaries with her, ensuring she understood her rights before he got started.

Four hours was all he was allowed under Queensland state laws. Within that time, he wanted a confession, but, also, burning in the back of his brain, he needed to know why Tina had lied about Kadie.

"We've been given medical clearance for this interview today. Are you feeling clear, lucid?"

She nodded.

"If you could speak up for me please."

"Yes. I'm much clearer."

"We'll get started here then. This interview is to expand on the conversation we had at the hospital."

She hesitated to respond. She didn't want to delve into her memories. As the substance in her bloodstream was expelled from her body, her recollection of that horrible morning had become stronger and sharper. Tears were already filling her eyes. Her stomach was sick with remorse.

"Okay," she whispered, wiping tears away with her palm.

He handed her a box of tissues. "I know this is difficult. Just try your best to answer the questions honestly."

A nod.

"I want to understand what was happening that morning before I found you in your car. Were you on your way to work?"

"No, I wasn't feeling well, so I'd called in sick. I was..." She lowered her gaze to the table, shook her head. "I was going to follow Isabelle to work."

"You had followed Isabelle to and from work for three days before that, is that right?"

"Yes."

"Why were you doing that?"

"To intimidate her. She'd been stalking me. I wanted to send a message that I knew it was her and that I wasn't going to put up with it."

"Describe what you did?"

"I waited on the side of the road for her each morning."

"Which road?"

"I think it's Grendell Street. I would wait for her to drive past, flip a U-turn and follow her."

"So, when you were parked on Grendell Street, you were facing the direction Isabelle would be arriving from?"

"Yes."

"And you had to cross the right lane, her right, and turn into the left lane to follow her car?"

"Yes."

"What changed the morning your car was involved in the accident?"

"I was a little later than usual and she was a little earlier, so we passed each other before the intersection."

"Who is *she*?"

"Isabelle." Her voice was a whisper. Tears filled her eyes.

"So, it was Isabelle's car you passed?"

Tina shook her head. "It couldn't have been."

"Why couldn't it have been Isabelle's?"

"It wasn't the right colour. Wasn't the same make. But it was Isabelle driving. I *believed* it was Isabelle driving."

"Do you still believe it was Isabelle?"

"I swear to you it was. In my memories, it's still her. But I've seen the news. I've heard the details of what happened. I know who was k-killed." Her lips were trembling. Hands shaking.

"But you still believe it was Isabelle you saw in that car?"

She nodded.

"Can you recall the make of the car?"

"A small hatch. It was silver, I think."

"And when you saw Isabelle in the car, what happened?"

"She was heading towards me, looking through her front windscreen with a smirk. She lifted her middle finger."

"Did that upset you?"

"Yes." Slightly defensive. "She'd been terrorising me. And now she was taunting me."

"How did you react to that?"

Tina sat back, her hands flat on the tabletop before her. She rolled her palms until they were facing upwards. Fingers shaking. "It's all hazy."

"Your memory?"

She shook her head. "No, my vision…" She lifted her hands and shimmied them up and down. "My vision that morning was wavy. I wasn't seeing things like I'm seeing them now." A hint of impatience. "I think I blacked out for a moment. I remember the sound of the crash, though. I wish I knew all the details because if we didn't crash…" She wiped fresh tears away with a tissue.

"When you came to, what happened?"

Tina lifted her head, met his gaze. There was a softness to her eyes and face, almost like resignation. "Isabelle climbed out of her car. She was angry."

"What was she doing that made you believe she was angry?"

Tina's fingers curled into fists as they sat on the table. "Her face was twisted. She was swearing and screaming." She placed a hand over her chest and fluttered her fingers. "My heart was racing so fast, it was frightening me. I thought I was going to have a heart attack."

"Did you speak to Isabelle?"

She shook her head. "I think, maybe, I was trying to, but everything was happening so fast. I know this sounds ridiculous, but her face was turning black like a demon thing. I was suffering from drug toxicity when I got to the hospital, so, I think, maybe, I was hallucinating. My doctor said the drug they found in my system—scopolam... scopo... it's in the nightshade family supposedly—is known for causing delirium."

"Scopolamine?" he asked.

She nodded. "At almost toxic levels."

McKenzie focused on his folder, already well aware that Tina was under the influence of drugs that day. But now he knew the drug he was dealing with.

Scopolamine had a bad reputation. He had read plenty of horror stories out of Colombia where wealthy-appearing men had their drinks spiked by young, attractive women and were then robbed. The drug wasn't an issue in Australia as it was only available by prescription and had less demand on the streets because it was certainly not a feel-good party drug.

He made a note to circle back later to this topic, but for the time being, he wanted to hold the line with his questions.

"So, what happened when Isabelle's face changed?" he asked.

"I screamed, and I sprinted back to my car. But she was following me. Still yelling at me with a terrifying voice. She was threatening me."

"How so?"

"She said she would kill me."

"Do you recall the words she used?"

Tina shuddered, shook her head, trying to toss the memory away. "It sounds ridiculous now, but at the time, I was so scared I could barely breathe."

"This isn't about judging you or your recollection of that day, Tina. This is about discovering the truth." His voice was calm, placating. "The more you can tell me, even if it feels absurd, the better it'll be for all involved."

Her eyelids closed briefly. She lifted her hands off the table, wrapped her arms around her stomach, shoulders hunching. When she spoke, her words were so soft McKenzie almost missed it. "I'm going to pull your womb out through your throat."

He leaned closer. "Pardon? Did you say, 'your womb'?"

She nodded, whispered. "Yes."

"How did you react to that?"

"I reached into my car for the wrecking bar I keep under the seat and held it up in warning."

His pulse quickened, realising he was a moment away from a confession, but he remained silent, face impartial, giving her the time she needed to continue.

She closed her mouth and didn't finish her sentence.

After the moment dragged on too long, he asked, "You held the wrecking bar up in warning?"

"Yes."

"What happened next?"

She couldn't look at him, went very still and silent, and focused on the chips in the Laminex tabletop.

He waited. Waited for long minutes with unwavering eye-contact. In a softer, warmer, more coaxing voice, he asked again, "What happened next, Tina, when you held the wrecking bar up in warning?"

A deep sigh. When she looked up, her eyes were red, rimmed with tears. Snot leaked from her nostrils.

McKenzie resisted the urge to offer a tissue, not willing to jeopardise the imminent confession, but after another long silence, it didn't come.

He tried once more. "Did Isabelle threaten you again? Did she try to hurt you?"

Tina broke down, sobbing and crying, shaking her head. She tore tissues from the box and wiped her eyes and nose.

"I understand that this can be difficult to talk about. Your honesty and openness have been commendable. I'm trying to find out what happened that day." He had one eye-witness statement—a jogger, the man who had first called emergency services—reporting that he had seen Tina strike Juliette. But he was a hundred metres away at the time. After door knocking, there were no homes or businesses with any video footage of the crime scene. Personal security systems were practically unheard of in a town like Gladstone.

"I need to go to the toilet please," she said.

He hid his disappointment. "Sure. Let's do that. Would you like a tea or coffee?"

"Some water please."

A female constable showed Tina to the bathroom, while McKenzie used the spare time to meet with Detective Jenkins in the office adjoining the interview room.

Jenkins lifted her head from the file spread out before her. "How do you think it's going in there?"

"Really well, until about fifteen minutes ago when she closed up." He held his thumb and forefinger apart. "This close."

Jenkins looked at her watch. "It's only been one hour and fifteen minutes."

He took a seat on the chair across from her, a desk between them. "Feels a lot longer."

"Tina's medical records have just come through." She stabbed the report with her finger. "Intoxication from high

191

levels of Scopolamine. The doctor questioned her over it and she claimed to have no idea of how she ingested the drugs."

"What are you thinking?"

Jenkins shook her head. "At this stage, I'm not sure. We need to dig deeper."

"Agreed."

McKenzie collected a bottle of water for Tina before he returned to the interview room. He placed it on the desk in front of her and resumed his seat, maintaining a respectful distance. Now wasn't the right moment to get into her personal space and exert pressure. His immediate goal was to get her talking again.

Tina sipped water from the bottle, then looked at him, expectant.

"You were married to Chris Brooks for a time?" he asked.

"Yes."

"How long for?"

"Fifteen years."

"But you divorced a few years ago?"

"Yes."

He cleared his throat. "When I spoke with you at the hospital, you mentioned a four-year-old girl called Kadie Brooks."

Her cheeks flushed. "I don't know why I said what I said that day."

"Which part?"

"That I was her mother."

"Why did you lie about that?"

She flinched. "I didn't lie."

"It wasn't the truth."

"I honestly thought I was telling the truth. I think it was the drugs. I think they've been in my system for a while." Her voice was strained, wavering with emotion. "Longer than just that day, because I've had some strange things happening and I wonder now if any of it was real."

"Were you prescribed Scopolamine for any reason?"

She shook her head. "I don't take drugs. Any kind of drugs. I never have."

"Could you have accidentally ingested it? I don't know, via some herbal remedy?"

"No. I eat well. I get sunlight. I stay fit. I don't take anything else." She leaned forward, her gaze meeting McKenzie's face unfalteringly. "I've started to remember the things that I've said and done over the past few weeks. Unusual things. Really, really unusual things."

"Like what?"

"I went to Kadie's grave on the anniversary of her death. I left flowers and a stuffed toy there and cried and felt grief so deep, as though she was my daughter. That's pretty messed up, don't you think?"

He didn't answer.

"Those notes I was finding around the house?"

"The one's you believe Isabelle was writing?" he asked.

She nodded. Her gaze was pleading. "I had put them into a resealable bag and left them in my desk drawer in the office. I checked and found ripped up pieces of white paper with nothing written on them. I'm not sure if the notes were even real. And now I don't know if I ever saw Isabelle at my window that night." Tears filled her eyes. "And here I am today, telling you that I stood face to face with Isabelle…" Her voice was strong even though she was crying. Her cheeks were red. "And yet, Isabelle is alive, and I'm being told I murdered her daughter. I now have to live with that. I have to live with knowing I killed a young woman."

Detective Inspector McKenzie went very still, though his pulse was racing. "So, when you raised the wrecking bar at Juliette, what happened?"

"She roared, so loud my ears almost burst from the pain of it. She lurched at me. I closed my eyes and swung…" She broke off with a sob, her lips trembling. "I was trying to bat her away. I was so scared. I threw the bar down and hopped into my car. I didn't look back. Just floored it out of there. But my vision got worse. The whole world was blurry and cartoonish. Waving around like I was underwater. That's when I turned off the road." A tremble so strong it almost knocked her off her seat. "But she was there, in the bushes, crawling towards me. I don't know what I saw, what was real, what wasn't real..."

"When you swung the wrecking bar and was batting Juliette away, did you hit her?"

Another tremble, a quick nod. "I hit her. I hit her over and over until she fell to the road."

McKenzie drew a deep breath in. "Tina Brooks, I'm placing you under arrest for the murder of Juliette Spencer."

* * *

McKenzie sank onto the chair across from his partner, wanting to feel good about extracting a confession from Tina, but a large, hard stone sat heavily in the pit of his stomach.

"Great work in there," Jenkins said.

He sighed. "I've been a detective for a long time. You know how it is, over the years you learn the ways and minds of suspects."

Jenkins crossed her arms over her chest and nodded.

"I couldn't find a hole in Tina's answers today. Her tears, her fear, had affected me. The hairs on my arms stood on end." At the end of the day, he was human with human empathy and Tina had evoked his.

Jenkins's brow furrowed as she leaned forward, elbows on the desk. "What are you trying to say?"

"Tina Brooks confessed to a serious crime today. I had to arrest her, but I'm not going to formally charge her yet. We've got a lot of convincing evidence and yet it's not enough. We're missing something. Something big."

"How did the Scopolamine make it into Tina's bloodstream?"

"Exactly," he said. "I think there could be another suspect out there."

Jenkins pushed her chair back and stood. "Well, without laying charges, there's only so long we can detain Tina. So, we better work out who that is and fast."

CHAPTER 26

"God, this is ridiculous!" Chris said as he paced the length of the floor. He'd barely managed more than a few hours of broken sleep last night. He kept waking from nightmares of Juliette, her face disfigured and bleeding as she laid contorted on the hot bitumen road.

He pulled his mobile out of his pocket, yet again, and checked for messages or a missed-call notification. Nothing.

Yesterday, after he phoned Isabelle, he'd sent a couple of follow-up text messages, but got crickets. He hadn't been able to wait a moment longer in that tiny hotel room, so he drove to the house. For all he knew, she may have had her phone turned off. But after knocking and knocking, no one had answered.

He had pressed his ear to the timber door and listened. She could have been inside and was avoiding him, so he slipped his key into the lock and went in to check. But the house was silent. No one was home.

A pang of guilt for doubting her. He had assumed Isabelle was most likely meeting with an undertaker, arranging the details of Juliette's funeral. A correct assumption. Meanwhile, he was snooping around expecting her to be hiding in her cupboard as though he was somehow more important than all else.

With his tail between his legs, he had driven back to the hotel and booked in for another few nights.

He shoved his phone in his pocket. "Screw it." He was going to drive over there again. He understood that she would be suffering right now, but he was her husband, and her silence didn't make sense.

Chris arrived at Isabelle's home and parked. He sat in his car for a while, engine running, looking at the house. He blinked back tears, then went to the front door and knocked.

An older woman answered. He took a step backwards, momentarily disconcerted. He gathered his wits and voice. "Jenny. Hi. It's Chris." His cheeks burned hot to be standing on the doorstep of his 'supposed' home and yet he'd had to knock.

"I know who you are," Isabelle's mother said. She had blonde hair like her daughter but cropped short. Shared the same petite build. He could have been looking into his wife's brown eyes.

"Right, of course." A polite but strained smile. "I've come by to see Issy."

"She doesn't want to speak to you."

"Well, that's too bad." He pushed past Jenny, through the door. She sidestepped in front of him to block his path, but he held her shoulders and gently shifted her to the side. "She's my wife. Isabelle?" he called out.

Isabelle strode into the living room, her father at her side. Chris's next breath vanished as he took in her appearance. Black, swollen rings sat beneath her bloodshot eyes. Her face drooped downward. Her hair was limp, oily. Her shoulders hunched like she was compelled to curl into a ball.

"Issy," he said and went to her, wanting to throw his arms around her and hold her tight to him.

She put her hand up. "Stop. Don't touch me."

He froze mid-stride. "I'm so deeply sorry about Juliette. I'm devastated. I can't believe it."

"I don't want you here, Chris. I don't want you anywhere near me."

"I don't understand," he said. "What have I done? I had to find out about Juliette from the police."

Her nose wrinkled, lips twisted as she pointed her finger at him. "If not for you, Juliette would still be alive."

He stumbled a step back. His mouth flapped open and shut. "I know you're upset, but that's one hell of an accusation. I can't even begin to make sense of that."

Her father, Richard, spoke up. "Tina was arrested today." His voice was deep and firm but wavered with emotion.

Chris narrowed his eyes, blinked, unable to process that news.

"For God's sake, Chris," Issy screeched. "They've arrested your ex-wife for bludgeoning my daughter to death and you still won't believe it. You're still sticking up for her."

"No, that's not it. I'm shocked. I didn't... I hadn't heard anything about Tina being involved, let alone arrested. It's a shock. That's all." He wiped his mouth with his palm. He was finding it difficult to breathe.

"I'm leaving for Tasmania after the funeral—"

"For how long?"

"Permanently," she said.

"What?"

"You can come over then and collect your things. I'm going to sell the salon. I can't stay here. I can't face this house and this town—"

"What about the baby?"

Isabelle's hand floated to her stomach, a strange expression coming over her. "My body. You've forfeited your rights."

"No way, Issy. It doesn't work like that. Not one bit."

"You need to leave," Richard said. "You've caused more than enough trouble."

"I'm not here to cause trouble. I'm here to console my wife. You're acting like I'm some sort of bloody criminal."

"You leave or I call the police and you can sit in jail with your ex and you can rot together."

"Jesus Christ." He tugged a hand through his hair. "This is ridiculous. I had nothing to do with Juliette."

"Get out!" Richard roared, his head shaking, eyes widening with his fury.

Chris held both hands up. "Fine, but you've got this all wrong. I'm just as shocked—"

Isabelle charged at him and slapped his face, over and over, his chest, his arms, his stomach. "You did this. You fucking did this," she screamed with every slap and punch, spit flying from her mouth. "You did this!"

He fended off the assault, careful not to hurt her, and turned, the blows now landing on his back. "I'm going." He marched to the door, each step like he was walking through glue. "I'm going. I'm going." He opened the door and shut it behind him.

His head was pounding as he fought to make sense of what was happening. He was panting. All the places Isabelle had hit him were throbbing. When back at his car, he sank into the driver's seat. For a while, he was unable to move. His world was no longer his own but some dark, twisted hell he had somehow landed in.

CHAPTER 27

Four days before the murder…

Maddison stood, pillow in her hands, and tiptoed around the bed until she was standing beside her husband, looking down at his sleeping frame. She lowered the pillow, smothered his face, held the ends down as hard as she could, then climbed onto him, kneeling on his chest.

A muffled groan. His arms came at her, trying to claw her away, but she would take all the ferocity for as long as she could. She had been preparing herself to withstand the pain of his defence for months and months.

He punched and pulled, kicked and squirmed, but she held tight, so damn tight. She was strong. Had endurance.

Maddison gasped as she snapped out of her daydream. She was sitting on the end of her bed in the darkened room watching her husband sleep. His breaths were loud and rhythmical. She stood, eyed the pyjamas she was wearing. Her hair was wet.

She had showered, but she couldn't remember doing so. It seemed like only a moment ago she was in the kitchen, drinking wine, posting pictures on social media and then…

No matter how much she tried to rack her brain for the right memories to fill in the gaps, she couldn't find them.

A cold rivulet of water dripped from her hair down her back and she shivered. She went to the ensuite for a towel but before she stepped inside, she jumped backwards. Blotches of red, very much like blood, were all over the white tiles beneath her feet.

Maddison flicked on the light, her eyes squinting against the brightness. Her vision was warped, her head spinning. But it wasn't blood on the tiles, rather pictures had been drawn over the floor in bright red lipstick.

She glanced around the room. An open lipstick sat on the basin's countertop. She stared at her reflection in the mirror; her lips were coated with red.

"Oh, God," she whispered. With a wet hand towel, she fell to her hands and knees and scrubbed the lipstick away. By the end, her white towel was stained red and ruined, so she carried it to the kitchen and threw it in the bin before Ben or the kids could see it.

She flopped onto a stool and sighed as she wondered if she had drawn those pictures. Of course she had, though she would never remember doing so.

Lucy, after their big night on the town, had been right about Maddison. Right to strike her from her life. Maddison's destructive efforts to block out that horrible day when Kadie had died were slowly making her lose her mind.

"Oh, Kadie," Maddison sobbed. "Why did you climb that stupid tree? Why?"

She spotted her phone sitting on the bench. Before she could stop herself, she had arranged an Uber. On her way out the front door, she grabbed a bottle of wine from the fridge.

The quiet, suburban street was still and dark as she waited on the footpath. No lights were on in any of the homes.

Good, hardworking people. Maddison was once that person. Now, she didn't know who she was.

If not for Ruby and Riley, she wouldn't willingly choose that pain every day when there was nothing else left to live for. Life was all about cost-benefit. She was teetering on the edge, trying to hold a balance between the two. If she were to allow the full force of her past to engulf her, the cost of her existence would outweigh all else.

* * *

Maddison stood in the backyard of her old property at Yarwun, looking up at the tree where Kadie was found hanging. She glanced behind her to the quiet house. Windows all dark. Once her home. A new family had moved in a few months after Kadie had died. They knew what had happened there and they hadn't cared; bought the place anyway because it was going cheap.

Maddison and Ben didn't sleep another night there after that horrible day. They had moved in with Maddison's parents until the property sold and they were able to buy another home. Having her parents to help had been a godsend because she and Ben were in no frame of mind to take care of Ruby and Riley in the months after the accident.

"Why do I keep doing this to myself?" she groaned. In the last three years, she had come to that spot a dozen times and each time she regretted it. Seeing that tree was enough to drag all the pain to the surface and overwhelm her. But as she stared up at the branches through the shadows, she was not only grief-stricken but angry. A dark force was vibrating beneath her skin and filling her chest. Rage. Violence.

The bottle of wine was still in her hand, opened, half-full. She tipped it to her lips, skolled the contents. It burned and made her gag, but she kept going. She didn't want to be there. She didn't want to feel anything let alone that excruciating agony.

* * *

"You bitch, you killed my daughter!" Maddison hurled the empty wine bottle at the side of Tina's house. It smashed into a million tiny pieces all over the grass. "Why couldn't you have stuck to your own husband. Why did you have to take mine! I hate you. I hate you."

A light turned on inside. She raced up the stairs to the front door and banged hard on it with her palms. "I know you're in there. I know you can hear me. You should hate yourself for what you did. You killed my daughter. You and Ben killed her. I hope by knowing that, your soul is destroyed. I hope you kill yourself you horrible, whore slut! I hate you. Everyone hates you." She scooted along the porch to the window and slapped it with her palms. "Did you hear me! You should kill yourself. That's all you deserve."

* * *

The sound of a child's voice. A poke at Maddison's ribs.

"Mummy, there's a lady here."

Maddison dragged her eyelids open, squinted against the blast of sunlight, and gazed into the face of a small girl about the age of six. Big brown eyes stared down at her. The girl smiled.

"Come away, Natasha. Hurry! Come on now," came a high-pitched older voice.

"Hello. You have priddy lipstick," the girl said.

Maddison sat up, her head pounding as she did. She glanced around. Grass beneath her palms. A swing set in the distance. The local park.

CHAPTER 28

Eighteen years ago…

Tina stood at the entry of the waiting room and called her next patient, "Chris Brooks".

Chris got to his feet, smiled at her and said in a deep, gruff voice, "G'day."

He was tall, broad, and as he followed her down the hallway, she was aware of every step he took. He had her heart racing double-time.

When in her office, she closed the door quietly behind them.

He reached for her hand and shook it. "Chris Brooks. Good to meet you."

A firm handshake. A hand so large it all but smothered hers. The rough friction of calluses met her palm, and she knew before he spoke that he worked a physical job. Not unusual in a blue-collar town like Gladstone, but something she hadn't known she appreciated until now.

Her first thought when Chris took a seat across from her and she gazed into his blue eyes was how rough-around-the-edges attractive he was. She checked his details; he was twenty-nine years old, five years older than her.

Her second thought was a question: *why did a strong, burly man like him need to see a psychologist?* But, of course, she was thinking about stereotypes. Stereotypes didn't exist, at least not once she delved deeper than the social facade.

For the next four months, Chris sat across from her once a week and spoke about his life. When four years old, his mother, Benita, died from pancreatic cancer. It devastated the family of five, but his father more so. Randall had sunk into a depressive funk and, when Chris was fifteen, had driven the family car into quiet bushland, put the barrel of a shotgun into his mouth and pulled the trigger.

To avoid the foster system, Chris's eldest sister, Jacinta, eighteen at the time, had taken him and his younger brother, Ben, into her legal care. For four years, the three of them lived together until Ben left for Rockhampton to study sports science at university. Soon after that, Chris was earning enough money while undertaking his apprenticeship as a mechanical fitter to move in with a couple of mates. A few years later, Jacinta landed a great job in Brisbane, so she moved there and settled.

Physically, Chris was a big, strong man with a beard and a gruff voice, and yet he was so gentle and careful. He often cried during his sessions, unafraid of his emotions. As someone who had been unable to access emotion since she was a young girl, Tina found that fascinating. Exhilarating.

As Chris continued to reveal the deepest parts of his soul, and she worked with him to shift him out of his grief and onto a path of healing, she developed a crush. That was the most surprising thing of all. Tina had never had a crush. She had never had a boyfriend.

From the age of thirteen, she had slept with a lot of boys, some her classmates, others from the competing schools in the district. She hadn't understood back then that it wasn't socially acceptable behaviour but, instead, something she later came to know as hypersexuality.

While studying for her psychology degree, she spent many nights with many different men until one evening she found herself in a play park with four guys she had met at a club. As they all took turns with her body, at no stage did they acknowledge she was human.

When done, they left her there alone and walked away laughing with each other as though Tina was nothing more than a big joke. She searched the ground for her jeans and underwear and slowly dressed, trembling from head to toe. She crumbled onto the grass, lowered her face into her hands and cried.

For three weeks, the tears wouldn't stop. She didn't attend her lectures. She couldn't get out of bed. The toxic residue from her past had rotted through her defences and contaminated her life. That was the first time she had discovered that her childhood couldn't be ignored. Immense and festering, it loomed over everything.

It was also the first time she had discovered she hated sex. Loathed it. She had never experienced pleasure from it. When she was in the arms of a man, her body was there, but she wasn't connected to it—fortifications she had built up to avoid pain, but it also meant she couldn't feel the opposite either.

In time, she clawed her way out of that black hole and for the next five years, she didn't touch another man. She had no desire for intimacy at all. Deep down, men frightened her, and she had always attracted those who could sniff out that vulnerability.

But there was Chris. And she was feeling something. Physical at first—a burst of chemicals in her brain and body each time she sat mere metres across the room from him.

Those lust chemicals were so new, interesting and unbelievably exhilarating. Mostly, she felt validated. All her hard work, years and years of picking apart her history and trauma and putting it back together with her new knowledge and adult perspective, had actually been helping.

She wasn't perfect. A child as broken as she was probably never could be. But she had chipped away at the compartments she had erected in her mind. The mechanisms that allowed her to float above her body, exist in her own safe, warm reality while grown men hurt, used and then discarded her.

That was why she chose to study psychology in the first place. She had wanted to fix herself. And as she trawled through the texts and information, she found herself in those case studies. She read about people who had also suffered sexual trauma as a child. Many, many people. When she watched their transformations, heard their stories of recovery, she held hope in her hands for the first time. Hope that she was capable of healing too. Hope for becoming a whole person again.

Tina was satisfied with the progress Chris was making, so she ended their sessions. She thought about him often but never saw him again after that until her friend Mandy's twenty-fifth birthday. Chris worked with Mandy's boyfriend, Trevor, and was invited to the same party. When he strode through the back doors, stepped onto the patio, where all the guests were gathered, and their eyes met, Tina had smiled so wide her cheeks hurt.

They sat in a quiet corner together and chatted for hours and hours. Those same desires were vibrant and strong. At the end of the night, she gave him her phone number. The next day, he called her.

Over the following months, they went to the movies together, for walks in the park, to the beach, out to dinner, for coffee, for drinks. She was falling in love with him. And he was falling in love with her; she could see it when his face lit up as he looked at her and in his bright smile.

Chris made her feel safe—a completely new experience. But to take the next big step was proving incredibly hard. He was patient, though, and after six months, she was finally ready to bare herself to him. Be intimate.

When Chris had held her in his arms, she was right there with him, and he didn't let her down. Not for a moment. His touch was full of veneration. He was understanding. Careful. Tender. And when he hovered above her body, elbows holding most of his weight, and finally entered her, it was slow, like he intuited he must ensure in every moment she was safe, comfortable.

She didn't disappear that night. No, she stayed right there, and she felt pleasure for the first time. As she laid in his arms afterwards, she knew with all her heart and soul that she loved him.

He had kissed her forehead, whispered into her ear, "I love you, Tina."

And without any fear, she said it right back. "I love you too."

CHAPTER 29

McKenzie ordered two takeaway extra-hot flat whites from his favourite coffee shop. The coffee was still scalding by the time he made it to the police station and met Jenkins to discuss the results from the house search conducted on Tina's home yesterday.

"How are you feeling?" Jenkins asked, noting the puffiness under his bloodshot eyes.

He swallowed a big mouthful of coffee, held his cup up. "Better after this."

"Not sleeping?"

He shrugged. "The usual."

She left the conversation there and opened the case folder. "First and foremost, Tina's DNA matched the samples gathered from the crime scenes, directly linking her to both. But..." She leafed through the paperwork until she landed on the right page. "The house search produced interesting evidence. This may be the key you were looking for."

His interest piqued, but his coffee cup was already to his lips, so he urged her to continue with a wave of his hand as he gulped a mouthful.

"Traces of drugs were found in Tina's espresso maker and the canister she stores her ground coffee. Both a match to the drug in her bloodstream." She handed over the toxicology report and photos.

McKenzie rested his coffee cup on the table and shuffled through the photos. The large espresso maker sat in the corner of the clean kitchen. A flap on the top could be opened, allowing ground coffee beans to be spooned inside each time an espresso was poured.

The accompanying report noted that a sample taken of the residual grounds tested positive for Scopolamine in powder form. The specific brand of the drug only came in tablet form.

He focused on his partner. "Someone would have had to grind the tablets into a fine powder before spiking the coffee. That indicates to me that this was an intentional drugging."

"I agree. Traces of this drug were also found in the splash of coffee left in a travel cup in Tina's car." She handed over another picture and report. "Latent fingerprints were collected from her house, most interestingly from the espresso maker and the coffee canister." She pointed to one of the pictures in McKenzie's hand, which showed a handprint. "See this here. This was found on the hallway wall."

Depending on Tina's cleaning habits, it wasn't necessarily incriminating to find fingerprints inside her home, because they could stay in place for years and she would have had many people come and go over that time.

"Tina was fastidiously clean," Jenkins said. "Shirts were ironed and hung in cupboards in colour-coded order. Shoes were perfectly aligned. Glasses were sparkling and in straight rows. The Tupperware cupboard was orderly. Forensics only found two sets of prints inside that house. One set was Tina's."

His brow arched.

"We ran the other set through the database. No match. But…" Jenkins turned her laptop, so the screen was facing

McKenzie, then opened a video file. "Hours and hours of time-stamped video footage recorded at Tina's residence was reviewed. You may find this interesting." She opened the file and clicked 'play'.

Footage showing Tina's front door. Night-time. A gaunt-looking woman wearing pyjamas runs up the stairs and pounds on the door. She yells something, hits the door again, and then rushes out of sight of the camera.

Jenkins opened a second video file and hit 'play'.

The footage is showing inside the house, looking down the long hall. Off the hall are several bedrooms and the main bathroom. The same woman walks along the hall. Wobbly legs. She sways into the wall with her hip, lifts her right hand to balance herself.

"That's the handprint?" McKenzie asked.

"Yep."

"All the prints belong to one person?"

"Yep."

"Who is she?"

"Maddison Brooks. Tina's ex-sister-in-law."

"Kadie Brooks' mother?"

"The one and only."

"Organise a warrant to search Maddison Brooks' home. If we find anything at all linking her to the drug, we make an arrest." He got to his feet, straightened his tie. "Meanwhile, I'm going to have another chat with Tina."

CHAPTER 30

Tina sat in the small interview room and waited. Her back ached. Her eyes burned. The emotional stamina required to endure that horrifying situation was rapidly emptying her.

The police staff had provided her with plastic cushions to rest on in her cell, but, by the morning, she had had no more than a few hours of patchy sleep and her ribs and hip bones were bruised.

Not that she would have slept anyway. Not without the help of sleeping pills or a lot of strong, hard liquor. She had never drunk alcohol in her life, nor taken sleeping pills, but she would make an exception if given the option.

The most difficult aspect for Tina was knowing all the details of the crime she had committed, yet her brain was telling her a skewed version of events. Trying to reconcile the two was impossible.

Not that it mattered. She deserved to suffer. Regardless of how much she wanted to change that day, sanitise it, turn it into something more palatable, she couldn't. The facts were: she had swung a wrecking bar repeatedly and with such force that she had crushed Juliette's eye socket, cheekbone and skull, exposing the brain and turning it to dogfood.

She wouldn't dull it down. She wouldn't word it politely or obscurely to make herself feel better. That's what had happened.

Not a second went by that those images were not appearing in her mind's eye like a nightmare on repeat. From the moment she was placed in her cell, she had sat on the stiff, cement bench and sobbed. Sobbed so hard she could barely breathe. She would never forgive herself.

By the time morning had arrived, and she was taken to the interview room to await Detective Inspector McKenzie, she had no more tears to give. Empty.

McKenzie opened the door and Tina flinched, her eyelids flickering. She had been expecting him, but her nervous system was set to panic, so the smallest noise or movement sent her fight-or-flight instincts into overdrive.

"Morning, Tina," he said. "I need a little more of your time to go over some details."

He still held the same casual I'm-your-friend tone that he had maintained all through their last interview. It unsettled Tina because she couldn't understand why anyone would be nice to her after what she had done.

He had maintained that tone right up until he had said he was arresting her. Then, his true feelings had shown on his face, in his timbre, and even though it was difficult being on the receiving end of such distaste, at least he was being honest. At least his emotions were matching the circumstances.

She opened her mouth, but the only sound she managed to make after a night of tears was so soft it was inaudible. She cleared her throat, swallowed, tried again. "Fine." The single syllable was hoarse, practically a whisper.

McKenzie sat down, eased back in the chair, his ankle resting on the opposite knee. His elbows were wide, fingers linked behind his head.

No one could relax in a situation like that. Except for someone who was pretending to. Knowing that, Tina wasn't quite so offended by McKenzie's facade of nonchalance.

She sank a little more into her seat, crossed her arms around her middle and sagged.

McKenzie's throat tightened when he noticed Tina's oily hair. The strands were clumping near her scalp. He looked away, gathered himself. When he met her eyes, his mask was on. "As was established by a forensic toxicology report, you had substantial quantities of anticholinergics—namely Scopolamine—in your system when you were found in your car on the morning of the incident."

She nodded.

"It's a drug that's not readily available other than by prescription. Have you recalled anything that might explain how you ingested it?" Medical records from Tina's GP, obtained under a warrant, showed that she hadn't been prescribed much of anything. The closest he found that even came close to a drug was a prescription for antibiotics six months ago to treat a urinary tract infection.

"I have no idea how I could have taken it," she said. "Zero."

"Tell me about this affair you had with Ben Brooks?"

She looked away.

"How long did your affair last?"

"It wasn't an affair," she said.

"You had sex with him while you were married to Chris, is that right?"

"Just once."

"Just once because Kadie Brooks, the girl you were claiming to be your daughter a few days ago, broke her neck after falling from a tree?"

Tina's next breath was rushed. McKenzie may have a cordial tone, but his questions were far from that. It was like dealing with someone with multiple personality disorder. "Yes."

"So, it wasn't the right environment to continue what was started that day?"

She cleared her throat. "You could say that."

He lowered his leg and his arms and leaned forward. "I want to know if *you* would say that."

"I would."

"Have you seen Ben since that day?"

She shook her head.

"The funeral?"

"I wouldn't have been welcome."

"I see," he said. "So, you've never accidentally bumped into Ben?"

"No."

"It's not a big town."

"No."

McKenzie added as nonchalantly as he could manage. "What about Maddison?"

She pursed her lips, glanced away from his solid eye contact. "What about her?"

"Does she ever come over to visit?"

"I wouldn't describe those encounters as *visits*."

"Do you ever invite her into your home to chat? After all, you were her sister-in-law for a long time."

"No. Never."

"Why not?" he asked.

"She hates my guts. She believes I killed her daughter. I'm not sure we'd have much to talk about." She fell silent for a long moment as she thought about all the times her ex-sister-in-law had stopped by her house. Maddison would scream and cry, tap on the doors and windows, hurling the most hateful abuse and Tina would try to drown out the noise with a pillow over her ears. "On dates important to Kadie, like her birthday, or the anniversary of her death, or even Christmas, Maddison always comes to the house."

McKenzie held still. "How so?"

"She arrives in a taxi or Uber. Wasted. She stands outside and screams abuse at me."

"Has she done this recently?"

Tina nodded. "Yes."

"I see. And what kinds of things would she say?"

"That I was to blame for Kadie's death. That I should kill myself. Things like that."

"And you never let her inside?"

She shook her head hard. "When she's like that, she frightens me."

"Why not call the police?"

"I'm not calling the police on a grieving mother. I've done enough, haven't I? Honestly, it's less than I deserve."

"You feel culpable for Kadie dying?"

"Every single day."

The fact that Tina was involved in the death of two people in a short space of time wasn't lost on McKenzie. He had studied the coroner's findings into Kadie, but there was not one indication that Tina was anything more than in the wrong place at the wrong time. An affair didn't equate to the crime of murder.

"Has Maddison ever threatened to harm you?"

She started to shake her head and then stopped. "Yes."

"During one of those encounters at your house?"

"Yes."

"What were the circumstances?" he asked.

"She was drunk again. Or high. I don't know exactly. Maybe both. She was slurring pretty bad. She had been in the front yard for about five minutes, just yelling and crying like she usually does. I climbed out of bed and locked the doors and windows, but I stayed inside, hoping she'd soon tire herself out. She usually did. But then she started rattling on the front door, trying to turn the knob. She was screaming that if she got in, she'd break my neck."

"Any other times?"

"No, that was the only one I can remember."

"And she has never come inside?"

"No. Unless she's broken in while I'm not there. That would be the only way. I've found little things in the yard that belong to her, so I think she's been around at the house when I've been out."

"What things have you found?"

"Vomit, mostly. A shoe once. Hairbands. Tissues. Things like that."

"Why didn't you ever think that Maddison could be your stalker?"

Tina closed her eyes and sighed. She was so exhausted, she didn't know if she could ever open them again, but she dragged her lids apart and looked at McKenzie's hardened expression. "It makes sense now. But I hadn't been thinking clearly. I thought Kadie was *my* child. Maddison didn't even exist in my world during the past month. Obviously in some subconscious way she did, but I wasn't *aware* of her." Her brow crinkled and she shook her head. "I can't explain it more clearly than that because it doesn't even make sense to me..." Her voice cracked and she broke off, trying to stem the tears. She had cried so much, it was now painful to feel that constriction in the back of her throat.

"You said someone had been coming into your home and leaving notes," McKenzie said.

"Yes."

"The police report you lodged stated that you were getting your locks changed."

"Yes. I got them changed."

"Can you recall the date?"

"Not off the top of my head. A few weeks ago. The locksmith probably has a record of it."

"Did Maddison have keys to your house?"

Tina racked her brain. "Um, yes, she would have. She and Ben used to keep an eye on the house if Chris and I went on holidays. We had a set cut for them."

"Were the locks changed before or after the cameras were installed?"

"Before."

"Tell me about the espresso maker?"

She frowned, shook her head. "I'm not sure what you mean?"

"Did you buy it second-hand off the Gladstone Classifieds, Facebook Marketplace or something like that?"

"Chris bought it new for my birthday a few years ago."

"You haven't loaned it out to anyone?" McKenzie asked.

"No. It's quite big. Not something I'd easily be able to lend to someone."

"Where do you buy your coffee?"

"Just from Woolworths. A cheap brand."

"Do you buy the beans whole and grind it yourself?" he asked.

"I buy pre-ground coffee."

"Every time?"

"I used to grind beans when I first got it. But the grinding mechanism is broken, so I don't do that anymore," she said.

"How long since you've ground the beans yourself?"

"Two, maybe three, years. I can't remember."

"Do you own a mortar and pestle?"

"No."

"A spice grinder?"

"No."

"A meat mallet?"

"No. I'm not sure why you want to know that."

"Where were you on the night of the eighteenth of March?" he asked.

"I can't—"

"Four days before the morning of the murder. Monday evening. Where were you?"

"At home. That would have been the night I saw my stalker, Isabelle."

"Did you invite anyone into your home that night?"

Goosebumps spread along her arms, up the back of her neck. "No, not that I'm aware of." Her hands flung to her mouth, finally connecting the dots. "Oh, my God, was Maddison drugging me?"

McKenzie leaned forward, linked his fingers. "That's unclear at this stage."

Even with this new fork in the investigation, he'd gathered enough evidence. It was his sworn duty to provide that evidence now diligently to a court of law, along with a suspect and a corresponding charge. It would be up to a jury to decide if Tina was guilty or innocent.

"Tina, I am formally bringing charges against you for the murder of Juliette Spencer."

CHAPTER 31

Maddison headed to the kitchen for a cup of coffee. She didn't have the urge to hide downstairs in her basement gym, working out until she couldn't walk. She hadn't worked out for a week. Her body was already thanking her for it—no crippling pain in every movement and each breath.

Her grief was still heavy, but she had confronted the biggest monster, and, in doing so, thieved some of its power. Reliving Kadie's death had been as unbearable as when she had experienced it three years ago. But she had done it, and she was still functioning.

That day in her therapist's office was the first time she had truly accepted that Kadie was dead and never coming back.

Over the years, Maddison had somehow believed that if she didn't look at that day again and fully acknowledge its existence, then it wasn't real. And if it wasn't real, it wasn't true. And if it wasn't true, then she didn't have to feel the full anguish of losing her daughter.

Ben was already in the kitchen, sitting at the bench, coffee beside him, newspaper spread out before him. He was breathing heavily. Concentrating hard as he read. He didn't even hear his wife come in.

"Morning," she said. It had been so long since she had spoken to her husband with kindness.

He didn't lift his head or acknowledge her presence, too engrossed in what he was reading.

"Morning," she said more loudly.

He blinked, lifted his gaze to look at her. His eyes were wide. "Have you seen the news?"

Brow furrowed, she shook her head. "Why, what is it?"

"Chris's stepdaughter was murdered."

Maddison gasped. "What?"

He turned the newspaper and tapped on the article. "Here. Right here. They've charged Tina with the murder."

"Tina? The Tina?"

He nodded.

"You've got to be kidding me. Seriously?"

"Read it," he insisted.

She yanked the paper towards her and speed-read the article. "Bloody hell," she growled and pushed the newspaper away. "I've always known she was a horrible person, but I never could have imagined this."

Ben disregarded the backhanded jibe. "I need to call Chris."

Her eyes widened. "Chris? What?"

"His stepdaughter was murdered. Of course, I need to speak to him."

"But it's been so long."

Kadie's funeral, three years ago, was the last time Ben had spoken to his brother. Ben had screwed up big time, in the worst possible way, and no matter what else was happening, it didn't take away from what he had done with Tina that day.

The fact that Chris had shown up for the funeral, spoke more about his character than it did to Ben's. Ben loved his brother. He had missed him so much over the past few years. He would be there for him now if Chris allowed him. And he would finally apologise.

He reached for his mobile and dialled his brother, hoping like mad Chris hadn't changed his number since they had last spoken.

"Ben?" Chris said when he answered. His voice was rough. A little older than Ben had expected.

"Yeah, mate. I just read what happened. I'm so sorry."

A long pause. "It's so messed up. I'm not gonna lie. I'm not doing too great. Issy's blaming me. Oh, God, I don't know what to do..." His voice cracked. Muffled cries through the phone.

Tears filled Ben's eyes, but he blinked them back. Breathed deeply. "Come over, mate, and we'll have breakfast and a chat."

Another pause. "You sure? Maddison will be okay with that?"

"Of course. We're family. I'm here for you. Come over." When he ended the call, he placed the phone on the bench. "Can you believe this?"

Maddison shook her head. "Not one bit. I better head out and pick up some bread, seeing as we're now expecting a visitor."

"Sure, better grab some more milk too."

Such horrible circumstances in which to reunite with his brother, and yet he was relieved to have broken the ice. In time, he hoped Chris would forgive him.

"I'll be back in fifteen minutes," Maddison said.

Maddison headed to the bakery for fresh croissants and milk. Despite her initial resistance, a flourish of happiness filled her chest to know Chris was coming over. She had always liked her brother-in-law. He was laidback, friendly. Unbelievably loyal to Tina. He hadn't deserved what had happened. He had loved Kadie so much. And Ruby and Riley. It would have been difficult when they were snatched from his life because of his wife's selfishness.

Murder was the last thing Maddison would have expected, though. She squeezed the steering wheel hard between her hands as she made her way home. Murder was reprehensible. Almost unbelievable.

A police vehicle and an executive sedan sat in the driveway when she arrived. Her heart thudded hard in her chest. She barely made it out of the car when Ruby and Riley's faces flashed in her mind, igniting a fierce fear that they may have been hurt in the time she had been out.

She raced up the front stairs, pushed open the door, and nearly crashed into the chest of Detective Inspector McKenzie who was dressed in grey slacks and a crisp, white long-sleeved shirt.

"What's going on?" she asked in a breathless rush.

Maddison looked around the room. Ben was seated on the couch. Chris was there, too, the children beside him. Detective Jenkins, wearing gloves, was placing a small cardboard box into a baggie. A uniformed police officer was holding Maddison's spice grinder, then placed it into a clear, sealable bag.

"I'm Detective Inspector McKenzie. Maddison Brooks?"

She nodded, unable to focus on anything for too long. A hot, tight ache in the centre of her chest.

"I'm placing you under arrest for unlawfully administering substances with the intent to harm."

CHAPTER 32

Maddison sagged lower on her chair when Detective Inspector McKenzie entered the room and sat opposite her. She had been processed, briefed, and locked in a watchhouse cell, where she had stayed for the past six hours until they allowed her out and led her to that small interview room.

She had the right to obtain a lawyer, but she didn't need one. She was innocent and as soon as she explained that, she would be going home.

McKenzie set his hard gaze on her and it was too much.

"I don't know why I've even been arrested," she insisted. "Let alone for giving someone drugs."

"For the time being, Maddison, I want to get some information."

Tears filled her eyes. She blew out a long breath. This wasn't the most difficult thing she had endured in her life, but it was coming close. She could feel that line being drawn in her mind, where if she were to cross it, she'd lose herself to panic. If she remained on that side, she could get through it. If she just told the truth, everything would be fine. It was simply a misunderstanding.

"Where were you on the evening of eighteen March."

She shook her head. "I have no idea."

"Think about it. It was a Monday."

She cringed as she realised that the eighteenth was the evening before she woke in the park. "I was at home with my husband. You can check my social media."

"You were at home *all* night?"

She lowered her gaze, swallowed hard. "Yes. My husband can vouch for that."

He leaned closer. "I'm going to make it clear right now that I know you were not at home all night. We have video footage of you very much not at home."

She gave a low, pained groan, scrubbed her hands over her face. "I don't know where I went that night. I woke up in a park. I don't remember anything other than having some drinks at home."

"You woke in a park?"

She nodded.

"Which park?"

"Henderson Play Park."

"Anyone to *vouch* for that?"

"A mother and her daughter," she said. "She called my husband to pick me up."

"And yet you just said your husband could vouch that you were home all night?"

Her jaw clenched tight, cheeks flushed with heat. "I was embarrassed."

"Have you arranged for your husband to lie about anything else?"

She shook her head. "I haven't asked him to lie. I just... I knew he wouldn't throw me under the bus."

"Under the bus for what?"

"For waking up in a park after a big night of prescription pills and alcohol. Other than that, I honestly have no idea how I even got there."

"A moment ago, though, you said that you could remember. And that you were home all night. And your husband could vouch for that."

"I know. I'm sorry. I won't lie again. I was trying to save face. It's not a good look for a middle-aged mother, you know?"

McKenzie settled back in his chair. "What's your relationship with Tina Brooks?"

"I don't have a relationship with that woman."

"At all?"

"None. Why would I?"

"You don't visit her property out at Yarwun?"

A stone in her stomach, falling, falling; the sensation almost took her breath away. "I have. A couple of times."

"What happens during these visits to Tina's residence?"

A long, airy exhalation and she slouched in her chair. "I cry. Scream."

"Do you threaten her?"

She shook her head hard. "No."

"You don't tell her to kill herself?"

"I don't think so."

"You don't tell her that you'll break her neck?"

Maddison jolted. "Oh, God." She lowered her face into her hands. When she sat up tall again, tears were in her eyes. "Yes, I've said that. I was trying to hurt her, you know?"

"Just so I have this clear, you threatened to break her neck as a means of hurting her?"

She winced. "I wouldn't follow through with it. I meant to hurt her with words. I wanted her to feel bad for what she'd done. I was angry and upset. How do you know about all this? Did Tina tell you?"

"I have a lot of information, Maddison, and so far, by continuing to lie to me, it's not working in your favour. Do you make a habit of threatening people?"

"Of course not. I was drunk. I was upset. She was screwing my husband when they should have been watching my daughter. You try coming home to that! Your husband still in the process of screwing your sister-in-law and then walking outside and finding your... my" – she broke off with a sob – "finding Kadie hanging by her head from a fucking tree. Of course, I'm angry," she screamed. Tears streamed down her face. She beat the desk. "Of course, I'm angry. And you're trying to make out like being angry is some kind of crime. I didn't do anything wrong. I didn't hurt Tina. I was venting."

"What about the nine-year-old schoolgirl you threatened to gut? Was that just anger?"

She froze, eyes widening. "That... that was a mother protecting her daughter."

He nodded. "But you didn't hurt her either?"

"Of course not. It was words."

"You never followed through?"

"No."

"Have you ever thought you'd like to hurt Tina? Maybe even kill her?"

She shook her head. "No."

"Even after what she did? What she put you and your family through?"

"Fine. I've thought about killing her a thousand times. But it doesn't mean I'd do it."

"Why were you in Tina's home on the night of the eighteenth?"

She went silent, looked to the side as she tried to access those stolen memories. "I wasn't."

"Maddison, you're lying to me. Again." His patience was thin, his countenance harsher. One thing he hated more than anything was a liar.

"Honestly, I'm not. I wasn't there. I don't think I was there." She groaned, slapped her head with the side of her hand. "Maybe I went there." A vision of her old house, the tree in the darkness. She could have walked to Tina's afterwards or before. "I don't know."

"Maddison, I have incontrovertible proof that you were there."

"What proof?"

"Video footage. Fingerprints."

Her mouth flapped open and shut.

"You were inside the house," he said.

"No. No, I wouldn't go inside. I wouldn't."

"But you did," he pushed. "I saw you dressed in pyjamas, red lipstick smudged across your mouth, banging on the front door. A moment later, more footage of you swaying down the hall."

"I don't remember any of that."

"Have you ever been prescribed Scopolamine?"

"I have no idea."

He slid a picture across the table to her. A photo of a Scopolamine packet. A prescription sticker on the outside in her name.

"Yes, um, I did. For a cruise a few years back. I get seasick. The doctor said this would help. But I didn't need them in the end."

"Did you take them later for any other reason?"

She shook her head. "I don't think so."

"This packet was found in your bedside drawer. Empty."

"I honestly don't know. Maybe I did take them. I can't remember specifically, though."

McKenzie shifted closer, right up in Maddison's personal space. His eye contact was solid. "Maddison, I need you to be straight with me. Did you go to Tina's house on the night of the eighteenth?"

A flash of bright lights. Tina's kitchen. The coffee machine. She shook her head. "I... yes." The detective was too close, invading her space. She wanted to shove him away or turn her head, anything but look into his eyes.

"Did you contaminate her coffee with Scopolamine tablets that you had ground into powder?"

"No."

"We found evidence of the drug in your spice grinder. We found the empty packet beside your bed. We found powder residue in your kitchen. Your fingerprints are on the coffee machine and canister at Tina's residence. We have video footage of you being there. So, I'll ask you again, did you drug Tina?"

Maddison lowered her face into her hands and shook her head. "I'm not saying anything more until I have a lawyer."

CHAPTER 33

The day of Kadie's death…

Tina knocked on her in-law's front door and waited. Her nieces and nephew were running around inside, their feet on the timber floorboards like elephants. A shout and a giggle sounded, and she smiled. She loved those kids so much she wanted to quietly steal them, take them home and never give them back.

She chuckled to herself when Ben's loud, slightly angry voice sang out. At times, she was sure Ben and Maddison would gladly send them to stay with her and Chris for a while. Three young kids were constant hard work. When Tina had them sleep at her house for a night, she was exhausted by the time she walked them back home.

Being an aunty was as close as she was going to get to motherhood, so she embraced it. She spoilt the kids rotten. Bought them expensive Christmas and birthday gifts, much to their parents' discouragement.

"You're going to turn them into rotten little shits if you keep spoiling them," Ben had said.

Chris laughed. "That's for you to deal with then, isn't it?"

Chris loved them just as much. A hollow pang in Tina's belly. She had fallen pregnant four times over her fifteen-year marriage. Many years of trying and failing in between. But not one pregnancy survived eight weeks. After that, she didn't have the will to endure the endless cycle of grief and disappointment anymore.

The door opened with a flurry. Ben stood there. "Tina. How are you?"

She smiled. "Good. Is Issy home?"

"Ah, no, she's out doing the grocery shopping. She shouldn't be too much longer if you want to come inside and wait."

"Sure. I'll say hello to the kids while I'm at it."

"They'll be excited to see you. Their favourite aunty and all."

She laughed. "The only aunty living close by, so I have no choice but to earn that title."

Tina followed him into the house. An old Queenslander, set upon a big plot of land. They had managed to renovate it meticulously over the years. Bigger than the house Tina and Chris were buying. Made sense with their brood of children.

She followed Ben down the long hall to the end. On the left was the living room. The kids were in there, cartoons blaring on the TV. Toys were strewn across the floor. The untidiness of children was the only thing that Tina didn't care for. She liked order. But she would have happily sacrificed her love of a neat and clean home for her own children, should the blessing have arrived.

Tina's nieces and nephew raced to her, throwing their arms around her and jumping up and down.

"Aunty Tina," cheered Kadie.

"Hi there, sweetheart," she said, stroking her fringe from her forehead and leaning down to kiss her cheek. "So good to see you. Are you having a good Saturday morning?"

"Yep."

Riley had raced away, picked up a paper aeroplane and was running back. "Look what I made?"

Tina's eyes widened. "All by yourself?"

He nodded with big, proud movements.

"You're incredibly clever. You should make me one too and we'll have a competition to see whose flies the furthest."

He grinned and ran into another room for paper and pencils.

Ruby was holding Tina's waist, had her head against her.

"Hello, gorgeous. Gee, I think you've grown in the three days I haven't seen you."

Ruby stood up taller, put her hand on her head. She had a huge smile on her face. "I feel taller."

"Well, there you go. It must be true then."

Ben stood behind them, watching. He appreciated how much Tina and Chris loved his kids. As someone who had his family ripped apart by death while he was so young, he had always craved a large family where Chris and his sister Jacinta played big roles.

He had a lot of sympathy for his brother in that regard. Not having a family cut him to the core. Though, Chris had only admitted to that the one time after he'd had too many beers at a barbeque.

Tina bent over to look at a Lego creation. She was wearing tight gym pants and they outlined the shape of her as though she were wearing nothing. He gave himself permission to look and admire.

Blood flowed to his groin. He readjusted himself quickly, so he could hide his growing erection. He had always been a sucker for a hot arse, though, and Tina's was proving to be exceptional. He wasn't certain if he'd ever known that about her before.

She stood up again, turned to him and smiled. He couldn't tell if she had meant to taunt him. He met her gaze. Her eyes held a teasing gleam, enough for him to suspect she had meant it. The heat between his legs grew.

But she wasn't teasing him. She had forgotten that she was still in her workout clothes and caught him ogling her as she had straightened. Her cheeks flushed, and she gave an embarrassed grin.

To fill the awkward silence, she said quickly, "Maddison offered to loan me a dress to wear to the work party Chris and I are going to tomorrow."

He nodded. "Right, yes, um… she did mention that. I think she left it hanging up in our bedroom if you want me to go grab it?"

"Yeah, that would be good. I'm keen to know if it fits. She's smaller than me."

He ran his eyes up the length of her, now certain she was leading him on with a comment like that. Arousal shot through him. He was as hard as a rock.

"Riley, how about you and the kids play a game of hide-n-seek?"

Ruby and Kadie cheered and clapped.

"Yes! I'm counting first. You two hide," Riley said excitedly to his sisters.

Ben tilted his head in the direction of the hall. "You better come with me, just to make sure we're talking about the same dress."

Tina hesitated. Going to the bedroom with her brother-in-law transgressed a clear line. Because of her childhood, her trust in men was low. She had spent most of her life trying to hide that fact because she had believed she was to blame for her abuses.

Her uncle had called her a devil. A demon. A little witch. Casting spells on him that made him want to do bad things to her. As an eight-year-old child, she had believed him. She was so scared to tell anyone what he was doing to her in case they, too, realised she was a witch.

Tina swallowed her intuition and followed Ben to his bedroom, not wanting to appear suspicious or rude. When she entered the room, he shut the door behind them. Her heart stuttered.

His smile was warm, sickly so. "The kids will be running in and out otherwise. Believe me, it will be faster this way." He went to the cupboard and hanging on the door was a long red dress.

"That's it," she said. "Beautiful."

He lifted it down and held it against her. "It'll look great. And will fit perfectly."

She smiled. "Thanks." And reached for the dress, but he held it tighter.

He was watching her. Chest expanding and deflating.

"I'll just go check on the kids. You can bring that out when you're ready." She spun to walk away, but he gripped her hand and yanked her back to him.

"Don't go yet. I reckon you should try it on first," he said.

"If it doesn't fit, I'll just bring it back."

He dropped the dress between them, took a big step closer and wrapped his arms around her. Kissed her mouth.

"No, Ben. No." She resisted, turned her head. But he didn't stop, kept trailing kisses down her face, to her neck.

She tried to wriggle out of his grip, but his muscled arms pulled tighter around her. Against her stomach was his jutting erection.

"Ben, don't do this."

"Don't act all coy now. You're not fooling me." Fast, forceful, he let her go, gripped her pants and yanked them down to her thighs. With strong, rough hands, he spun her, pushed her in the back and she flung forward. She twisted her wrist painfully as she caught herself against the hard floor. Her knees thudded.

Before she could move, he was there, shoving her down hard, her stomach flat to the floor, face squished. His insistent hand smothered her mouth, stifling her scream. His forearm was hard and heavy over her lower back, pinning her there. Within a second he was inside her.

A muffled scream as pain almost blinded her. She whimpered against his hand, tears falling down her face.

No longer was she human.

She had to get away from there. From him. She squirmed, twisted, but Ben was relentless. Much too strong. The pain overwhelmed everything. She could barely breathe. She squeezed her eyes closed, needing to escape.

All those old defensive barriers flooded back and without needing to try, she left her body, flew to that place in her mind where there were beautiful flowers and ice cream. Sunshine and butterflies. She lay on that grass, the sun beating down on her face.

Safe.

When she opened her eyes, Ben's weight was easing off her. Someone had screamed.

Unbeknownst to them all, that moment was when little Kadie had crawled along the tree branch, her toes gripping the smooth bark, her hands holding on tight. She stumbled and tried to gain her balance but tilted too far backwards and fell feet first. She clawed at the slippery tree limb but couldn't find purchase and plunged between the two branches. A sharp yank, a crack and a pop and her short four years on the earth were over.

But the world didn't miss a beat. It didn't pause for a death that would have ramifications for years after. Even the thoughts taking place in the bedroom didn't hesitate for even a fraction of time.

Maddison, Tina thought. *Maddison is home.* At first, relief flooded her body because she believed she would be rescued.

"Ruby, Riley, Kadie, come here please. Right now," Maddison yelled as she rushed from the room.

Ben leaned down, close to Tina's ear and growled, "Now look what you've done."

He stood tall again and followed his wife out of the room.

For a long moment, Tina lay there, unable to move, trembling all over. "You can do this. You've done this before. Get up, get dressed, and go home."

Like a robot, she slowly got to her feet, pulled her pants up. She could feel the wetness between her legs and her stomach convulsed. She swallowed hard. Breathed deeply, slowly.

"Butterflies. Rainbows. Warm sun. Grass," she repeated as she walked down the hall, then silently in her head as she strode to the front door and left.

When she arrived home, she stripped out of her clothes and ran the shower. There she stayed, washing with soap, and staring at the tiled floor as she meticulously, expertly, reframed the entire morning.

It had been a lovely day. Warm sunshine on her face. She had stopped by to see Maddison, but she wasn't home, so she had a nice cup of tea with Ben as she waited. Ruby wanted to show her how big she had grown and had prepared the tea all by herself. She had done a great job too. It had tasted delicious. Riley made her a paper plane and coloured it with bright flowers and butterflies. They laughed and chatted as they flew them across the blue sky. Then she built a house with a pink roof out of Lego with Kadie. When it was time to leave, she kissed her nieces and nephew on the cheek, waved, and walked home in the sunshine.

Tina startled and gasped when she realised the shower water was stone cold, beating against her body. She hurriedly turned off the taps and dried herself. Shivering all over, she dressed into her winter pyjamas, climbed into bed, and pulled the doona high over her shoulders despite it being thirty-odd degrees outside.

* * *

Chris arrived home around nine o'clock that night. A small part of Tina's brain knew this wasn't right. He was meant to be home tomorrow. But Tina barely existed anymore, at least not in the real world.

The front door tinkled as he opened the locks and came in. "Tina," he called out.

She didn't answer.

He found her in bed, her face hot, hair dripping with sweat. And yet she was shivering. "Are you okay? I've been trying to call you all day."

She attempted to meet his eyes when he turned on the bedside lamp, but she couldn't focus. He pulled the doona down, reached for her pyjama top, but she flinched and pushed him away.

He felt her forehead with the back of his hand. "You're burning up. How long have you been like this?"

She shrugged.

"Will you let me get you paracetamol? It will help lower your fever."

She didn't say anything. He rushed out of the room, came back later with two paracetamols and a glass of water. Without thinking, she swallowed them down.

He sighed. "I know you hate taking pills, but, honestly, Tina, you're so hot. I can feel the heat radiating from you. I didn't know you were sick."

"I'm not."

He sat on the bed beside her like he weighed a ton, lowered his face into his hands and rubbed his eyes. "I can't believe Kadie is gone. I just can't believe it. I couldn't get a straight story out of Ben when he rang me. Maddison was inconsolable. Ben said you were there. What happened?"

Tina blinked. "I don't understand."

"Kadie. She fell out of the tree."

She sat up slowly, shook her head.

"Kadie broke her neck. She died. Ben is…" Tears filled his eyes. "I can't believe it."

"Kadie is dead?"

His brows arched. "You didn't know?"

"No."

"Ben said you were there."

"I was. But I left. I didn't—" Something broke inside Tina then. Something silent but big and so significant. She disappeared to that place she had dwelled as a small child. The good place. The kind place. In that happy world, she created an entirely different life and floated above her real existence as a contented, whole person.

She no longer had the capacity for love. Not in the real world. When Chris looked into her vacant eyes then, he had intuited that. His wife was no longer there. And no matter how much he searched for her, tried to find her, amidst his grief and pain and rejection, he never could. The walls were up, and each brick was rigidly fixed into place. He would need a sledgehammer to get through.

He lasted six months more in that lonely home, lost somewhere between resentment, pity, and grief. He had given Tina every chance to stop him from leaving, but she never tried. Never raised her voice, let alone a fist to fight him. He hated himself for quitting.

But Tina didn't hate him. And she certainly didn't blame him. She was emotionless. Numb. A meat body without a heart. Her husband needed to heal and that required love. Touch. Feelings. All the things she could no longer give him.

And so, Tina was left alone, comfortable in her fabricated world. She didn't re-emerge into reality again until years later.

CHAPTER 34

Isabelle drove through the frosty streets of Launceston, heater set to high. A pretty, old, undulating city that held onto many historic buildings. The sunlight was muted, not like bright Queensland days, and it dulled the hue of the flanking structures and cloudy, grey sky above.

Not that Isabelle noticed any of that. Since arriving nine weeks ago with her parents, in the deepest, darkest depths of her grief, where her body was consumed by a pain she had never believed possible let alone bearable, where she had to actively choose to keep going each second, she hadn't noticed much at all.

Life was a series of motions. Every one of them had a steep mountain at their foot. She stayed at her parents' home, the same house from her childhood, the same bedroom, and she went about her day barely receptive to the happenings around her. Her mum tried to get her out of the house for walks when the sun was doing its best to shine. But nothing stopped the relentless cold that wouldn't leave her bones. Her Dad tried to cheer her up by cooking her favourite childhood meals. But nothing had taste.

Isabelle gently gripped the steering wheel and drove, adhering to the commands of traffic lights and stop signs and giving way when needed. But she wasn't present, not completely. Her mind was protecting itself from the truth. Mostly, her mind was protecting itself from the injustice. The injustice of Juliette's death was the most difficult aspect of it all. Of all the people to have suffered such a pointless, heinous death, it had to be the person who least deserved it. Juliette.

Juliette had been such a great kid. A diligent sleeper from the moment she was born. Isabelle had often marvelled at how lucky she was to have a baby like that. Juliette had been the kindest of children. Social. Happy. A good, loyal friend. The most loving daughter. She had worked hard and never expected life to hand out favours.

She had been Isabelle's whole world from the time she felt her little feet flutter against her belly for the first time. Isabelle didn't know anything else but Juliette. Even with Chris there, it had been a way to fill the void that was imminent once Juliette moved out and started a family of her own. She hadn't known that, until the biggest, darkest void had opened up beneath her feet and she realised that Chris never could fill it. Not at all. Not one bit.

Now she had to navigate her world without the only person who ever anchored her to it. And that was, most days, impossible.

Isabelle looked at the long street ahead of her and blinked. She didn't know where she was going. After five minutes of driving around in circles, she found an empty park and pulled in. She stared, existing somewhere between the realm of life and death, awake and asleep, conscious and unconscious. She hovered there, her gaze filled with an out-of-focus blur of muted colour.

A small flutter—subtle at first and then more insistent—beat in her belly. Her hand floated to her stomach, but the baby was too small to feel from the outside yet. As though her tiny child had sent her a message, she remembered the purpose of today's outing—her eighteen-week-scan.

Isabelle sighed. The shine on her pregnancy had dulled since her daughter was violently stolen from the world. Her pregnancy had taken a back seat to the immensity of emotions that loomed over everything. Almost a chore to pretend to be okay for the few moments she had to interact with doctors during scheduled appointments.

To even envision mothering another child shone a light on the insidious loneliness left by Juliette's absence. New motherhood was too momentous, too great a task for someone who couldn't even remember where she was going.

Isabelle steered her car out onto the street and headed to the women's imaging office her doctor had referred her to. When she arrived, she went inside and sat in the small waiting room avoiding the other patients' eyes.

She didn't want to be spoken to, didn't want to speak. She didn't want to act like a normal human being because she wasn't normal. Not anymore. She was a broken, barely pulled-together replica.

A middle-aged female sonographer stood at the head of the waiting room and called, "Isabelle Spencer?"

Isabelle had already dropped her married name. Mostly because it added another layer of anonymity, but also because her marriage was over, so she wasn't about to pretend otherwise. She stood and met the smiling woman's gaze but couldn't bring herself to smile back.

In a private room, once Isabelle was directed to lay back on the padded table, shorts pulled low, shirt lifted under her breasts, the sonographer applied some gel to a transducer.

"I'm very sorry, I know that's a little cold," she said as she pressed the tool onto Isabelle's stomach.

Isabelle shrugged; she had barely noticed.

"Did you want to know the sex of your baby today?"

"Sure."

The transducer slipped across her stomach and came to a stop. An image of a tiny being, heart thumping away, appeared on the monitor.

"There she is," the sonographer said.

Isabelle's eyes widened. "A girl?"

She smiled, nodded. "Congratulations."

Isabelle turned back to the image as the transducer continued a path over her stomach, stopping here and there as the sonographer clicked her computer, taking measurements of body parts and organs. The baby seemed to move as though knowing she was being watched. Her little heart was strong, determined and insistent, the rhythmical beating filling the room.

At that moment, something shifted inside of Isabelle. As though a tiny spark had been ignited and it was slowly waking her up from her nightmare ever so gradually.

"Life," Isabelle whispered.

The sonographer smiled. "Sure is."

What a revelation. What a shining beacon awaiting on the shore of this swamp of death, loss and grief she had been wading through.

There, in her very womb, was life. Creation. A future.

Her lungs ached. Her throat was tight and painful. "Her sister is going to love her," Isabelle whispered.

"And what's her sister's name?"

"Juliette. She's been super excited about this pregnancy and will be so happy to know she's going to have a baby sister. She's going to be the best big sister." A watery laugh. "Said so herself."

The sonographer chuckled. "Self-professed best sister in the world."

"Absolutely."

"How old is Juliette?"

"Twenty-two. She turned twenty-two last week."

"That's a big age gap."

Isabelle sniffled, wiped the tears from her cheeks. "Took me that long to get my act together again."

"Better late than never."

A few more minutes of silence as the sonographer continued with her ultrasound. All the while Isabelle stared at the screen and marvelled at her daughter.

"Well, everything seems to be in order here. No signs of abnormalities. No markers present for any genetic disorders. By all accounts, you have a healthy baby girl."

Isabelle breathed in and her lungs inflated fully— something she hadn't managed for too long now. A brief moment of levity.

The sonographer wiped the gel from Isabelle's stomach. "All done."

"Thank you," Isabelle said.

When she made it back to the carpark and sat in the driver's seat, looking out at the other cars and nearby businesses, colours were brighter, shapes sharper. A subtle but profound alteration of her perceptions.

For months, Isabelle had been trapped in her tight skin, her focus directed inward. When she had stared at that ball of life in her belly, she had glimpsed the world outside of her. What she saw didn't dwell in the realm of grief. Her baby was like the sun—full of life-giving warmth. Her heart had cracked and through that fissure, a love that was bigger than her seeped in.

The future she had been unable to consider stretched out before her. Her hand floated to her stomach and she sighed with relief. That small spark of life in her womb was all the reason she needed to keep going.

Chris filled her mind and she reached for her phone. She should call him to let him know that they were having a baby girl. She should.

She turned her mobile on, scrolled through her contacts. Her finger hovered over his name, but no matter how much she forced herself to call him, she couldn't do it. Even with time and physical distance between them, how she felt about him hadn't changed.

Juliette's death was an enormous blow and Isabelle had been unplugged from that life she once existed in, with all its delusions, and woke up in another. A darker place. But a more real place.

There wasn't room in her heart or head in this new world for Chris. She hadn't the wherewithal, the energy, the desire to patch up or prolong what was barely real to start with. She clicked her phone off, sat it in the centre console and drove home.

CHAPTER 35

Christmas Day – three months before the murder…

T ina accelerated along the darkened streets of Yarwun towards home. She was on her way back from Mandy's where she had spent Christmas day with her friends and their families.

A long, hot summer's day. The first Christmas she had celebrated since the sexual assault and Kadie's death.

In the past few months, she had been poking her head out of her imaginary world and existing in reality for a time. Those moments were becoming more and more frequent. Finally, she was letting that horrible day go. Her defences were dismantling.

She hadn't been sure if she was ready to socialise in a group situation, but she had no excuses left to deny her friends her company yet again.

What she had been fearing, actually turned out to be great fun. She had swum, laughed, sung Christmas carols, reminisced and feasted on ham, seafood and salads. An ideal day until Trevor had mentioned that Chris was getting married next month.

Over two years had passed since he had walked out. Nearly a year since their divorce was finalised. She had known he had a girlfriend and a stepdaughter, but this was different.

She gripped the steering wheel tighter. She had always assumed their separation was temporary. Just a blip until she was strong again. But with Chris marrying someone else, it revealed that he didn't see matters the same way. He was moving on.

Tina's hands were shaking by the time she pulled into her driveway, speeding the car along the gravel and sticks and screeching on the brakes as she approached her carport, barely stopping in time before running into the water tank.

She climbed out and headed to the front door, stopping when she noticed the debris left on the doorstep. Her eyes darted around the yard, suddenly alert.

"Maddison?" she called out, but there was no answer. She couldn't see anyone.

Her shoulders relaxed and she sighed. She had dodged that drug-fuelled visit from Maddison. She hadn't had to hear her cry, yell and hurl abuse at her from the top of her lungs. Tonight, of all nights, she wasn't sure she could have handled it.

"Geez, Maddy, you must have been in a state tonight," she said, bending over to pick up the sole shoe lying near the door. A little further over was a packet of tissues. A few wet and scrunched tissues beside that. A hairband. A full box of prescription tablets.

She sighed as she picked up all the rubbish.

Maddison, only an hour earlier, while screaming and crying on the front porch, had tipped her bag over, dropped the contents everywhere, and was so useless from insobriety, she hadn't even noticed.

Tina marched to the garbage bin, sitting out the front near the carport, opened the lid and threw the shoe inside with all the force she could muster.

She resented Maddison. To not be able to recognise that Tina had lost so much that day as well came from a place of stubborn ignorance. The pain of losing Kadie still stung her. The shame. The sense of responsibility.

The loudest emotion was guilt. She should have fought Ben off. She should have fought him instead of cowering, avoiding, disappearing. If she had fought back, then she could have saved Kadie. She could have saved her marriage. All their lives could have continued as normal instead of being destroyed and lying in tatters around them.

She needed Maddison to stop blaming her. To stop reminding her of what had been thieved from her life and her soul.

Tina threw the tissue packet, hairband and dirty tissues into the bin. She held the box of tablets up closer to her face and read the name through the shadows. Scopolamine.

"Bloody hell, Maddison, why do you have these?" She had only been reading an article a few weeks ago about these drugs.

With a sigh, she lifted her hand, started to lower it with force, only to stop herself when a thought hit her.

"What if I *had* fought back?" she whispered, her body going very still.

Tingles fanned down the back of her neck, spread along her arms. A revelation was occurring. A tilting of reality. A shift in her perceptions was taking place right at that very moment.

All her life, she had been viewing the world from the wrong angle. She had always, regardless of the circumstances, positioned herself as the victim. When watching the news, she would listen to the graphic details of some girl who was raped and murdered as she cut through a park on her way home, and Tina would put herself in the victim's shoes. She would imagine the fear and suffering in the girl's final moments. She would think about how the young girl's family would feel.

Or when a patient had poured their heart out to her about a tragic moment in their life, she would be consumed with such empathy because she would be viewing the circumstances from her patient's point of view.

And even when a friend experienced loss or downfall, she would be right in there with them, living it as though it was happening to her.

She did that because to not be the victim meant she had to be the perpetrator. They were the only two roles. And perpetrators were the worst kind of people. They inflicted pain. They made others suffer. She never wanted to be that. Never.

But that always meant she was the one who got hurt.

Barely a minute ago, she had been wishing for Maddison to please stop blaming her. How wrong that was. What Tina should have been saying was that *she would make* Maddison stop blaming her. *Make* Maddison stop reminding her of Ben's assault. *Make* Ben learn the consequences of his misbehaviour. *Fight*, until she was the last one standing, to get her life back.

Yes, that was the right mindset. She slid the box into her pocket, shut the bin lid and went inside.

CHAPTER 36

Callous Housewife Convicted for Juliette Spencer's Murder.

The Gladstone Housewife Trials came to an end Monday when the vengeful housewife and mother of two, Maddison Brooks, was convicted of manslaughter, closing the eighteen-month-long case.

Maddison Brooks was given the maximum sentence of twenty years in prison after a jury unanimously found her guilty of intentionally drugging her ex-sister-in-law, Tina Brooks, which led to Tina viciously beating Juliette Spencer to death with a wrecking bar.

The jury said that though Maddison Brooks didn't intend for Juliette Spencer to die, it was proven beyond reasonable doubt that her 'callous' involvement directly led to the heartbreaking death.

Maddison Brooks was also convicted of a battery of additional charges including unlawfully administering a substance with the intent to cause harm, stalking, and breaking and entering.

This comes only months after Tina Brooks had her charges dismissed. Her initial murder charge was downgraded to manslaughter when Diminished Responsibility was argued due to Tina's unwitting intoxication at the time of the murder.

The jury returned a not guilty verdict after the defence team, over five long days, provided proof of Tina's mental demise, paranoia and eventual delirium directly caused when her coffee supply was intentionally spiked with Scopolamine, a drug documented for causing altered states of mind when consumed in high doses.

Lead defence lawyer, Robert Gennaro, who represented Tina Brooks, stated about the outcome, 'Tina's compromised mental state was well-substantiated and with her good standing in the community, lack of prior convictions of any kind, dedication to counselling since the incident, along with her obvious remorse, we were always confident she would be found not guilty'.

Not the case for Maddison Brooks who was noted as appearing 'shellshocked' when her guilty verdict was handed down. Her defence team didn't wish to comment when approached outside the Brisbane Supreme Court soon afterwards.

Isabelle Brooks, the mother of Juliette Spencer, made a short statement thanking all involved in the trial. Through tears, she said, 'I hope people will remember my daughter for the vibrant, beautiful, happy young woman she was, not the tragic way her life was ended'.

As for Gladstone residents, after their town was made famous for all the wrong reasons, it is understandable that many in the community would like to put this horrifying incident behind them.

CHAPTER 37

C hris stood outside the Brisbane Supreme Court and watched Isabelle speak to a horde of reporters. Her voice was soft, wavering, and her eyes were red and wet from tears. His wife's face was pale. Her shoulders stooped. Her long blonde hair had been cut to just below her ears. Chris hardly recognised her.

Maybe he had made the wrong decision flying to Brisbane to be there today. Maybe he was wrong to put her through any more pain, any more punishment, after a long, excruciating trial. But he had to see his child.

He kept Isabelle in his sight as she finished her statement, her parents at her side, then rushed to a waiting car. He hailed a taxi and followed.

A few minutes across town and their car turned into a hotel driveway, stopping outside of the ground-level reception. Chris directed his taxi driver to quickly pull in and park a distance behind them.

Isabelle and her parents climbed out of the car and disappeared into the hotel foyer. He hastily paid the taxi fare and followed after them.

Through the foyer, past reception was a large bank of lifts. Isabelle and her parents were waiting there. Chris hung back out of sight. A lift door opened, and they stepped inside. A *whoosh* as the heavy metal doors closed.

He rushed to the small room and watched the numbers above the lift flick from one up to eight, where they stopped. He jabbed the 'up' button of the adjoining lift. When the doors slid open, he raced inside, hitting the button for the eighth floor with his palm. He zoomed up the levels, impatiently tapping his foot until the lift stopped.

The doors opened and he exited into the hall. Looked left. Nothing. Looked right. A door up the end of the hall shut. That had to be them. He jogged towards the door until he was standing outside it. After a deep breath in for courage, he banged hard with his fist.

A few seconds passed, muffled voices from inside, and then the door opened with a rush.

Richard stood there. Hunched. His eyes were dull. "What the hell are you doing here?"

Chris pushed the door hard and charged into the room. "I'm here to see my kid."

Isabelle stood in the middle of the room, wide-eyed. Her mother was beside her. An unfamiliar woman sat on the bed, holding a baby dressed in a pink frilly outfit to her shoulder.

For a moment he was distracted, unable to think. A daughter. He had a daughter. His eyes focused on Isabelle. "Is that... is she...?"

A long sigh. "Yes."

A step closer and Isabelle's stance stiffened.

"What's her name?" he asked.

"It doesn't matter."

He squeezed his eyes closed, balled his fists. "It does matter. She's my daughter," he ground out through gritted teeth with all the whispered venom he could manage.

Isabelle recoiled. "Her name is Sarah."

"Sarah," he said with a nod, calmer now. He took a few steps closer to Sarah.

"I'm calling security and the police," Richard barked, went to the desk and picked up the telephone receiver.

Chris turned to him. "Stop!" He pointed his finger. "I've done nothing wrong here. Nothing. You don't get to fabricate who you think I am. You don't get to judge me based on the actions of someone I happened to be related to through marriage. I am not Maddison. We do not even have the same blood. She was a disturbed, messed-up woman and she did the most horrible, horrible thing. Ruined so many lives. But she is not me. I never hurt anyone. So, stop acting as though I have." He was angry, his tone was harsh, but he kept the volume low, aware of Sarah watching on. "Now, I am going to meet my daughter because that is my God-given right."

Richard exchanged a glance with his daughter. Isabelle nodded with resignation. With a sigh, Richard placed the receiver back down.

Isabelle lifted Sarah from her nanny's shoulder, who had been watching her throughout the trial. With Sarah resting maternally on Isabelle's hip, she carried her closer to Chris.

Sarah would be ten months old, assuming she had been born on time. He hadn't heard a word from Isabelle to know. No matter what Chris had done, short of hiring an investigator to find her in Tasmania, he had been unable to contact her.

When he looked at his daughter, his face softened. She had his blue eyes. Her skin was soft and creamy coloured. Slightly pink cheeks. Her hair was dark like his, not blonde like Isabelle's. Tears filled his eyes, and he couldn't blink them away. She was the most beautiful child he had ever laid eyes on. Ever imagined.

"Hi there, Sarah, I'm your dad. I'm so happy to finally meet you."

Sarah's big blue eyes looked at him with curiosity.

He smiled as he reached for her face and stroked a finger down her soft cheek. "You are truly something else."

She grinned, all gums.

He laughed.

She laughed too.

He loved her already. He had only known her for one minute and he was deeply in love. Unlike anything he'd ever felt before. "How old is she?"

"She came a month early. From stress I presume. She turned eleven months old, two days ago."

"A year-old next month," he said with a shake of his head. So much time he had missed out on.

"Chris. Listen to me please." Isabelle's voice was pleading, and it thieved his attention. "I have lost" – her eyes watered, bottom lip trembled – "I've been through hell in the past eighteen months. I'm not sure you could even begin to understand how hard it's been to get out of bed each morning. If not for Sarah, I wouldn't be here." Her eyes implored him. "Please, please, Chris, walk away. I just want to get on with my life and I feel like if you're hanging around wanting custody rights or holiday visits, I won't ever be able to do that. I'll always be connected to Gladstone. To the place that took my daughter from me. I'm hanging on by a thread here. I just need to get on with my life. With Sarah. In peace."

His forehead was lined with his incredulity. "You can't."

"I can."

"I have rights."

"You do. That's why I'm appealing to you, as a man."

He shook his head. "You can't ask this of me. I've already missed a year of her life. I've been through hell too. I've lost absolutely everything. Everything."

"I know. I know," she said with more sympathy. "But please, Chris, I'm asking you to let us go." Her voice was so soft. Eyes filled with tears.

All the air spewed from his mouth and it came out as a tortured groan. He closed his eyes and a tear rolled down his cheek.

"Please," she pleaded. "Please, let us go. Walk away. Don't look back."

He stood there, glancing between his wife and his daughter.

After a long, tortured moment, he leaned forward and kissed Sarah's forehead. He allowed his gaze to roam over the soft lines of her face, trying to remember everything about that moment.

Exhausting every ounce of strength within him, he lowered his head, turned and walked out of the room.

When he burst outside into the hall, his shoulders shook as he fought back tears. By the time the lift doors closed, he was sobbing. He didn't stop as he made his way across the foyer and into a taxi.

"You okay, mate?" the taxi-driver asked.

"Take me to the airport," he managed between sobs.

That, right there, was the hardest thing he had ever had to do.

CHAPTER 38

Four days before the murder…

"You bitch, you killed my daughter!" Maddison screamed, followed by a clang at the front door, a few moments of silence, then glass exploded.

The small town of Yarwun was quiet. Not a car on the roads. Barely a light on in the homes, except for a few dim bedside lamps still shining as their owners tucked beneath covers reading deep into the night.

Tina was awake now. "Bloody hell," she growled, sitting up in her bed.

"Why couldn't you have stuck to your own husband? Why did you have to take mine? I hate you. I hate you."

Tina flicked on her bedside lamp, checked her clock. Almost midnight. Maddison was late to her pity party.

A loud banging at the front door.

"I know you're in there. I know you can hear me. You should hate yourself for what you did. You killed my daughter. You and Ben killed her. I hope by knowing that, your soul is destroyed. I hope you kill yourself you horrible, whore slut! I hate you. Everyone hates you." Banging against the front window. "Did you hear me! You should kill yourself. That's all you deserve."

Silence. Then crying, which crescendoed into wolf-like howling sobs. Silence again.

Tina rested back against her pillow, turned off her lamp, settling in for the long night ahead.

Tap. Tap. Tap.

Tap. Tap. Tap.

She reached for her torch on the bedside table and crept to the window. Sparks of excitement were zooming through her bloodstream. She bit back a grin as she waited for another tap.

Tap. Tap. Tap.

She pulled the curtain back and shone the torch at Maddison.

Maddison shrieked, blinked, stumbled four steps backwards and landed on her backside on the grass. Tina lifted the heavy window. Humid wind gushed in. She poked her head out, looked at Maddison sprawled below. "Aren't you finished already? Seriously, how much more do I have to take?"

Maddison wiped her cheeks. "Until you feel so bad for what you've done." Her words were slurring much more than usual.

"That's the one thing you're not quite getting. I do feel bad. Every. Single. Day. I loved Kadie. I loved her—I know not as much as you, her mother—but I did love her. I miss her too. I wish I could take back that day every single moment of my life. But I can't. And with you coming here and screaming and saying what you say, it only makes it worse. For us all. Seriously, look at you, you're a mess."

Who Maddison once was—self-assured, determined, funny, loving—didn't resemble that dishevelled, drunk, blithering woman slumped on the grass.

Maddison tried to sit up taller. "I am not. I'm perfectly fine."

Tina rolled her eyes.

"I just want my baby girl back. I can't do this anymore. I can't. I just want her back." She lowered her face into her hands and sobbed. Shoulders shaking.

Tina sighed. "Come inside. We'll make a coffee to sober you up a little bit. Then I'll drive you home. You can't be out there in the dark like that."

Maddison lifted her head, wiped her tears. "Why are you being nice to me?"

"Because you're my sister-in-law. And we were once really good friends. And that hasn't changed in my heart."

"Really?" she hiccupped.

"Really. Now get up. The back door is open. I don't want you heading around the front in the dark and breaking your ankle. Better yet, wait there and I'll help you inside."

Tina undressed out of her pyjamas, threw on a pair of shorts, a bra and a t-shirt, slipped on a pair of shoes, then climbed out the window.

She reached for Maddison's cold hand and helped her off the ground. She was so light. Even in the darkness, only the moonlight above them, the wiriness of Maddison's limbs was obvious. Hard bone and muscle—nothing else.

"Around here." Tina led the way over tufts of grass onto the concrete path.

Maddison swayed to the back door and went inside.

"The coffee machine is there," Tina said, pointing to the corner of the kitchen. "The canister is there. Do you think you can manage?"

Maddison put her hands on her hips and rolled her eyes. "I'm drunk, not mentally challenged." She staggered into the kitchen, pressed the machine's power button with the dexterity of a slug and lifted a flap on the top.

"The grinding function is broken. There's pre-ground coffee in the canister."

Maddison wouldn't be able to make coffee. She could barely get a sentence out. Barely walk. But that wasn't the point.

"I need to pee," Maddison whined as she crossed one leg in front of the other.

"Here, let me finish these coffees," Tina said. "You head up to the toilet. You know where it is. Call me if you need my help."

Again, with the eye roll. "I've been peeing my entire life. I don't need your help."

Tina waved her hand in a shooing motion. "Fine. Off you go then. I don't want any accidents on my good floorboards."

"They're scuffed and scratched anyway."

By the time Maddison wobbled back down the hallway, almost falling over and using her hand against the wall to keep balance, the coffees were made.

Tina handed a disposable travel cup to Maddison. "Here you go. You can drink this in the car on the way home." Not that she ordinarily allowed any food or drink in her car, but she had to make an exception.

She shuffled Maddison out the backdoor.

"Why are we going this way again?" Maddison grumbled.

"Because you shattered glass over the front lawn. I'm not having you cut your feet so you can bleed all through my car."

Maddison turned to her under the dim light of the moon and sighed. "I still hate you. Even though you're being nice to me."

"I wouldn't expect any other reaction."

Maddison never managed to drink one drop of her coffee, merely placed the travel cup in the centre console, rested her head against the side window, and fell into a deep, deep sleep.

In silence, along the dark, quiet roads, Tina drove into town. Maddison didn't move. Not even an eyelid fluttered. Her slow breaths continued unabated.

Tina didn't go anywhere near Maddison's home. She had no intentions of dropping her off there. Instead, she drove to a park that was a few minutes across town. One with little light and no possibility of cameras. When she stopped the car, she climbed out and peered around the shadowy field. No one was there. The road lining the park had sparse streetlights casting a dull glow, but the bordering houses' windows were all dark.

She opened the passenger door and Maddison tilted over. Mustering all her physical strength, she heaved Maddison upright before she splatted onto the street. Tina half carried, half walked her across the dew damp grass. Her arms and back strained as she helped Maddison onto the ground under a tree.

Without opening her eyes again, Maddison curled into a ball on her side and her hands slid beneath her head, taking the place of a pillow.

Tina jogged back to her waiting car, climbed inside, and drove away, not looking behind her.

Twenty minutes later, she arrived home, trudged around the back of the house and stood outside her window. It appeared higher than when she had climbed from it earlier. Three big jumps until she managed to land her waist on the window ledge, her ribs grinding against the hard timber. Like a half-dead caterpillar, she wiggled and heaved her way forward until she fell over the other side, taking her weight on her hands on the bedroom floor.

When she slithered the lower half of her body over, grunting and straining, she finally got to her feet again. Her stomach was sore. She was puffing. But it was a small sacrifice to make for the greater good. *Her* greater good.

She closed the window, changed into her pyjamas and climbed into bed. Before turning out the light, she reached for her phone and opened her contacts. The electronic data trail she had been working on would assist in shaping the evidence. Evidence that would back up her narrative. A narrative that would soon be pulled apart by prosecutors, so it had to be flawless.

Tomorrow, she would clean her car until it was immaculate. She couldn't have any traces of Maddison left behind. But for now, she typed out a message for Chris, a slow creeping smile on her lips.

TINA: *Tell your wife to stay the hell away from me!*

CHAPTER 39

Present-day...

Tina made a cup of tea, carried it outside along with her phone and sat on the front step. She placed the cup beside her and gazed at her yard. Rain had fallen during that month, and everything was vibrantly green, almost as though the earth knew all had been righted. Life was returning to the status quo.

Beyond the perimeter, a single car was driving past—a mango farmer from a property a few minutes up the road, his Kelpie yapping in the back. He thought about Tina as he passed. Many people in the town had thought about her over the past eighteen months. Some felt sorry for her. Some believed she should have been punished somehow, but when they imagined themselves in the same situation, they realised the right decision had been made.

That's why it was time for Tina to sell up. Well, it was the excuse she was about to use. She was more isolated there than ever and yet, strangely, more visible. Like all the eyes of Yarwun and its neighbouring town of Gladstone—the streets of which she drove along every weekday, knocking on residents' doors—were ogling her. Judging. Everyone knew her delivery van now. The gossip mill had spread the details. She noticed the stares, the pointing, the sympathetic frowns.

She didn't want anyone's sympathy. She just wanted to get on with her life. Eighteen months had gone by since she had last spoken to Chris. His house payment still made it to their shared loan account every month, on time, like always. She hoped that meant he didn't completely hate her.

But she needed to break the ice now because his signature would be required on any sales contract, or maybe he would buy her out and keep the place for himself.

She picked up her phone, dialled his number. He was in his car on the opposite side of Gladstone, heading to a hardware store. When her name appeared on his dash, he almost smiled because he had been thinking about her that very moment, wondering if he should call her to see how she was. He couldn't imagine what she had endured these past eighteen months as the Gladstone Housewife Trials played out.

For a long time, he had been so angry with her. He had been angry with himself for ever loving her. But then the facts started to emerge and that small hope he had kept secret inside of him, grew. She was still the woman he fell in love with. A love greater than any other... until his daughter had come along.

But even now, one month after meeting Sarah for the first and last time, the memories of her face were less vivid. Distorted. He didn't know when he conjured Sarah's face if it was hers and not some child's image he had seen on television.

His yearning was still there, though. That would never leave. But when he had decided to grant Isabelle the peace she demanded and deserved, it had to be a firm decision, or he would always be wondering if it was the right one.

What he didn't know, and what was probably best for his sanity, was that Isabelle had gained a new respect for Chris at that moment. She understood the selflessness of what he had done for her and their daughter. She witnessed the pain and sorrow in his eyes. The space in her heart that had once loved him grew warmer. But she never spoke that out loud, only thought about it from time to time as she tried to drift off to sleep at night.

Chris answered the phone. "Hi, Tina."

"Hi." Her voice was hesitant. "I'm not sure if you even want to speak to me—"

"Of course," he said. "It's fine. How are you going? Considering."

"A lot better than I have been."

"Yeah, I bet you're glad it's all over, hey?"

A small smile. "You have no idea."

"I'm really sorry you had to go through that. It must have been some kind of hell. I'm sure it still is."

"Sometimes, I think hell might have been a nicer place to have landed in."

"Geez. I can't even... just the most horrible of circumstances."

"Yeah. But, um, Chris, I was calling to see if you would agree to sell the house."

"Oh?"

"I feel like I need a fresh start," she said.

"Of course. I can understand that. But it's a good property."

"It is. You can buy me out if you like. If you want to keep it."

"Can you give me a few days to think about it?"

"Sure. No rush. Just thought I'd run it by you before I made any fast decisions."

A small silence. "How about I head over there? We could talk about it. I could check the place out."

"That'd be nice."

"I could come over now?"

"I'm not busy."

Another silence.

She rubbed her forehead, closed her eyes, giving him time.

"I'm sorry I haven't been there for you," he said.

"It's okay. I think it's something I had to get through on my own anyway. It was out of my hands. Out of your hands."

"I know, but I could have mowed the lawns at least. Or made you dinner."

"Don't fret," she said. "I'm out the other side."

"Glad to hear it. I'll head over now. Be there in about twenty minutes."

"See you soon."

Tina hung up, placed the phone beside her and sighed. She drank her tea as parrots, crows, kookaburras and magpies chirped and carolled in the treetops. That was the most peaceful she had felt in a long time and for that she was grateful.

When her cup was empty, she stood, dusted the back of her shorts and went inside. As she was rinsing her mug under tap water at the kitchen sink, Chris's ute turned into the driveway.

For a moment, just briefly, it was like times of old, as though the years between then and now had never happened.

Chris parked and headed up the front stairs. The door was open, so he walked straight in. When he met Tina's gaze as she dried her cup and returned it to the cabinets, only then did he realise he hadn't knocked. But his intuition hinted that it was meant to happen that way. The way he used to come home. The way a husband would ordinarily enter his house.

He couldn't put words to it, but a spark was glowing in Tina's eyes. He was looking at the woman he had married all those years ago. The woman he had loved. She was there again.

He drew a deep breath—the first in a very long time it seemed. The tightness across his chest eased and the relaxed man he had always been in her presence returned.

She smiled. "Hi."

"Hi," he said.

"You want a cup of coffee?" She had bought a new espresso maker but hadn't been able to bring herself to drink coffee again, so it hadn't had much use.

"I'd love one."

She gestured to the dining table. "Good. Take a seat."

The familiar way they had always interacted played out between them—the easy rhythm of their roles. Tina was imitating that life where all she had to do was love this man and take care of him. And all he had to do was love her in return and know that he was in good hands.

When finished, she joined him at the table, placing his coffee down before him and her tea in arms reach.

"The yard is so green," he said. "I'm not sure I ever remember it being this green."

She looked out the front windows. "I know. It's all that rain we've had. The whole place is renewed."

He sipped his coffee. "And you're sure you want to sell up?"

"I don't know." She sighed. "Maybe I'm running away. I love it here. I do. I just feel like everyone is judging me. I'm not sure anyone can understand what it's been like..." Her voice cracked and she looked away.

He reached across the table and rested his hand on hers. "People understand more than you know. No one in their right mind could blame you, let alone punish you, for what happened. It was tragic and incredibly sad. A shock for a town like this. But you're not to blame for what Maddison did to you. It's punishment enough to have to live with what happened."

Tears filled her eyes as she placed her free hand over her chest. "I'm not sure I will ever forgive myself."

He frowned. "I can't know exactly what it must be like, but I do understand it was very, very hard."

"So hard," she whispered. She sat up taller, cleared her throat, blinked the tears away. "But I'm not going to dwell on it. I've done enough of that. I just want to look towards the future."

He nodded, a deep sadness moving through his chest, reaching up the back of his throat. "Me too". He removed his hand from on top of hers. "I filed for a divorce last month."

"That's a shame. I had read in a newspaper Isabelle was living in Tasmania."

"She hasn't wanted anything to do with me. She doesn't want me to have anything to do with our baby."

Tina managed to hide her flinch at the blatant way he had spoken about his child. Vicious jealously curled around her heart and squeezed. "That's a very cruel thing for her to do."

"Yeah. Looks like we all have our crosses to bear."

She didn't comment, remained focused on her teacup.

"So, how the hell have you been coping through all this?" he asked.

A small, embarrassed smile. "I've been seeing a therapist."

His eyes widened. "Wow. You finally caved."

"Honestly, she's helped me so much. Having someone to talk to and guide me through the ups and downs has been a godsend."

"I'm really glad to hear that."

Tina shifted in her chair, kept her gaze lowered. "Chris there's something I need to tell you. Something my therapist felt would be good for me to get off my chest."

He leaned closer, softened his voice. "Sure. What is it?"

"That day when Kadie died."

His nod was stiff.

"The story Ben and Maddison told you wasn't entirely right."

"How so?"

"Maddison did find me and Ben in her bedroom, engaged in…" She cleared her throat.

He held tight, barely breathing.

"It wasn't consensual. What Ben did to me that day wasn't consensual."

His mouth opened and shut. "What are you saying?"

She shook her hands, blew out a breath. Tears brimmed. "Your brother raped me."

Chris's chair flung back, scraping against the floorboards and he lurched to his feet. "What the actual hell?"

She held her hands up, palms facing him. "Please. Sit down. This is so hard to speak about. I need you to be seated. Please."

He was breathing heavily, but he nodded and slowly sat. Inside his chest a storm was brewing. A tight, hot, violent storm. "I'm going to kill him!" He pointed in the direction of their former house. "He did all of this. All of this started because of him. I lost everyone I have ever loved—Kadie, Ruby, Riley, and now my baby. Not to mention you."

Tina tried her hardest to stay calm, to keep Chris calm. She wouldn't be able to get through this with much more emotion. "Chris, I'm not about to tell you how to feel or react. You have every right to be angry. Every right. But it's not going to help either of us now. In any way. Can you understand that?"

A resigned sigh. "I guess."

"I've told you about my childhood. A little of it. The sexual abuse I suffered."

He nodded, frowned.

"Well, it seems all that was sitting beneath the surface waiting to blow up in my face. What happened that day with Ben, broke me. Mentally. Physically. I can barely remember three years of my life. It's been a long, hard road trying to claw my way back. Trying to get" – she tapped her chest – "*me* back. I didn't deserve what happened to me. I sure as hell didn't ask for it. But what happened had consequences that went beyond me. That includes our marriage. I want to take responsibility for that side of things. I regret that I didn't fight harder that day. Fight Ben off me. And fight to keep you. You didn't deserve what happened either."

"You're not seriously blaming yourself?"

She shook her head hard. "Absolutely not. At least not anymore. I did. Once. I blamed myself for a lot of things. But I know better now. I'm apologising for what happened to us. And to our marriage. That's one of the biggest regrets of my life. Not fighting to keep you."

He slumped in his chair, scrubbed his hands over his face. "Bloody hell, Tina. If only I knew. I would never have left. Never. I could have helped—"

"It's too late for all that. The past has happened. I understand why you left. Roles reversed, I would have done the same. Any rational person would do the same. This isn't about trying to change anything, but rather acknowledging, for my closure, and for my healing, the part I played. I know better now. I'm in a better place. A stronger place. I won't ever be that person again."

He rubbed his mouth with the back of his hand, looked up to the ceiling. "What an absolute mess this is." His fist came down hard towards the table, but he stopped before he made impact. "Ben destroyed our lives."

"You think that?"

A derisive laugh, as though it was self-evident. "Of course. I was a wreck for years. It almost killed me when I left you. I wanted you so badly to tell me to stay and say that you still loved me. But I was insecure. I thought you wanted someone more than me and that's why you slept with Ben." His nose wrinkled with his distaste. "I blamed myself for not being here enough. God, and then I went and married the first woman who even looked my way, thinking that would make me feel better about myself. But it didn't. It just screwed everything up so much more."

Heat blasted his cheeks for admitting to that. But it was the truth. Isabelle was young and pretty and he was aching for validation and reassurance that his wife didn't screw his brother because he wasn't enough of a husband for her.

Now that he knew the real truth about what had happened to Tina, he wished the reasons for the indiscretion were as petty as he had first believed them to be.

As though reading his mind, she reached for his hand and held it. "Ben is suffering in more ways than we can ever imagine for what he did. That's enough for me."

His jaw tightened, head drooped. "I know he would be. But he did the wrong thing. I'm sick of giving him concessions. He's had more than enough."

"I know. But I'm not going through another trial. I'm not digging up that day all over again just to make it official."

He pursed his lips and eventually nodded.

"We look forward," she said. "You don't have to be nice to him. You don't even have to talk to him. But I can't handle any more police. Any more hurt. Any more trials, okay? I just want to move on. But I needed to let you know the truth. You deserve that. For your own healing."

He pushed to his feet, took her hands and helped her from her chair. He wrapped his arms around her and held her tight. "I am so sorry for the pain you've been through. I wish I could take it all away from you."

"Don't worry, Chris. I'm strong." She wiped the tears from her eyes. "As I said, I've come through to the other side. I have a bright future ahead of me now."

After a long moment, she pulled herself out of his arms and collected her teacup from the table. "Grab your coffee,

I'll show you the fruit trees." She smiled. "They're blooming again."

"Really?"

She led him outside to the mandarin tree. It was full of big, bright orange fruit.

"Wow," he said. "I remember when we first planted this. I got so sunburnt. I looked like a cooked lobster for days afterwards. I copped so much stick at work for that."

She laughed. "And I put aloe vera leaves in the fridge to cool before rubbing them on you. But it was so cold against the heat of your burn, you were in agony."

As they inspected the mulberry tree, Chris pulled a ripe, fragrant berry off its stem and popped it into his mouth. "They're better than I remember. You really can't get fruit that tastes like this from the shops."

"The mangos were amazing this summer. Tasted like a spoon full of sugar."

"I haven't had a decent mango for five years," he said with a wry smile.

"There's always next summer."

He grinned. "Yeah, there is."

She took him around the property, discussing things that might need mending—a fence paling, a bent letterbox, a rusted panel on the carport.

"Yard needs a good mow," he said. "I can come back and do that tomorrow. Get it all neat and tidy."

"Geez, if we keep going like this" – she giggled – "I may not want to leave here."

He shrugged. "Don't. Maybe give it a little time first and see what happens. Things will calm down. The goldfish brains around town will soon move on to other things."

She kicked at the grass with the toe of her shoe. "Perhaps you're right."

They headed back inside and rinsed their cups in the sink.

"Stay for dinner," she said.

"You sure?"

"I'd love the company."

He smiled. "I would too."

At that moment, he remembered something he had seen there, on the fridge, before everything went to hell. A box of prescription tablets. He looked at Tina, trying to process the new thoughts that were pounding his brain. Connections were forming like chain links on a long fence.

He wasn't entirely sure what made him do what he did next, but it would make more sense later on after he'd had time to process it. A step towards her. His breaths were deep. Eyes glossing. He leaned over and pressed his lips to hers.

With her warm mouth against his, all their shared memories came flooding back. All the joy, all the love. None of the pain. They had been so happy once. An ache in his chest as he realised he wanted that again so much.

When her arms slung around his neck and she floated closer, her warm body against his, he had the overwhelming sense of finally coming home. She took his hand, gazed into his eyes and led him to her bedroom. He didn't hesitate. In her arms, in her bed, in their home, was where he belonged. Had always belonged.

Tina lay back, letting Chris climb on top. Everything she had ever wanted was wrapped in her arms. Big. Strong. She breathed him in as she kissed his neck. He smelled so good. Her hands roamed over his strong arms, down his chest.

Potent desire, only he could evoke, was surging through her body as he slowly undressed her. She wanted to cheer, to laugh, to sing that *she* was back.

And when he finally entered her with care and tenderness, she almost cried with relief. He was still Chris. And she still wanted him.

Validation, triumph, bloomed in her soul because everything she had done to bring them both to this exact moment in time had been worth it.

CHAPTER 40

The morning of the murder…

The opportunity to murder someone didn't arise every day. Electricity sparked through Tina's veins as she dressed into the outfit she had chosen to wear for that occasion—a flattering skirt and blouse—and applied a little makeup. Her tummy was fluttering. She couldn't discern if those feelings were nerves or excitement.

Happy with her appearance, she hummed as she went to the kitchen and unsealed her bag of powdered Scopolamine.

After trailing Isabelle to work yesterday, she had stopped by Ben and Maddison's on her way home. As anticipated, the house was empty—both parents at the gym and the kids at school.

She had parked a distance away, wearing her parcel delivery uniform, and, while carrying a big white package, strode up to the front door and called, "Delivery".

Of course, no one answered, so she quietly slipped around the side of the house to the backyard that was shielded from the neighbouring properties by tall fences and shady trees. She rummaged through her pockets for three clear plastic shower caps and a pair of latex gloves.

She placed two of the caps over her shoes and slipped her hands into the gloves. Her hair was tied back, plaited, but she fitted the last plastic shower cap on her head and dusted her shoulders and clothes before she went to the back door, testing the lock. It was open.

It had taken no more than ten minutes to sneak inside, plant the empty prescription box in the drawer of Maddison's bedside table, then find the spice grinder to crush the tablets, slipping the powdery substance into a resealable bag before placing the grinder back in the kitchen cupboard.

Ignoring her growing jitteriness, Tina poured some of the scopolamine powder into the canister of pre-ground coffee beans, then set about preparing a double-shot flat white. She added a heap of extra powder to an empty travel mug before pouring the hot coffee into it. Ready to go. Once she started drinking that, she had twenty minutes before it kicked in.

That was the part Tina was most anxious about. She didn't take medications usually. So, she had tested her response to smaller doses to see how she would cope, but to also have physical evidence to support her story that she had been drugged over a few weeks.

She had handled the smaller doses well, but she had no idea what to expect when she would consume almost toxic levels later on. All she could hope for was that she gained quick medical attention, her concocted version of events was so well rehearsed that she didn't blow it while delirious and that she didn't accidentally overdose.

Tina had created a bulletproof story and practised it over and over again as she drove for eight hours each day delivering packages. She could run the details backwards and forwards, inside and out, up and down, without missing a step. She had patched any holes, any forgotten particulars, and created a trail of evidence to back it all up.

Now, all she had to do was kill Juliette.

Tina cleaned the kitchen, being sure not to disturb the espresso machine and canister, then headed to her car, travel cup in hand. Instead of turning right onto Gladstone Mount Larcom Road that would take her into town, she drove straight through the intersection onto the barely used Targinnie Road. A road bordered by tall trees. No residential houses, only the odd rural property here and there.

For a distance, she followed that quiet route until she could park to the side in obscurity. Using a small spade, she dug into the soft dirt and buried the contaminated resealable bag inside, along with the shower caps and gloves, then covered them over, ensuring her hands didn't get dirty. When done, she pitched the spade hard and deep into the thick scrub, then slid into the driver's seat, flipped a U-turn and made her way to Gladstone.

For the past three mornings, Tina had tracked Juliette's schedule. All the while, she had trailed Isabelle to and from work—a mere cover story to add substance to her stalker theory and provide traceable evidence that she was slowly losing her sanity.

She almost smiled as she recalled Chris's face when she had told him his wife was a stalker. For a flicker of time, in the set of his features, she had wondered if he had believed her rather than Isabelle. For a flicker of time, he had.

Juliette was always whom Tina intended to kill. The police would never know that, though. They would be expertly lied to. Manipulated until they believed Tina's version of events. She would swear black and blue that the woman she was beating to death with a wrecking bar was her stalker, Isabelle.

The only unexpected spanner in her plan was the baby. Her fingers gripped the steering wheel tight, her knuckles turning white. A baby could complicate the dynamics between Chris and Isabelle. Could strengthen their bond and create a hopeful future, resilient enough to counteract what Tina hoped was about to play out.

Chris and Isabelle's romance had happened too fast. A rebound relationship. The fact that Chris didn't agree to a proper wedding, indicated he had reservations about marrying again. Isabelle had been single for so long. Predictably, she would be too set in her ways and content with her independence to fully appreciate her new live-in husband. Add Tina into the mix—the murderess. No relationship that flimsy could withstand such horrendous circumstances.

But the baby added unpredictability.

Too late to turn back now, though. Tina would carry this through, exactly as intended.

She reached for her coffee and gulped it down, leaving a little in the bottom. The timing had to be exactly right, or her plan would unravel.

Ten minutes later, Tina slowed as she neared the road she had been parked at for the past three mornings. She watched the time on her dash. Barely thirty seconds away from when Juliette would rush out her front door, skip to her car, and drive down the street in Tina's direction.

Soon enough, there was a flash of silver in the distance. Adrenalin sparked making Tina's hands slightly jittery. Her senses were already beginning to alter. Her world a little dreamlike. But she knew what she had to do. She just hoped she had left enough time.

Juliette drove closer. As she passed, Tina yanked her steering wheel hard to the right and smashed into the small hatchback's frontend. She slammed on the brakes, shifted her car into park but kept the motor running. She reached under her seat for the wrecking bar, hid it behind her back as she opened her car door and stepped out.

"Hurry up," Tina whispered under her breath.

Juliette was visibly flustered, taking too long as she turned the motor off, unclipped her seatbelt and climbed from her car. Her expression was apologetic. Her eyes glossing with tears.

But Tina didn't have time for weak theatrics. Already her vision was starting to change, turning black at the edges. Juliette's face was warping.

"I'm so sorry, I don't know how that happened," Juliette said, coming closer. She was a beautiful young woman. Looked so much like her mother.

Such a shame.

Tina didn't hesitate as she lurched towards Juliette, lifted the bar and unleashed until she was panting, covered in warm blood, and Juliette's body fell like a sack of oranges to the road below.

Dizzy. Tina's heart was racing out of control. She threw the wrecking bar to the ground with a clang, then slid into the driver's seat, buckled her seatbelt, and sped away, driving until she couldn't drive any longer.

CHAPTER 41

Time moved slowly in jail. That day, it had almost stalled as Maddison awaited her family. Her leg bounced as she sat in the visitors centre at a set of table and chairs in a newly built high-security women's correctional centre that still smelled like fresh paint, located south of Brisbane.

She wore a standard-issue uniform of blue shorts and a collared t-shirt. White trainers. Her hair was tied back with little care. No makeup. No jewellery. No watch. She had already put on weight since arriving nearly three months ago, her face filling out, the hard lines of her limbs softening. An inevitable side effect of spending seventeen hours each day locked in her small cell.

At last, Maddison spotted Ben through the heavy glass windows. She smiled, anticipating her children walking beside him—not quite tall enough yet to be seen through the high window—and yet she felt like crying too. Always dissonant emotions.

Her family had visited three times before, but only for one-hour non-contact visits. Maddison couldn't bear to see her children from behind a clear shield again and not touch, smell and hold them in her arms.

Ruby and Riley consumed her mind in every moment she was there. Six-minute phone calls were not enough to fill the aching hole in her heart. Initially, the jail had been unbearable. Knowing she had at least twenty years ahead of her, the claustrophobia, the sheer panic, almost broke her. She sobbed, shook and pleaded for the first week, alarming the correctional officers enough to put her on twenty-four-hour suicide watch.

Killer Housewife, the other prisoners named her before she had even stepped foot in the jail. Taunted her with it. They had watched her trial play out on prime-time news and had bets on whether or not she would be convicted.

In the early days, she would beg them to believe her innocence. But they would laugh at her and say, "Yes, yes, we're all innocent in here."

The guard opened the door. The thought of cuddling her children was making her shake. A big smile filled her face as she watched Ben and the kids stride into the room. She lurched to her feet, held her arms open wide. Ruby and Riley ran to her. Tears filled her eyes as she drew them into her arms, kissing their faces and head, holding them so tight. She never wanted to let them go.

"Oh, my gosh," she said, gripping Riley by his shoulders. "You've grown in the month since I saw you last." His thirteenth birthday was in a fortnight, but she was trying not to think about missing such an important milestone.

Riley wasn't meeting her gaze and was blinking fast, trying to be brave and hold back his emotions, but a mother could see behind that facade.

"It's okay, Riley," she soothed, stroking a hand through his hair. "You can feel upset about all this."

Tears flooded his eyes. "I just don't know why you have to be in here."

Maddison didn't have the answer to that. She always maintained her innocence for her children's sake, but, deep down, she couldn't definitively say if she had drugged Tina or not because she could not remember. The evidence during the trial proved that she had, so that's all she could rely on.

"I know. I know. It's hard, but this will start to feel better soon. I haven't gone away forever, okay? We still get to spend time together. I'll always be here for you, no matter what."

He nodded, angrily wiped the tears from his eyes with the back of his hand. She kissed his forehead. "You're such a strong boy, Riley. And I'm proud of you. I love you so much."

"I love you too," he whispered.

She hugged Ruby who was hiccupping with sobs and held her against her chest, stroking her fringe from her forehead, until she eventually calmed down. Maddison's children were her entire world. They were who got her through in those first few days and weeks. She had to be strong for them.

Enough of her life had been wasted wallowing in her self-inflicted insobriety. Even though she was now tucked away behind prison walls, she was still their mother and they needed her. Not an ideal situation. Not one she even remotely liked, but nothing she did was going to change her circumstances. She had to do the best she could with the hand she'd been dealt.

Maddison took a seat. Ruby settled on her lap and Riley sat beside her on the chair, her arm around him.

"Hi, Ben, thanks for bringing the kids again." The strain of the last two years was evident in the deepening lines on her husband's face. The dulled colour of his eyes. Greying hair. He was thinner.

"That's okay."

"Did you get to fly here?" she asked Riley.

He nodded. "We got little muffins this time."

She smiled. "That would have been yummy."

"It was."

"And you're staying with your Aunty Jacinta?"

"Yep," Ruby said. "Aunty Jacinta is going to take us to Australia Zoo tomorrow."

Maddison's eyes widened. "Wow, well that makes the trip more than worthwhile. You'll have to tell me the best parts when I call you next."

She had petitioned in advance for two hours of contact time this weekend, an hour today with the kids and an hour alone with Ben tomorrow. She didn't want Ruby and Riley to know about Ben's solo visit. They wouldn't understand.

"So, what's been happening at school?" she asked Riley. He was coming to the end of his first year of high school. Her stomach swirled with the realisation that she would miss every major event in her children's lives for many, many years to come. She squeezed her eyes closed for a moment, forcing that thought away. If she allowed it to fester, it would devastate her.

"We've been cooking this term," Riley said. "And I got to make lasagne, fried rice and san choy bow."

"Keep that up and you'll be taking over dinner duties." Her heart ached, as she wished with all her might that she could be at home with her family preparing the evening meals for them.

He grinned. "Dad said that too because it tasted really good. Didn't it, Dad?"

"Sure did," Ben said. "I've had him prepare lasagne three times since."

Maddison laughed. "And what about you, Ruby? Not long and you'll be in grade six."

"I have to give a speech next week to the whole school to see if I can become a student leader."

"Have you prepared the speech already?"

"Yep, Dad's been helping me." She rolled her eyes. "He made me read it to him three times for practice."

"You know what they say about practice?"

"Yes, I know. Practice makes perfect."

"Exactly."

"My teacher says I have a good chance. But then my friend Juniper told me that the teacher said the same thing to her too."

"Well, you can only try your hardest and we'll see what happens."

For the rest of the hour, Maddison held it together as she listened to her children talk about their lives—school, sports and friendship dilemmas. It spawned a craving inside of her so strong, she thought it might eat her whole, no bones left to spit out.

When the guard announced the hour was up, she fought back her tears as she cuddled and kissed Ruby and Riley and held them both so tight to her body in an embrace she couldn't bring herself to end. That was the real punishment. Maddison could handle being locked in a small cell for most of the day. She could deal with the substandard meals, the schedules, the uniform, the company of criminals, but she was hanging on by a thread when it came to her children. Not being able to exist full-time in their lives was the worst kind of torture.

But it wasn't death. She was still there. Still a mother. As brief as the visits were with Riley and Ruby, they were more than she had with Kadie, so she would not take what little time she did have with her children for granted.

Eventually, the guard was forceful enough that Maddison let her children go. She didn't cry because she summoned all her courage to show them that she was strong, and she would get through this and they didn't need to worry about her. When the door closed behind them, she burst into tears and couldn't stop.

Maddison was led back to her cell and locked inside. She bawled all afternoon until she finally fell asleep. When she woke the next morning, she was herded out for muster, ready to repeat the same day.

When Ben arrived for the one-hour contact visit, nerves beat in her belly. This was a long-overdue conversation. One that if had five years ago, could have prevented the path she had stumbled onto.

Ben was dressed in a pair of jeans and a t-shirt—still the most handsome man she had ever laid eyes on, but none of that had mattered for a long time. He sat on the chair across from her in the visitor centre. His smile was small, strained.

"How were the kids this morning?" she asked, desperate to hear that they weren't suffering because of her.

"They were fine. Excited about going to Australia Zoo with Jacinta."

A sigh of relief. "It's great that she lives nearby, so you can all stay there when you come to visit."

"She's a godsend."

Maddison nodded. "I know." She wished now they'd had more to do with Ben's sister for the kids' sake, but the six-hundred-kilometre distance between them had hindered that.

"She's loving having Ruby and Riley visit so often," he said.

"That's so good to hear." One thing Maddison wanted for her children was for them to continue with a normal existence and that meant family connections.

"She suggested we move to Brisbane, to be closer to her and you. Give the kids a fresh start where nobody knows their history."

Maddison tensed. "Are they getting teased at school?" She held her breath as she awaited the answer.

A small shake of his head. "No, not at all. The school has been incredible. Taken control of the situation. Riley has a small group of really good mates, and they don't seem to care one bit that you're" – he gestured around the grey, cold walls – "in here. Ruby and Juniper are like two peas in a pod. I think it would be harder for them if I moved them away from their friendship groups."

"Then don't. I know it's a pain to have to travel here all the time, but we need their lives to stay as stable as possible. I mean, if it's too hard, maybe you could reduce how often you vis—"

"No way. The kids need the visits as much as you do."

Her shoulders relaxed. "And you still haven't spoken to Chris?"

A sad shake of his head. His eyes focused on the table. "Nah, that's gone cold. I've tried to call him a few times, but he doesn't answer."

"It's complicated."

"Yeah."

She pressed her palms to the tabletop. "Look, Ben, there was a reason I needed this private time with you today."

His eyes widened as he nodded, urging her to continue.

"I'm going to file for a divorce."

He shook his head. "That's a bit hasty, don't you think?"

"No, it's not hasty at all. We should have had this conversation five years ago. Staying in our marriage—a marriage that is based on some twisted arrangement where I dish out as much punishment as I can, and you take it—is not even remotely healthy. For me, living that way was a prison. No different to where I am now. And I'm certain it was for you, too."

"I just... I know you're upset. I am too, but we need to keep things stable for the kids. You said that yourself."

"What we have isn't stable. It hasn't been stable for a long time. Look where I am for Christ's sake."

He sighed, shoulders sagging. "I don't know. It feels like the wrong thing to do. The wrong time."

She reached across the table, placed her hand on his. "Ben, I should never have blamed you for Kadie's death. Never. That was the worst thing. The lowest, most horrible accusation to make. And to have blamed Tina as I did... No wonder I ended up in this mess. The lives I've destroyed because of my blame and anger is unforgivable. I'm so sorry for ever putting you through that. You loved Kadie so much. You would never have intentionally hurt her. It was just a horrible, horrible accident."

Ben wiped the tears from his eyes with his free hand.

"I want you to get on with your life. You and the kids. I'm not getting out of here anytime soon. Find someone new. Give Ruby and Riley a mother figure. A happy family. Somewhere they're glad to arrive home to. I'll always be their mum, no matter what. But all I want is for them to be happy, okay? That's it. If I know they're happy, then I can endure this place." Her voice wavered with emotion. "Please, Ben, it's all I have to hope for."

Ben sniffled. Used his shirt to wipe his eyes. His bottom lip was trembling.

"Please," she whispered. "If you can give me one thing, this is it."

His exhale was shaky. "I don't deserve your forgiveness."

"Of course, you do."

"No, I don't. Look, Maddy, I need to tell you something."

Her hand drifted away from his and she leaned back against her seat, arms crossed.

"Tina isn't to blame for what happened when Kadie died."

Maddison's head twitched. "What are you saying?"

A tortured groan. "I forced myself on her."

A long silence as her gaze flickered over Ben's face. A hot ball of shame in Maddison's stomach as that reality found a home inside her. Memories and emotions knitted together, and she finally confronted the truth.

She recalled the lack of reaction from Tina that day. The way she was slumped on the floor, detached and unmoving. She remembered the dazed glaze of her eyes, the paleness of her face, as she silently strode out the front door afterwards.

Maddison, at long last, forced herself to see her husband for who he was back then. The violent way he had gripped

Tina's head. The ferocity of his movements. The brutal twist of his features.

But so much destruction happened after that. For Maddison to admit that her husband was capable of rape on top of everything else, would have been the end of her. As difficult as it was to admit, it was easier to blame Tina. To punish her husband. To pretend that it was simply an affair. She wasn't proud of that, but she also couldn't change it.

When she spoke, her voice was weak. "I think, in some way, I've always known that, but I couldn't accept it."

"I'm so sorry. I'm to blame for all this. I don't ever deserve your forgiveness."

"What you did that day is your burden to carry," she said. "Not mine. I can't. Not anymore. Everything I said, still holds because I need to forgive you to be able to move on. I'm doing it for me. Whether you can forgive yourself, that is totally up to you."

His bottom lip trembled, face crumpled. He lowered his head into his hands and burst into tears.

"You owe it to yourself to make this right, Ben. For the kids. And for me."

After a long while, he sat up, wiped the tears from his eyes, sniffling. "I'm doing my best."

"Then you keep doing that." Their best was all they could do. There was no other choice. Because, the reality was, the past was in the past. It was dark and horrifying and it created consequences that were still impacting them to that day. Maddison was ashamed by some of the things she had done, but she had been dealt her punishment. She would pay for her crimes.

Blame, shame, guilt and grief had never done her any favours. Maddison wasn't going to keep all those emotions in her heart anymore. It was too soul-destroying. No way could she buckle in and shoulder her long future in jail if her oppressive past was still riding her. She had to let all that go. Make a clean break from Ben. And get on with life.

If only she had done it sooner.

CHAPTER 42

Tina sat in her therapist's office. Her defence lawyers had said it would look favourable if she received mental health help during the length of the trial. She certainly hadn't been about to argue with the experts. But now that it was all over, there was no need to keep up the charade.

Heather, her psychologist, sat in the chair opposite Tina. She was young. Reminded Tina a little of herself all those years ago, believing she could make a real difference in people's lives.

"You must be feeling very relieved," Heather said conversationally as their session started.

"Yes, but I think I always had hoped for this outcome. Truth, in the end, prevails, doesn't it?"

Heather smiled. "Yes, truth, I think, in most instances, is always the winning path." She frowned then, sympathy shaping her features.

Tina resented that look. Sympathy was strangely patronising once she had stopped playing the victim. As though she were so broken, so incapable, she needed someone to pity her and champion on her behalf. She was almost at her wit's end with it.

If not for the trial, she wouldn't have lasted a single session with Heather. Nothing Tina spoke about during her sessions was ever truthful anyway. She didn't delve into her childhood trauma. She couldn't risk Heather's files being subpoenaed and her history blaring from the pages like a bright red flag. A history that could indicate a damaged child cum revengeful adult woman, perhaps capable of murder.

Tina didn't hate Heather for doing her job or for choosing that profession. She was once very much the same herself at the start of her career. Human nature was innately empathetic, but she'd had too many harsh lessons, too young, about the realities of life and the human condition.

Well before any person should ever butt against such truths, she had learned that there were two types of people in the world: those who were good-natured, kind and empathetic, and those who took advantage of those who were good-natured, kind and empathetic.

She had never earned brownie points for being moral. For being a good little girl. Life didn't care about such trivialities. A serial rapist could live their long life in the lap of luxury, existing in their self-built Utopia. While a hardworking, virtuous man, doing good in his community, could be struck dead at forty-two from a stroke, left to wither away in hospital as his grieving family gathered around his bed, wondering how that tortured end could ever come to such a good man.

Tina had read all the news articles about Juliette. How it was so unfair that a beautiful, young, blonde woman with such a gorgeous smile, who never hurt anyone, could succumb to a terrible, horrifying death. Especially in a town like Gladstone where murder was rare.

Juliette's shield of virtue was nowhere to be seen when Tina stood before her, wrecking bar poised like a tiger snake, ready to strike. Nowhere because virtue was only a story people told themselves to elevate their sense of self above others around them.

The endless battle between victim and victor. But even victims used their victimhood as power, otherwise, there would be no reason to stretch that mindset out, sometimes across years, even decades. There had to be some twisted, irrational underlying benefit, even if it were subconscious and hidden.

Tina had been like that once. She still didn't know why she had maintained that mentality for so long. But what she did know was that a victim, despite the benefits, was still a victim. She lost more than she had ever gained by being that person.

All the manipulators, the opportunists, the deviants, had gravitated to her like she was a black hole for their perversion. They could see what Tina hadn't been able to see in herself—her vulnerability, her weakness. But then she had decided, in a single moment, that she wasn't going to be 'her' anymore, and she fought like a rabid dog to get her life back.

"Did you want to talk about the investigation and trial, Tina? The emotions you might be feeling?" Heather asked. "Perhaps you hold some resentment towards Maddison?"

Tina pursed her lips, suppressing her smile for Heather's naivety. She sat back in her chair, finding a comfortable position. "You know, I never told you this. But when I was about your age, I worked as a psychologist. For about eight years all up."

Heather leaned forward, her eyes widening. "No, you didn't mention that."

"You remind me a lot of myself."

Heather looked down at her notes to avoid Tina's eyes.

"The very last patient I had taught me a valuable lesson," Tina said.

"Really? What was that?"

"He was an older man. Nearly seventy. His wife of forty-five years had died eighteen months earlier and he was grieving her loss. He was also worried about something else that was happening. Desires that were swelling within him now that the one person who suppressed those feelings was gone. He was attracted to young boys and it deeply disturbed him.

"He swore black and blue that he had never acted on those impulses in any way. Not a pornographic picture. Not even an innocent picture. He looked away when he passed children at the shops or in the street. He was cautious to never be alone with his grandchildren. But he was having thoughts and he believed while they were just thoughts, he could nip it in the bud before it got worse. Before his thoughts turned into actions."

Heather nodded, moved her hand in a way that prompted Tina to continue.

"I was quite experienced by the time he came to me, but I was still gullible. And, honestly, I'd never worked with someone who suspected they were a paedophile. I spoke with my boss about him. We did all the assessments to check if he was a risk. Informed all the correct channels. I was permitted to proceed with his therapy. I genuinely believed that if I could just help this guy, then I could stop him from ever hurting children." She didn't mention that he had hit a raw nerve with her. She thought if she could 'fix him', all his potential victims would never have to suffer like she'd had to.

"He hadn't committed a crime. He genuinely wanted therapy. So, I worked with him for eighteen months. We delved intensively into his childhood. He had suffered horrible, horrible sexual abuse. I felt the deepest sympathy for him, and this made me want to help him more. He was doing well. Making progress. Completing his homework—you know, the hard, gritty work patients have to do on their own between sessions."

Heather nodded.

"And then I received a subpoena for his files. The police had found the skeletons of three boys buried in the ground beneath the crawlspace of his house. He was charged and convicted of their sexual assault and murder."

"How did you feel about that?"

A brow rose, her head tilted to the side, then straightened again. "Like a fool. Betrayed. Mostly, I was embarrassed. He had completely manipulated me. Lied to my face and I had believed him. But, as I said, I learned a valuable lesson. One I have carried with me to this day."

"And what is that?"

"Monsters are made. But they're still monsters. You can never forget that no matter what disguise the monster is wearing, how sweet their voice sounds or how foolproof their story is."

Heather's eye twitched. She crossed her leg in the opposite direction. "What do you mean by that?"

Tina smiled, got to her feet, and slipped her bag over her shoulder. "Some monsters are past saving."

"What does that mean?" Heather asked, more demanding now, her tone higher pitched.

Tina didn't look back as she strode to the door, opened it and walked out of that room for the last time.

CHAPTER 43

Yarwun was experiencing a sunny Sunday morning. The growl and chug of lawnmowers and whipper snippers could be heard on the wind as men across distant properties tried to tame the unruly explosion of lawn growth.

Tina rolled out of bed and opened the curtains. She was naked. The sunlight rushed in, warm and yellow. She glanced over her shoulder at Chris. He was smiling at her, running his gaze over the length of her body. Not in an ogling way, but with reverence.

He patted the space beside him. "Dressed like that, you might want to come back to bed."

Outside, the chickens were clucking. The rooster was crowing. The gardens were blossoming as spring stretched its arms and the fruit trees were full and ripe.

Tina crawled on her hands and knees across the bed towards Chris and straddled his lap. She kissed his face, his lips, lingering at his mouth before trailing her lips down his strong jaw to his neck. Rough stubble against her soft mouth.

No remorse or indignity for what she had done. Not when this was who she had fought for. Love conquered all. That was how the fairy tales from her childhood had ended. What those stories forgot to mention, though, was that sometimes you had to fight to the death to get your happy ending. You had to be your own hero. And a little bit of revenge didn't go astray.

Tina had wanted Ben to lose everything, exactly like he had done to her.

And she had succeeded.

Maddison, Isabelle and Juliette were nothing more than collateral damage.

After making love with Chris, fully experiencing the wonderment, the pleasure, of every moment, Tina showered, dressed, kissed Chris's cheek and promised she'd be back soon with a surprise.

While she was gone, Chris mowed the lawn. He was returning the ride-on mower to the shed when Tina arrived home. The scent of petrol and freshly cut, fertile grass lingered as the Mini Cooper roamed up the gritty drive and parked in the carport.

He met Tina beside the car, kissed her cheek. Boots encased his feet; the soles were now bright green from treading over the lawn.

"Hey," he said, eager to know where she had been, and mostly, what the surprise was.

She lifted onto tiptoes and pressed her lips to his, kissed him slowly, delighting in the moment. For the past few weeks, as she had drifted off to sleep, his big, warm body beside her, she had never known a time she was happier.

Maybe because she'd had to climb so high, fight so hard, to reach that summit. Or maybe because she knew the agony of losing her quiet, simple but rewarding life, so to have it, once again, in her grasp, meant so much more. Any complacency was gone. Chris was a treasure to her. A real treasure. And she loved him so very much.

Tina wasn't sure how Chris would react if he discovered she had done all this for him—for *them*. But she would never take that risk. No, she'd keep to her version of events. A version so well-practised, so well-planned and executed that the details were almost real to her now.

Occasionally, when she reflected on the past, for just a moment, she would forget that Kadie wasn't really her daughter. That she hadn't actually visited her grave and cried. She would recall the night Maddison appeared at her bedroom window and would see Isabelle's face in her memories instead. She would forget that those were just stories. A concocted narrative. A means to an end.

But then again, she was always so good at that. Dissociation. Of building new worlds to exist in when reality was too much. The plan she had executed to get away with murder was no different. A twisted kind of truth. Lies repeated so many times that they took on the shape of reality. And slowly vanishing behind the lies was all that was left unsaid.

"I've felt like a boy at Christmas this past hour," Chris said.

"Me too," she squealed and reached for a box sitting on the passenger seat. She carefully picked it up and carried it into the house. Chris took his boots off at the bottom of the stairs and followed her inside to the living room.

She sat on the floor, the box between her legs, and opened it. Chris hadn't had a chance to sit when a black, white and brown shaggy puppy jumped out into Tina's arms.

"A puppy?"

She smiled, nodded. "An Aussie Shepherd. We've got a big yard for her and time to groom and care for her. She'll be a challenge, but I think we'll appreciate having her around."

"I thought dogs were too messy?"

She shrugged. "Yes, but, hey, it's time."

He reached for the puppy and lifted her into his arms. Her furry tail wagged, and she whimpered with excitement. "Hello there, gorgeous little girl. My God, you're adorable."

Tina watched Chris, unable to wipe the smile from her face. "You can name her if you like."

He grinned so wide as he held the puppy up to his face and touched his nose to her snout. "I think I'll call you Sarah."

Tina's stomach wrenched with pain. But that was the whole purpose of the dog. A way for Chris to move on from all that life he lived between Isabelle and now. If he wanted to call the dog after his daughter as a way to cope, she wasn't going to complain.

"Perfect," she said. "Sarah it is."

"I think I'm in love already."

Tina laughed as she got to her feet and dusted the fine puppy hair from her clothes. "Me too."

His smile faded and his eyes softened as he came closer. With Sarah still against his chest, he bent his head and kissed Tina. "Thank you."

"My pleasure."

A teasing glint in his blue eyes. "No, I mean, thank you, for everything you've done for us."

She flinched. "Pardon?"

"I'm happy again. For the first time in a really long time. You always seem to know exactly how to save me. From that very moment, all those years ago, when you called my name in your office. I'm not sure you can understand how good this feels."

A sharp breath inward. "What are you saying?"

"Since when have you ever allowed a travel mug of coffee in your car?"

She lowered her gaze, bit down on her bottom lip.

"And I saw the prescription tablets on the fridge. I'm much taller than you. It may have been out of your sight, but it wasn't out of mine. I know you down to your bones, Tina. They weren't for you—well, not for the usual reasons someone would have medication. But I'd forgotten about it until that day I came here. And it all made sense. I knew I should be" – he shook his head – "I don't know, upset."

Tina tensed, waited without breath.

"But I wasn't because it was at that moment, I realised how much you love me. No greater sensation exists than knowing with absolute certainty that you love me and that you'd go to such lengths, and risk everything, to prove that." He kissed her lips, lingering at her mouth for a long moment. "Just so you know, I love you that much too. More than I can ever show."

A gentle flush of her cheeks. Her heart was blossoming with warmth. "I love you too."

"I know. I know you do." He pretended to zip his lips. "That's why we won't ever speak of what really happened again." He reached for her hand and threaded his fingers with hers. "Come on, let's give Sarah a run around her new yard."

She smiled. "Yes, let's."

MORE FROM THE AUTHOR

Thanks for reading *All That Was Left Unsaid*.
I hope you enjoyed it.

If you'd like to know more about me, my books, or to
connect with me online, you can visit my webpage
www.jacquieunderdown.com

Reviews can help readers find books, and I am grateful for
all honest reviews. Thank you for taking the time to let
others know what you've read, and what you thought.

If you liked this book, here are my other books:

Women's fiction/psychological thrillers

The Perfect Family
The Secrets Mothers Keep

Contemporary small-town romance

The Stockman's Daughter

Wattle Valley Series
Catch Me a Cowboy
Meet Me in the Middle

THE PERFECT FAMILY

Three everyday couples, from one ordinary family ... and an astonishing murder plot.

Outwardly, The Radcliffes are a typical suburban family. But anyone close enough to them will know that it's all for show.

Matt and Nikki's life is perfect. They're happily married, work great jobs, and are raising two loveable teenage sons.

Anthony and Belinda have it all—the looks, the big house by the water, and a successful business.

Vaughn and Paige couldn't be more in love; they can't wait to start a family of their own.

But underneath, each couple is in crisis and there is one root cause. Out of options and their backs against the wall, they discover that murder isn't a tool reserved only for criminals.

The Perfect Family is available worldwide from Amazon stores.

THE SECRETS MOTHERS KEEP

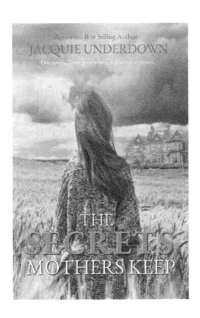

One Family. Three generations. A common goal to unite them. A lifetime of secrets to divide them. But could uncovering the truth be the only way that this family can finally heal?

Three generations of women find their way back home to Tasmania. They embark on a project together to renovate the family manor and convert it into a bed and breakfast.

After a tumultuous life of pain and betrayal, Mary swore she'd never let anyone hurt her or her family again. But in order to keep her word, she must guard a secret she swore to keep fifty years earlier.

But with the family now under the one roof, and the past tampered with, the foundations of this secret are shaken.

Mary always believed that hiding the truth was protecting the family, but when all is exposed, she finds that by keeping her secret, she was the one hurting them all.

The Secrets Mothers Keep is available worldwide from Amazon stores.

ABOUT THE AUTHOR

Jacquie is an Australian author who lives in Central Queensland, Australia, where it's always hot, and humidity coats the skin, summer or winter. After writing her first story over a decade ago, it didn't take long for the writing bug to take her over completely, and she happily did away with her business career. Now she spends her days wrapped up in her imagination, creating characters, exploring alternative realities, and meeting a host of characters who occupy her mind at first, then eventually her books.

Her novels, *Bittersweet* and *One Hot Christmas*, were finalists in multiple categories in the Australian Romance Readers Association awards in 2019 and 2020. *Bittersweet* was a finalist in the Romance Writers of Australia Romantic Book of the Year Awards in 2019.

Jacquie has a business degree, studied postgraduate writing, editing and publishing at The University of Queensland, and earned a Master of Letters (Creative Writing) from Central Queensland University. But all that means is that she's super-dedicated to writing the best books she can for readers to enjoy. With well over a million words published, be sure to check out her many published novels, novellas and short stories. You can find out more about Jacquie on her website: https://www.jacquieunderdown.com/

Made in the USA
Monee, IL
31 July 2021